Krysty tugged gently

The bell tolled immediately, its booming note echoing across the morning's stillness.

"Leave it," Ryan snapped. "Want to rouse the whole bastard country against us?"

He noticed something lying on top of the altar. It was a multithonged whip, with tiny metal barbs knotted into each lash. All of them were stiff and stained black with what looked like old, dried blood. A sense of threatening danger became much stronger.

"Come on," he called. "Something's not right about this place. It's not a proper church. Let's get out before someone comes and brings trouble."

Neither of them heard the door whisper open, but they both recognized the audible click of the twin hammers being drawn back on a scattergun.

"Welcome, pilgrims," said a rich, jolly voice.

D1358985

Also available in the Deathlands saga:

JAMES AXLER

DEATH LANDS®

Circle Thrice

A GOLD EAGLE BOOK FROM

WORLDWIDE®

TORONTO • NEW YORK • LONDON
AMSTERDAM • PARIS • SYDNEY • HAMBURG
STOCKHOLM • ATHENS • TOKYO • MILAN
MADRID • WARSAW • BUDAPEST • AUCKLAND

If you purchased this book without a cover you should be aware
that this book is stolen property. It was reported as "unsold and
destroyed" to the publisher, and neither the author nor the
publisher has received any payment for this "stripped book."

This is dedicated to Kathryn, Stevie and Laurie,
with all the love I have to give.

First edition June 1996

ISBN 0-373-62532-4

CIRCLE THRICE

Copyright © 1996 by Worldwide Library.

All rights reserved. Except for use in any review, the
reproduction or utilization of this work in whole or in part
in any form by any electronic, mechanical or other means,
now known or hereafter invented, including xerography,
photocopying and recording, or in any information storage
or retrieval system, is forbidden without the written permission
of the publisher, Worldwide Library, 225 Duncan Mill Road,
Don Mills, Ontario, Canada M3B 3K9.

All characters in this book have no existence outside the
imagination of the author and have no relation whatsoever to
anyone bearing the same name or names. They are not even
distantly inspired by any individual known or unknown to the
author, and all incidents are pure invention.

® and TM are trademarks of the publisher. Trademarks indicated
with ® are registered in the United States Patent and Trademark
Office, the Canadian Trade Marks Office and in other countries.

Printed in U.S.A.

When Chuck Berry asked long-distance information whether he was through to Memphis, Tennessee, it was a question that arrowed straight into the heartland of the American myth. While Memphis lives, then rock and roll will truly never die.

—From *Trying to Tell a Stranger,*
by Larry "The Fox" Burrell,
published by Banbury Press of
Oxford, 1996

Prologue

The companions' sojourn into the remnants of old Japan had drawn to its inevitable, horrific conclusion. Ryan and his friends retreated to the house that hid the gateway, intent on making a hasty jump back to Deathlands.

Ryan led the way toward the airlock door, through and along to the elevator.

"Where are we going to put the grens?" J. B. Dix, the Armorer, asked.

"They've only got 20-second timers, haven't they? Not all that long."

The Armorer nodded. "Right. We don't really know how long it takes for a jump to be properly initiated. Feels like thirty seconds or so before we become unconscious. Might be a deal more than that before we actually get to jump out of there."

"Grens could go off while we're in midjump," Mildred Wyeth cautioned. "That what you're saying, John?"

"Right, love. Could put them in the elevator shaft when we're down there. Seal it off tight and also bring the house down on top of everything."

"That would bury us snugger than a pharaoh in his sarcophagus, would it not?" Doc Tanner asked.

"Sure would," Ryan replied.

"And if something malfunctioned with the mechanism? What then? Then it will be a long goodbye and a big sleep for us all. As Mr. Chandler would have said."

Ryan didn't know who this Chandler guy was, but Doc had a point.

It could be rather like sawing off a branch that you were sitting on.

"Mashashige won't be invading Deathlands," he said. "Nor will any of his men. Nor his brother."

"But there'll always be someone else who'll find the house and the gateway," Krysty Wroth protested.

Ryan sighed. It was tempting to take the grens with them back to Deathlands, where they could always find a use. But Krysty was right. Everything that they'd seen in what remained of Japan pointed toward lethal problems over the next few years. And if the gateway should still function...

There was an obvious risk to themselves, but a greater risk for the future if they didn't act now.

"Use them in the house," he decided. "Last burner and an implode. Last pair of implodes can go up in the elevator at the final moment before we go to make the jump. We can check that everything seems all right in the gateway first."

Nobody argued against the plan.

When they stood in front of the elevator, Ryan pushed in the code: six, two, eight, three, four and one.

The door slid open and he stepped in, pressing the button to hold it open. "J.B., use your burner and the implode. Jak, keep yours for the last minute. Set them for the full twenty and then get in quick."

The Armorer set the timer on the scarlet-and-blue implode and lobbed it out through the internal door into the hallway, following it immediately with the burner. Then he closed the doors and stepped smartly into the elevator.

Ryan pushed the Down arrow and the cage began to drop.

"Quake now and we're deep in the ordure," Mildred commented.

Ryan was looking at his chron, counting down the seconds. It was on eleven when they reached the bottom of the shaft and the door hissed smoothly open.

As they were entering the mat-trans control area, the tiny digits flickered to twenty.

There was a faint vibration from above them, and a few flakes of plaster fell from the cracked ceiling. Ryan noticed even at a cursory glance that the control area had suffered from the recent quakes, with some consoles dark and several ceiling lights off.

One thing that had been worrying him was how they would actually jump to Deathlands, whether the ordinary Return code would do the trick.

But he noticed something they'd missed on the way out. There was a piece of cardboard taped to the door by the control panel that listed several American regions.

"Want me to do the last grens?" Jak asked.

"Sure." The earth trembled and another light went off. "Do it now. Krysty, we could copy this list, take it with us and see if it operates from other gateways. Give us control over where we want to jump to."

Doc shook his head. "I fear, my dear friend, that it would be fruitless. The codes differ from redoubt to redoubt. I remember that from my time with the whitecoats of Cerberus. Just pick a place and enter it.''

Jak Lauren came running back. ''Sent them up in elevator,'' he said. ''Got about fifteen. Closed outer door. Give protection. But should go quick.''

''Right.'' Ryan scanned the list. ''How about Tennessee? Haven't been there for a while.''

''Do it lover,'' Krysty said nervously. ''Got a bad feeling that something's going wrong.''

Like an echo to her words, they all felt a rumble that made the floor shake.

''Grens,'' Mildred said hopefully.

Jak sniffed, counting to himself. ''Not time. Coming up...now.''

Chapter One

They all heard the distinctive roar of the pair of implode grens far above them, though it was muffled by the sec doors that led into the gateway. The sound was overlaid by the thunder of a quake, the noise all around them, as if the walls were about to crumble at any second.

"In," Ryan snapped, punching in the digital code for Tennessee. Not waiting for everyone to sit on the floor of the orange-walled chamber, he stepped in and slammed the door shut to trigger the jump mechanism.

Everyone knew what to do.

J.B. had taken off his fedora and placed it on his lap, carefully folding his glasses and slipping them safely into a pocket. The Uzi was in his lap, the scattergun within reach. He held Mildred's hand, and she reached out for Doc Tanner, who had slowly creaked his way down, laying the ebony swordstick at his side, stretching out his aged knee boots.

Jak, his red eyes swollen from crying at the sudden and shocking death of the little geisha girl, Issie, sat next to Doc, pressing his skinny back against the armaglass wall.

The rumble was becoming much louder and more

insistent as Ryan finally seated himself beside Krysty, having unslung the rifle and placed it by his side.

"Here we go," he said.

"*Sayonara,* my friends," Doc whispered, his voice sounding small and faraway.

The disks in the floor and ceiling were beginning to glow brightly, and the familiar white mist was gathering above their heads. Ryan felt as if his brain were being scooped out of his skull and whirled around and around.

"Tennessee," he breathed, his last sentient thought one of pleasure that they would very soon be home safely in Deathlands again.

At that moment the big quake finally arrived.

A HUNDRED FEET ABOVE the mat-trans unit, in the ravaged and polluted remains of Japan, the quake brought down the remnants of the burning mansion that had been built by the Americans. Erected well before skydark, it had been used by them as a safe hiding place for the secret gateway.

The place had been set on fire by a burner gren and three implodes as Ryan and company made their way toward the safety of a jump.

Now it was a mountain of glowing ashes in the darkness of the Oriental night, roof beams tumbled on top of the hidden elevator that ran down the reinforced-concrete shaft to the gateway.

A column of smoke, with glittering ruby sparks, soared high into the sky. The ground shook and churned, solid rock becoming liquid under the unimaginable pressures of the earthquake. Nearly a hundred years after the missiles darkened the skies and the ultimate war began, there were no longer any scientific instruments left in the world to measure quakes.

But if there had been any, then the movement would have pushed the needle skittering across the roll of graph paper, indicating a gigantic tremor that would have been measured at something like 7.8 on the Richter scale.

It caused immense damage on the southern fraction of old Japan that remained, nearly wiping out the population and triggering a series of tidal waves.

The six-sided chamber with its sturdy wall of fiery orange armaglass only resisted the force of the quake for a handful of seconds. In the room beyond, desks and comp consoles slid sideways, shorting out the nuke-powered electrics. The whole system failed in less than a dozen heartbeats.

As the walls splintered and a torrent of fluid stone flooded into the chamber, Ryan and the others had already left it.

Just left it.

Their bodies had been disintegrated, coded by the mat-trans digital controls by the door, to be reassembled in a similar gateway in the heart of old Tennessee, in Deathlands.

But the process was crucially interrupted by the quake.

Chapter Two

The mat-trans units were highly sophisticated pieces of equipment, the finest that the whitecoat scientists of the predark times could design and manufacture. In the last year or so before skydark, and the transition of the United States of America into Deathlands, with the deaths of around 99.4 percent of the population during the nuke holocaust and the long winters that followed, the government had been working on a number of ultrasecret projects.

The Totality Concept was the blanket name for all the differing branches of research. Within that Pentagon-controlled umbrella, there was Operation Chronos, dealing with time travel; the Genesis Project, which dealt with genetic tampering and DNA research; and Overproject Whisper, which had a number of arcane, mysterious and murderous subdivisions. One of these was Cerberus, which covered the installation of matter-transfer gateways in a number of specially built military complexes called redoubts.

The greens and liberals and conservationists at the end of the twentieth century had been enraged at the way the government had chosen to site these redoubts, riding roughshod over all objections. Many of the redoubts were located in idyllic and isolated parts of the country, remote from cities. In many cases the deep-buried complexes had been located in national parks.

In the apocalypse that followed the skydark mega-cull, some of these redoubts had been destroyed. But others, abandoned, had been maintained by superbly engineered nuke power plants that kept the gateways functioning.

Ryan and his friends had stumbled on one of these long-hidden redoubts and accidentally triggered the mat-trans unit, finding that they had miraculously ''jumped'' to somewhere else.

Since then, they'd made a number of such jumps, generally with safety and success, but not always. The big problem was that all scientific data had gone with the missiles, and nobody knew the codes that enabled the users to choose a specific location.

All Ryan knew was that when you shut the door of the hexagonal armaglass chamber, you triggered the jump mechanism, became unconscious and woke up some other place.

That was what was supposed to happen.

But the timing of the devastating earthquake had proved crucial to the jump.

The dissolution of the molecular structure of each of the six companions had taken place, but the reassembly was abruptly interrupted.

The reception unit in Tennessee was on alert, the initial mechanism functioning.

But there was nothing to receive.

The microcomps were searching the void, making tens of millions of calculations every second, seeking the physical parameters for the six humans in order to try to complete the assembly and conclude the jump.

Ryan Cawdor. Male. Late thirties. Seventy-four inches. Two hundred and five pounds. Eyes negative. Left eye missing. Right eye pale blue. Skin dark. Hair curly and black. A dozen or more scars all over his body, including one that ran from eye to the corner of the mouth on the right side of his face.

A myriad list of endless details covered every aspect and measurement of Ryan, from the length of his stubble to the condition of his fingernails.

It went on to describe the clothes that Ryan Cawdor had been wearing—the long coat and the white silk scarf weighted at the end with silver dollars, blue denim shirt, dark blue pants, combat boots.

The comps searched for comparisons, weights and calibers for his weapons. The Steyr SSG-70 fired a 7.62 mm round and was mounted with a laser image enhancer and Starlight nightscope. A SIG-Sauer automatic was holstered on his hip, the P-226 model, carrying fifteen rounds of 9 mm full-metal-jacket rounds. Length was 7.72 inches. Barrel length was 4.41 inches, its weight 25.52 ounces. An eighteen-inch panga was sheathed on the other hip, with a blade honed to a whisper of death.

There were similar details for the other five friends, concentrating on the unusual elements that made them the individuals that they were.

John Barrymore Dix. Male. Similar age to Ryan. Sixty-eight inches tall and one-forty pounds soaking wet. Hair thin and dark brown. Complexion sallow. Eyes brown. Lean build. Wire-rimmed spectacles. Clothes included jacket and pants with endlessly capacious pockets filled with all manner of miniature tools, picklocks, wrist chron and microsextant. And his beloved fedora hat.

He had two blasters, the M-4000 Smith & Wesson 12-gauge scattergun with a folding butt, pistol grip and its unique ammo, eight rounds of Remington fléchettes. Twenty of the lethal inch-long darts were in each shell. His Uzi automatic machine pistol held twenty rounds of 9 mm ammo.

Krysty Wroth. Female. Midtwenties. Seventy-one inches and one-fifty pounds. Green eyed, with fresh complexion. Well built. Long red hair. Nearly a century after the nukecaust there was still residual genetic damage throughout Deathlands that led to all manner of mutations in animal and vegetable life. The comps were thrown by Krysty Wroth's fiery hair, puzzled by its sentience. In times of stress it would seem to shrink and curl closer to Krysty's skull, almost like a cap. When things were going well, then it would flow luxuriantly across her shoulders.

White shirt. Blue pants and jacket. The system reproduced precisely what she'd been wearing. The unusual boots, Western style, dark blue leather, with chiseled silver points on the toes and embroidered with silver spread-winged falcons.

Her weapon was a Smith & Wesson double-action Model 640, 5-shot, .38-caliber blaster with a stubby two-inch barrel.

The unseen mutations that were an integral part of Krysty's persona were also duplicated. Her strange gift of "seeing" a threat of danger. Or "feeling" when there was any life force in the immediate area.

Krysty's other mutie talent had been inherited from her mother, Sonja, back when she'd been a teenage girl in the ville of Harmony up in old Colorado. At times of direst need, Krysty could draw on the power of Gaia, the Earth Mother, which would briefly give her phenomenal, almost supernatural strength. But she would pay a dreadful price for utilizing this power and would collapse, utterly drained and barely conscious.

The mat-trans system had some problems with Jak Lauren. Male. Late teens. Only sixty-four inches tall and barely tipping the scales at one-ten pounds. Deep facial scars. Hair of purest white. Skin white. Eyes of ruby red. Full-blown albino. Very athletic build.

Leather-and-canvas camouflage coat over ragged fur jacket. Denim pants. Combat boots.

Satin-finish Colt Python Magnum, .357 caliber. Six round. Six-inch barrel. A man-stopper. A cannon of a blaster for the skinny albino teenager. He also carried a number of leaf-shaped throwing knives, with heavy taped hilts, concealed all about his person.

Mildred Winonia Wyeth. Female. Age indeterminate. Either late thirties or one hundred and twenty. The comp found that aspect of Mildred difficult to handle. It had no way of knowing that she had been born in Lincoln, Nebraska, on December 17, 1964. A doctor and expert on the medical freezing of human beings, she had gone into hospital for minor abdominal surgery a few days before skydark, on December 28, 2000. Ironically things had gone badly wrong, and to save her life it had been necessary to freeze her cryonically.

She had been plucked back from eternal sleep by Ryan and the others.

Skin, black. Hair, black, in beaded plaits. Height, sixty-four inches. Weight, one hundred and forty pounds. Eyes, brown.

Wore quilted denim jacket, reinforced military jeans and calf-length boots of black leather. Mildred's weapon was typical of the woman and her unusual skills.

In the last-ever Olympic games, held in Atlanta in 1996, she had won the silver medal for the free-shooting pistol event. She had scored three ninety-eight from four hundred and was arguably the finest shot in Deathlands.

She carried a target revolver, a ZKR 551, made at the Zbrojvka works in Brno, Czechoslovakia. Designed by the Koucky brothers, the blaster held six .38-caliber rounds. The beautiful handblaster had a solid frame side-rod ejector and short fall thumb cocking hammer.

With it Mildred could put all six rounds into a three-inch target at fifty yards.

Last of the six was Dr. Theophilus Algernon Tanner, whose genetic makeup was so unusual it completely freaked out the computer. Most of Doc's mat-trans facts were simple and reasonably straightforward.

Male, height of seventy-five inches and weight of around one hundred and fifty pounds. Very skinny for his height. Hair, grizzled and shoulder length. Eyes, pale blue. Face, deeply lined. Oddly perfect teeth. Deep voice.

The clothes weren't a problem. Old-fashioned frock coat, faded and stained coppery green with age. Cracked knee boots. White denim shirt.

And the weapons weren't common, but they could be found in the infinite data base of the mat-trans system.

His blaster was a reproduction of a famous handgun from the days of the Civil War. The J. E. B. Stuart commemorative Le Mat, engraved and inlaid with gold. Peculiar for a pistol, the Le Mat had two barrels. One fired a single round of 18-gauge grapeshot. A quick adjustment of the hammer accessed nine .44-caliber rounds, on the cap-and-ball system.

The other weapon that Doc always carried was a long ebony swordstick, with a silver lion's-head hilt. The black wooden cane concealed a rapier of superb-quality Toledo steel that bore the engraved message *No Me Saques Sin Razón; No Me Envaines Sin Honor— Do not draw me without good reason and do not sheathe me without honor.*

It was when the computer came to Doc's age that the powerful comp nearly blew its fuses.

Data does not compute was its message to itself, seeking to find some way of rationalizing the contradictory information that it received.

Doc's actual birth date was February 14, 1868, which made him something like two hundred and thirty years old. He had married pretty little Emily Chandler on June 17, 1891. They had two children: Rachel, who was three years old, and Jolyon, who was just one when their father completely vanished.

Operation Chronos had been working in ultrasecret conditions to try to achieve time travel with a view toward utilizing it against the Russians. Assassinating Joseph Stalin was just one of the aims of the project.

Sadly the whitecoats could never get it right.

They began by trying to trawl people from the past. Judge Crater was one of their spectacular failures. The writer Ambrose Bierce was another. They disappeared from their pasts, but what emerged in the secret laboratories in Virginia bore scant relationship to anything human. After they had thrown up at the hideous abortions of humanity that they had trawled into the present, the horrified whitecoats ordered that the remnants be hastily burned.

Their successes could be counted on the fingers of one hand. And the prize of them all was the eminent scientist and philosopher, Dr. Theophilus Tanner, one of the leading academics of the Victorian era.

They dragged him forward to 1998, where he proved so difficult and uncooperative a study that they were glad to get rid of him by pushing him forward again in December of 2000. The scientists, who had destroyed his life, died days later in the nightmare of skydark, and Doc found himself stranded in the heart of Deathlands, nearly a hundred years in the future.

For reasons that nobody could understand, this man, who was only in his midthirties, resembled a man in his sixties.

The experiences had also taken their toll on his mind. Doc wasn't always in absolute control, but then no one was in control when consigning the body's particles to the mat-trans process.

But eventually all the physical elements were resolved and the process of reassembling the six humans in the redoubt in Tennessee began.

A NORMAL JUMP, under the best of circumstances, was extremely trying for the participants, always leading to a period of mental blackness and, not unusually, some degree of trauma.

That happened in even the best of jumps. And the jump from the burning house in Japan to the redoubt in Tennessee wasn't the best.

Not by a country mile.

The interruption to the process of matter transfer compounded the usual nightmares.

It was bad.

Chapter Three

Jak Lauren was walking through the heart of a huge, sprawling ville. He didn't recognize it, though it reminded him a little of the outer suburbs of ruined Newyork. It was an endless tangle of rusting metal and rotted concrete, the streets littered by old cans and broken glass, so that every step crunched under the heels of his combat boots.

He was holding the sticky hand of his two-year-old daughter, Jenny, and they were trying to find Jak's wife, Christina. The little girl had been toddling bravely at his side all day, but now she was starting to complain that she was becoming tired and hungry.

"Want eat, Daddy..."

"When we find Mom," Jak replied, tugging a little harder at the child, almost pulling her off her feet, making her whine unhappily. He stopped and knelt by her, wiping her face with a spotless linen kerchief embroidered with a flying dragon in vermillion silk.

"Nearly fell," she protested.

"Sorry, honey. Daddy's tired and hungry, as well."

He thought they'd been walking for days, though Jak couldn't recall when they'd actually begun their trek. Nor could he remember precisely where he and Christina were supposed to meet. Where or when.

It was passing strange that there was nobody around in the ville.

He was sure that earlier they'd been pushing their way through bustling streets, going against a faceless, silent throng, making them battle for every yard, like salmon fighting up a succession of foaming torrents.

It seemed as if he had almost lost his grip on Jenny's tiny fingers and nearly lost her, turning to see the little figure being washed away amid the human breakers.

But he still had her.

From the poor light that spilled between the shattered, grounded hulks of skyscrapers, Jak guessed that it had to be late afternoon or early evening.

Jenny stopped and reached up to her father, and he stooped and plucked her from the street, cradling her safely in his strong, lean arms. Somewhere in the vast stillness, Jak was aware of the distant rumbling of a powerful war-wag engine.

"Where's Mommy?"

"Around, Jenny. Don't worry. Find her."

It had been raining and the chill streets were dark and gleaming, with coiling snakes of steam billowing up from deep below the city.

A rat appeared from the open doorway of an antique deli, as big as a terrier, its eyes glittering like gold as its head turned slowly to consider the human invaders into its territory. Jak's hand dropped to the butt of his Python, but the holster was empty.

"Fuck off," he grated.

The rodent seemed to hesitate, its narrow mouth opening, showing threads of bloody mucus dribbling from the needle-sharp teeth.

Reluctantly it turned away from Jak and the little girl, padding across the street into the shadows that spilled from a ruined office tower.

"Nasty," Jenny whispered.

"Right," Jak agreed.

The noise of the engine was roaring closer.

Riding above it, the teenager heard the unmistakable sound of someone walking along a side road, someone who had a severe limp, the steps uneven.

"Christina?" he said, puzzled at how flat and dead his voice sounded, with not a single echo from the concrete pinnacles that surrounded them.

"Mommy?" the little girl queried.

"Could be her. Must be her. Will be her. Will be good. Will be very good."

"There's Mommy!" Jenny's whoop of delight took him by surprise, and the little girl wriggled free from his hands, stumbling as she landed, then toddled off at a surprising speed toward the shape of a woman that had appeared on the corner of two streets.

The silhouette was limping toward them, waving a hand, encouraging the child toward her, beckoning her across the wide avenue.

The roar of the war-wag engine was louder.

Much louder.

It raced in a low gear at high speed, screeching like a midnight voodoo demon in a Louisiana graveyard.

Jak opened his pale mouth to shout a warning to both wife and child, but the words became trapped in translucent bubbles that caught the sound and muted it, floating away, high into the evening air, catching the last bright rays of the setting sun, far off among the stone canyons of the ville.

The wag turned a corner, huge in camouflage browns and greens, sparks trailing from its rumbling exhaust, wheels skidding on the damp tarmac.

The woman stopped, reaching out for the toddler.

Jenny's mouth was open in delight, her eyes wide and sparkling, her little legs pumping.

Jak stood frozen to the spot, his fingernails digging bloody furrows in his white palms, trying to scream.

The impact was surprisingly small for the extinction of a human life. There was a dull thud, and the child hurled through the air, arms and legs limp, her head hanging loose on her neck, hair flying. A veil of blood fountained from her open mouth.

The body landed a good twenty yards in front of the powerful war wag, which made no visible effort to stop. It clattered on, its huge wheels crushing the helpless little body, pulping it into the pavement.

Jak closed his ruby eyes, great tears coursing down his ivory cheeks.

The wag carried on without even attempting to deviate or brake, vanishing around the next corner and rumbling off into the distance, the smell of its exhaust overlaying the bitter tang of fresh-spilled blood.

The woman hadn't moved, staring at the crumpled corpse, her face in shadow.

Lifting her head, she revealed the smooth complexion and almond eyes of the little geisha, Issie, her rosebud mouth pursed in distress. "So sorry," she lisped. "To save the child would have been difficult."

Jak couldn't stop crying.

MILDRED LAY ON A TABLE of polished glass, naked, in a room of glittering chrome walls and ceiling and floor.

Her breath was slow and steady, pluming out into the freezing air around her. Her body was covered in a sheen of ice crystals, fragile and delicate.

A range of gleaming surgical instruments hung limply from the ceiling, the concealed lighting bouncing off the steel. There were various probes, drills, strange whirling blades and spring-loaded devices that looked as if they were designed to stretch the intimate orifices of the body.

Mildred couldn't move.

She wasn't dead.

Was she?

There wasn't a shred of feeling in any part of her body, no sensation of life.

But she could see her own breath.

There was a faint tinkling sound, and some of the remote-controlled equipment above her began to move in a way that seemed sinister and threatening to her.

A long probe, the size and shape of a pencil, lowered itself over her face, hovering as if it were trying to select a target, going toward her right eye.

Mildred struggled to close her eyes, to protect them from the steel, but nothing happened.

The probe delicately tapped on the surface of the eye, and she heard a faint clicking sound like metal on glass. The knowledge that the surface of her eye was frozen solid was somehow more terrifying than anything else, and she wanted to vomit.

But that was closed off from her, as well.

Another of the surgical devices was moving toward her, aiming itself at the junction of her spread thighs.

There was a whirring noise, and it began to revolve very quickly, the sharp teeth on its end spinning with a vibration like a tiny chain saw.

As Mildred felt the machine enter her, with a sudden warmth over her thighs, she fought to scream in revulsion and in protest at the gross invasion of her helpless body.

But there was no sound from her.

The blackness that swam up over her mind was a great mercy to her.

J.B. STROLLED through a dense forest of pine trees, with a bright, dazzling sun that broke through like golden spears into the occasional clearing, filling the still air with the scent of balsam.

The path wound its way gently into a steep hollow, the close-packed trees making it hard to see more than a few yards ahead.

The air was oppressively warm, and he hadn't seen any wildlife. Nothing scurried across the trail. No bird soared in the gaps in between the upper branches.

As J.B. reached the bottom of the track, he found himself in a clearing, surrounded on all sides by a dense hedge of thorns. He pushed through the undergrowth, glancing behind him as the brush sprang back to close the opening, sealing him in.

At the center of the clearing was an irregular block of stone, roughly rectangular.

The Armorer pushed back his fedora, blinking in the dusty light. He took off his glasses to polish them on his sleeve, then peered at the boulder, realizing that it was some kind of altar.

It had a dark, ancient, ominous stain crusted on one side, and there were deep incisions on all four sides, visible as shadows. J.B. knelt to look at them, vaguely conscious that anyone watching him might think he was performing some secret act of worship to this god unknown.

There seemed to be some kind of writing hewn into the granite. The Armorer couldn't read it, but he felt a vague unease, a feeling that his hands had suddenly become contaminated and sticky. He wiped them on the dry grass around the altar.

He blinked at the carvings, feeling that there was something wrong about them. They seemed to contain blasphemous suggestions of entities beyond time and space. The meaning was barely concealed from him by a ragged veil. If it was removed, then J.B. might understand all things.

And he might well go mad.

He leaned his back against the sun-warmed stone and slithered into a deep sleep.

And as he slept, they came gibbering for him.

He fought to wake himself from the living nightmare, but all in vain, trapped forever in the heart of a pitiless and relentless darkness.

SUSPENDED BETWEEN the two malfunctioning gateways, Krysty dreamed of a great fire that dropped from the sky and scorched the face of the earth.

Up in Harmony, her old home, she was a young girl. Barely past puberty, with tender, budding breasts, she was playing softball with friends on a high, flat expanse of cropped turf above the buildings of the ville. She was out in left field, shading her eyes against the sun, near the edge of the playing area, marked by a steep bank that rolled down into a ditch that held a clean, fast-flowing stream of pure water.

Patti van Onselen was at bat and had just cracked an enormous hit over Krysty's head, the ball rolling down the incline and splashing into the water.

"Go get it!" called an older girl, sitting in the shade of some white-thorn bushes.

Krysty started after it, hearing the distant sound of an airplane way, way overhead. Part of her mind thought that it was strange, as there were no longer any planes in Deathlands. But part of her accepted it as perfectly normal.

The noise of the chattering stream was loud in her ears as she slithered over the edge, making her way down on her denimed rear toward the white ball that was bobbing along fifteen or twenty yards away.

There was a faint whistling from somewhere above her, but Krysty ignored it, focusing her attention on the softball, shutting out the yells and shrieks of her friends on the field behind her.

She darted along in the shadow of the steep bank, finally seeing the ball trapped in a small pool between shallows. Krysty splashed out to reach for it, gasping at the icy bite of the meltwater.

Her fingers had just touched the ball when the world seemed to explode.

There was a flash of light, so bright that it blinded Krysty, making her drop the ball as she pressed her fingers to her eyes, crouching by the stream.

While she was still there, paralyzed by shock, there was a great wave of noise and heat, like the horsemen of the apocalypse racing close overhead, with a blast of fire and a rumble like a thousand peals of thunder all rolled into one.

Krysty cried out, falling to her knees, smelling her hair scorching in the inferno that roiled above her.

Several long seconds drifted by, and the noise and the rushing, fiery wind all passed over. She came to her senses enough to realize that the steepness of the bank above had protected her from what had happened.

It took several long minutes before she recovered enough to stand on shaky legs and crawl up the slope toward the softball field.

The grass at the top was gone, replaced by a dark, powdery ash, and the air was filled with an overwhelming stench of scorching, like the time in the fall when the farmers burned off the stubble from their fields.

Very slowly Krysty pushed her face over the brink of the slope until she could see all around her.

Until she could see that there was nothing all around her.

Everything had gone.

She gazed out at an unrelievedly gray landscape, like a far-off planet. There was no color except gray, shades of gray, close to black in places.

Nobody.

Except that the gray of the burned grass held strange blacker silhouettes, human shapes, distorted, hands high, running, falling figures. Nothing remained of her friends except those smudges on the smoking ground.

Krysty cried out once and collapsed in a dead, mindless faint.

DOC HAD PLUNGED directly into a black pit that held a lake of freezing black water.

He felt too tired to struggle and submitted to the icy embrace, letting himself sink.

RYAN SAT BY A GRAY SEA, where sullen breakers washed slowly over rounded boulders. Farther along the bleak shore he could see two saddled horses standing in the edge of the water, side by side.

He looked around the other way, and wasn't surprised to see a tall, slender figure in a long black cloak, the hood pulled up over the shadowed face.

"You come for me?"

"I come for everyone, Ryan Cawdor."

"I didn't expect you yet."

"It is rare that anyone expects my arrival. They always look for me on the morrow."

"Somewhere else?"

"Perhaps in Somarra."

The figure moved toward him, seeming to float over the restless shingle, the cloak widening until it filled half of the horizon.

"I thought I could play you at chess," Ryan said, gesturing toward the board that stood open on a large flat stone in front of him.

A spark of interest lit the deep-set eyes beneath the hood. "How did you know I played chess?"

"Seen the movie."

"Ah, yes. The weary knight. That was so very long ago, Ryan Cawdor."

The one-eyed man arranged the pieces on the board, taking off a pair of pawns, concealing them behind his back, then offering them to the cloaked figure, who tapped the left hand and smiled at Ryan.

"Black. Appropriate, is it not?"

They began to play, accompanied by the ceaseless whispering of the waves on the beach.

"This is the place where ignorant armies clash by night," Death commented.

Ryan stared at the board, realizing with a shock of horror that he didn't know how to play the game. The pieces weren't familiar to him. Instead of knights, bishops, pawns and queens, there were dragons, monks and razors.

When he looked up from the board, the dark figure had gone. So had the beach.

Now he was standing in a ruined ville, with fireworks exploding in the distance in showers of cascading reds, yellows and blues. Ryan walked through a gaping doorway, finding himself in an open place, filled with lines of washing, endless rows of white sheets, making it impossible to see more than a few paces.

He could hear someone sobbing, panting, ragged breaths that flowed with pain.

"Hey, there," Ryan called softly, sensing that he was in a place of danger.

A hand came around the edge of one of the sheets, close by him, pressing it against the body of whoever was hiding behind it. Immediately there was a spreading patch of dark blood, black against the starched white of the sheet.

A face, young, with curly hair, wearing heavily tinted glasses, peered at Ryan.

"Can I help you? Looks like you stopped one there."

The handsome youth didn't answer, but staggered away from Ryan, through another gate on the far side of the area. He stumbled and fell into what looked to Ryan like the biggest garbage heap in the world.

The youth held both hands clasped to his stomach, where Ryan could see a hideous gash had opened him up. Loops of intestines, gray and yellow, streaked with pink, were tumbling from the wound, trailing in the fly-covered filth.

It was a most dreadful way to die.

Ryan had closed his eye for a moment, not wanting to watch the agonized death throes.

As he opened it again, the world had changed.

The garbage heap had vanished.

Now he was riding alone in the back of a filthy cart, his hands tied tightly behind his back, wearing some triple-weird old-time clothes with a brocade frock coat and stained lace at his throat and cuffs.

A spavined nag pulled the cart over uneven cobbles, through a jeering crowd that cursed and spit at him. They heaved rotting vegetables at him, calling him an aristo and screaming that he would soon be kissing Madame.

Most of the scruffy men and women wore ragged clothes, and all sported ribbons or caps of red, white and blue. Ryan couldn't understand where he was. Or when he was. The lath-and-plaster houses that lined the narrow street were packed close together, with mullioned windows, half-timbered fronts and thatched roofs. Beneath the iron-bound wheels of the cart bubbled a noisesome open sewer.

The stench of the foul air was almost too much for Ryan, and he gagged, trying to breathe through his mouth to minimize the smell.

Now he could hear a different noise above the bedlam of the hostile mob. There was a pattern to it, repeated again and again, louder as the car drew nearer to the center of the action.

It was a drumroll, then a voice calling out what sounded like a name. A howl of derision rose from the crowd, then came the strangest noise of all—a high whistling like a sword slicing through the air, then a dull thump, like a huge butcher's cleaver striking squarely at a carcass.

Another loud cheer erupted, then the whole thing was repeated over and over.

The mob grew thicker and noisier as the cart pressed on, the man leading the horse having to strike out with a short whip to keep them back. The flavor of a lynching lay heavy in the bright sunlight.

Ryan tested the cords, but they'd been tied by someone who knew his business. They had been pulled so tight that he could feel blood trickling from around his fingernails.

The street turned a sharp dogleg corner, and Ryan could see what was waiting for him.

Suddenly he was out of the cart, being pushed up a short flight of steep stairs, standing on a wooden platform that was awash with blood and urine. Below it was a pile of straw sodden with more dark blood.

An old woman had been sitting on the steps, her hair and clothes splattered with crimson, calmly knitting. "May ye rot in Hell, citizen aristo," she hissed at him.

There was the rattle of the drum, and the name of a marquis was called out. The great steel blade was hauled to the top of the guillotine by a team of four men, its angled edge dripping scarlet.

The press of people on the platform prevented Ryan from seeing what was happening, but he saw the blade drop and heard the thunk of the impact and the cheer from the huge, swaying crowd at the gout of blood that sprayed into the sunshine.

"You're next, citizen," muttered an old man in a stained frock coat and cracked knee boots, pushing at him with an ebony stick with a silver lion's-head hilt. "All over soon. By the Three Kennedys, it will."

Ryan recognized the voice and tried to turn, but he was gripped firmly by the elbows and marched to the foot of the guillotine.

His feet slipped in the blood, and he nearly fell.

There was a long, broad plank, with a semicircular notch roughly cut in one end, the whole thing soaked in blood. It was tilted toward him for ease of handling, and he felt himself lifted bodily and slid along, the sticky liquid cold and clammy against his skin. Another piece of wood was clamped over the back of his head, holding him still.

"For treason against the body and heart of France and for dealings counter to the righteous ideal of the revolution, sentence of death is hereby pronounced against the person of the duke of Glamis, marquis of Cawdor."

"Who should have been king hereafter," whispered the old man with the ebony cane.

The drum was beating, very fast and high, like a staccato heartbeat.

The cheering that had greeted the announcement of Ryan's name was hushed, dying away into a great, sighing stillness that filled the square of the town.

The rope creaked as the ponderous blade was hauled to the top of the execution machine.

"This is a cruel and unnatural punishment under the constitution," Ryan said, but a cloth gag had been thrust into his mouth and he nearly choked on his own words. All of his senses were swamped with the sensation of blood, soaking into his clothes, reeking in the warm air.

If Krysty and the others were going to rush to his rescue, then they were cutting it close.

"Hangman, hangman, slacken the noose," Ryan whispered to himself.

There came a snapped command and the strange whistling noise that had puzzled him earlier, followed by that same sickening thud as the blade severed his head. His dimming eye took a close-up picture of bloodied straw into eternal darkness.

Chapter Four

Coming around from any jump was unpleasant.

For each of the six friends, this particular interrupted jump.had been the worst.

Doc was twitching like someone suffering from an ague, blood trickling from his nose and from both ears, matting in his silver hair.

Jak had been violently sick. The pool of vomit had congealed at his side and streaked his shining white hair. His nails had dug so hard into his ivory palms that they had also drawn half moons of dark blood.

Krysty had been crying, gobbets of tears streaking her pale cheeks. She had bitten the end of her tongue, and blood smeared her chin. As she started to recover consciousness, she was shuddering violently.

Mildred was trembling, the beads in her plaited hair rattling on the armaglass floor of the gateway chamber. Her hands were pressed between her thighs, and she was huddled in the fetal position.

At her side J.B. was on his way back from the blackness. His eyelids were moving rapidly as though he were dreaming, and his fingers kept clenching and opening, as though they were trying to grasp the butt of a blaster. Like Doc, he had suffered from a bleeding nose. The blood trickled down his face, onto the floor, where it was already beginning to clot.

Ryan was the first to manage to open an eye, promptly closing it again as a tidal wave of sickness swept up from his stomach. He clamped his mouth shut and swallowed hard, tasting the iron of blood on his tongue.

He had a pounding headache, and his good eye felt as if someone were holding a red hot dagger behind it, trying to push it from its socket.

The air felt neutral, flat and stale, which generally meant that they were in a redoubt that was still sealed from the days of skydark.

Ryan risked another brief glance, checking the color of the armaglass walls of the six-sided chamber. Back in Japan they had been a vivid orange.

"Purple," he whispered to himself. "Deep purple."

It meant that they'd made the jump safely, even though it had taken a toll on everyone's health.

"Fireblast!" The agony seemed to be slowly abating from his head.

Ryan coughed, feeling the bitterness of bile rising in his gorge. He cleared his throat and spit on the floor in the corner of the gateway, seeing the phlegm was flecked with blood.

He finally felt able to look around to see how the others were doing. It looked as though everyone had either been bleeding or had been sick.

Or both.

J.B. was closest to coming around, his eyes blinking open, showing only the whites. His hands were gently touching his face, as though he were trying to find some unguessable wound.

Doc had rolled on his back and was snoring like a blast furnace.

The others were still deeply unconscious.

Ryan was relieved that his young son, Dean, hadn't been with them. The boy had often suffered from previous jumps.

He wondered how Dean was getting on in the boarding school up in the high country of Colorado. Nick Brody, owner of the school, had seemed a good and honest enough person, and the place's reputation was sound.

Ryan had promised that he would visit the boy when it was possible, though Dean had lived long enough and hard enough in Deathlands to know that it might be quite some time before such a visit was practical.

"Dark night! Been rolled and tolled like a bell. Now I'm feeling just like Hell."

"Good day, John Dix," Ryan said. "Sounds like you feel about as well as you look."

"If I look as well as you look, Ryan, then I'm looking twice as well as I feel."

Krysty's voice was as weak as a newborn kitten's. "Gaia! I can tell you that I feel twice as bad as both of you put together. That was a mean mother of a jump."

In the corner Jak struggled to his knees and then puked again, bringing up a watery, yellow grue, shaking his head and moaning. "Anyone get number of wag?" he asked. "Or was it mule kicked me in balls?"

Ryan had managed to drag himself onto his feet, fighting a wave of vertigo that threatened to send him back to his hands and knees. He closed his eye again and took several long, slow breaths. "If there's any day-old rabbits looking to kick my ass, tell them from me that I surrender right now."

Krysty was sitting now, running her fingers through the tight coils of her bright red hair. "Think that Doc and Mildred are all right?"

The black woman answered for herself, without opening her eyes. "Don't know about that stringy old buzzard, but I think I'm still the right side of the dark river." She paused. "Though the way I feel, I might prefer it if I was dead and free from suffering. That was just about the worst jump I've known."

"Must've been because of the quake just as we started the matter transfer," J.B. said, carefully removing his glasses from his pocket and wiping them before placing them back on his narrow nose.

Doc groaned, sounding like a man in the last stages of some fearsome terminal disease. He wiped his hand across his face, peering myopically at the smear of blood.

"By the Three Kennedys! Holy Mary, pray for me now, sinner that I am."

"Too late for repentance, Doc," Mildred said, sitting up and pressing her hands together.

"Not too late for penalties, though, madam. I fear that I must be the most wicked of sinners. The punishments of Damien are as nothing compared to what I am suffering. All that happened to him was that he had all the joints of his body cut through and hot lead poured into them while he was being ripped apart by a team of horses. A mere bagatelle to the agonies that I am barely managing to endure here."

On the opposite side of the chamber, Jak was noisily sick again.

"I had a horrible dream," Krysty said. "Makes a bad jump worse."

"Me too, lover," Ryan agreed.

There was a general nodding and muttering of agreement about the nightmares, though nobody was prepared to tell the others what his or her own particular horror had been.

"Think we've landed in Tennessee?" J.B. asked, replacing the fedora and brushing down his thinning hair.

"Didn't catch the Japanese out in any lies over stuff like that." Ryan sniffed. "Air feels right for an old redoubt." He looked at the others. "Be nice if we found a place where we could all clean up some."

"I'll second that," Mildred said, leaning on the purple wall of the chamber.

Behind her, Jak was throwing up again.

"REMEMBER, WE'RE ON RED, everyone," Ryan cautioned, easing open the heavy, opaque, armaglass door of the mat-trans unit, hearing the lock click.

They stepped out of the chamber, everyone holding a blaster cocked and ready, and faced a small anteroom. There was no door on their side of it, and the frame was scarred and chipped, with splinters of wood hanging off.

"Looks like there was violence," Krysty observed.

"Bullet holes," Jak said, pointing with his Python at pockmarks in the far wall.

"Semiautomatic, 9 mm," the Armorer stated. "Way I read it so far, it seems like there was a firefight down here, likely in the last day or so of the nukecaust."

"Last hours," Ryan suggested. "Minutes?"

"Hours. Door's missing, so there was time for someone to do some tidying."

"Something written there," Mildred said, indicating a neat line of graffiti in the otherwise empty room.

"'James Burton will live forever,'" read Krysty. "One of the soldiers here?"

Mildred shook her head. "No. One of the greats of rock and roll. Lead-guitar man who played with Elvis and Ricky Nelson and all the best. Nice to see someone appreciated him."

"They signed their graffiti," Ryan said. "Someone called Rog wrote it."

"Must've been a rock-and-roll man." Mildred smiled at the thought. "They always used to say that rock and roll would never die."

THERE WERE MORE SIGNS in the control room of a violent skirmish. More bullet holes had been stitched along one wall, running up into the sloping ceiling, taking out two strips of neon lighting and one of the probing sec cameras. There was also an ancient stain, showing almost black on the pale cream floor, that looked remarkably like old blood.

"Couple of the consoles been blasted from here to perdition," Doc observed, leaning on the corner of a desk to steady himself.

Ryan looked around the room. "Rest are all working fine by the look of it."

"No bodies," Krysty said. "Shows there was time to do some cleaning after the shooting."

"Doesn't seem to have affected any of the main controls." Ryan glanced at Doc. "Any idea what those two comp consoles would have done?"

"The broken ones?"

"Yeah?"

The old man walked and looked at them, his head to one side. "I believe that the one on the left was an Awac Subcomm 14. The other one was an Andromeda Suff 84."

Ryan waited for a further explanation. "Yeah? So, what did they do? What aspects of the mat-trans unit did they work? That's what matters."

Doc sighed. "I fear that it would take greater wisdom than I possess to answer that, old friend. All I can do is tell you what they were called."

"How do you know that?" Mildred asked. "I'm grudgingly impressed at your memory, Doc."

"Ah, well, I cannot truthfully take the credit for that. There are neat little labels attached to the desks in front of each of the comp screens."

"READY?"

Ryan knelt on the cold stone floor, up against the massive sec door that sealed off the mat-trans section from the rest of what he assumed would be another redoubt. Jak, still looking a whiter shade of pale, was standing by to operate the green handle that controlled the raising and lowering of the door, waiting for the word.

"Take her up six."

Jak eased the lever upward, and they all heard the familiar noise of hydraulic gears operating behind the thick, reinforced walls.

After a moment's hesitation the door began to move slowly upward.

"Stop," Ryan ordered, flattening himself and squinting out to check for any obvious sign of danger.

All he could see was the most familiar of redoubt sights—an expanse of bare corridor, curving away to the left and right, brightly lit.

"Up another six inches. Hold it."

Now Ryan could see farther in both directions. He breathed in, tasting the air, savoring the flatness and dull quality that normally indicated that the military complex hadn't been broken into over the century since skydark.

All of the redoubts had been powered with the finest examples of twentieth-century American scientific knowledge, nuclear power plants that were designed to be self-maintaining, controlling every aspect of the redoubts: temperature, humidity and air quality; filtering, cleaning and recycling automatically for close to a hundred years without a mortal hand being laid on the controls.

If there was any problem, then there were automatic cutouts and bypass arrangements so that the whole complex would carry on running at a minimally low level, ticking over, waiting for the humans to return once the nuclear threat was done and passed.

But the nuclear threat had destroyed the world. The events of skydark killed all but a tiny handful of the planet's population, irrevocably shattering science and industry forever and a day. The long winters set the country back to its Deathlands status, similar in some ways to the dark times of the Middle Ages in Europe, with a number of larger and smaller villes, some of them ruled by their own barons.

So the humans never returned.

But the redoubts continued.

Some—it would never be known how many—had been destroyed by the first strike, wiped away at ground zero. But a surprising number had survived, relatively unscarred.

"Take it all the way up," ordered Ryan, rising to his feet, still gripping the SIG-Sauer.

The gears hissed and whirred, and the huge sec-steel door rose ponderously to vanish into the ceiling of the control room, halting with a slight grating jar.

"Feel anything, lover?" he asked Krysty, who stood at his elbow.

She shook her head. "Just a great age of nothing. Can't sense any kind of life reading."

"Good."

"But there's always the possibility of my power being thrown off by all the steel and lead shielding in these places. Bear that in mind, lover."

"Sure."

The passage beyond the open door gaped smooth and silent. As in most redoubts, the ceiling was curved, with recessed lighting and a number of tiny sec cameras fixed at the junction of concrete wall and ceiling, ceaselessly roaming, a glowing red light showing when they were actually transmitting pictures back to some long-abandoned central control area of the complex.

"We going out?" Jak asked.

"Sure. Skirmish line, and everyone keep it on condition triple-red."

Chapter Five

Ryan led the way toward the left, though experience in many other redoubts made him guess what he might find. Almost universally the passage to the left of the entrance to the mat-trans unit ended in a blank wall, as though the original, long-dead builders had deliberately made the gateway in the deepest, most secure part of the complex, as far away from the surface and potential danger as possible.

Above the sec door was a notice that he'd seen before in a variety of forms: Entry To This High-Security Section Of The Redoubt Is Absolutely Forbidden To All Personnel Below The Security Clearing Of B12.

The corridor wound gently, ending after about a hundred yards in a blank, unfinished wall of raw rock. The stone crystals glittered brightly in the stark overhead lighting.

"Like gold," Jak said.

"More like the gold of fools, son," Doc stated. "Iron pyrites, unless I miss my guess."

"No point standing looking at it," Ryan said. "About-face and let's move on out."

IT WAS A BIG REDOUBT, nothing like some of the smaller, concealed buildings that they'd come across in their travels. This one was seriously substantial. You could sense it, even if you didn't have any special mutie powers.

"Feels like being buried at the bottom of the deepest mine shaft in the world," J.B. commented, his voice falling flatly into the endless space of the wide corridor.

"We must be careful not to risk a mine-shaft gap, *mein* President," Mildred said, laughing. She looked at the others, grinning at their puzzled faces. "I haven't gone crazy. Sort of a quote from a movie. *Doctor Strangelove.* Had a long subtitle. 'How I stopped worrying and learned to love the bomb.' Think that was it. Never thought about that until now. Amazingly prophetic movie. Kind of a black comedy."

"Never heard of it," Ryan said, shaking his head. "Didn't survive skydark."

The woman nodded. "I somehow think that the director might have liked that irony."

They moved toward the right, the corridor winding in a big circle, rising slightly as it went upward.

"Like being inside the shell of a huge snail," Krysty commented. "Going to get dizzy if this goes on much farther."

They passed a number of side passages, but all were blocked off by immovable sec doors. Each had a digital panel at the side, but the letter and number codes had vanished in the nuke haze of a century earlier.

Each time they came to one of the green painted doors, Jak wandered over and punched the keys at random, shaking his mane of stark white hair in disappointment.

Doc laughed. "I would hazard a guess that the odds against your stumbling on the right combination to open any of the doors is something in the order of... Let me see." He closed his pale blue eyes as he did the calculation. "Six to one. No, that cannot be correct. Of course. I had forgotten that the decimal point should..." He tapped the twin barrels of the massive Le Mat on the side of his head. "One hundred and eight million, six hundred and forty thousand to one. Very roughly. To the nearest ten thousand or so. Somewhere in that vicinity. Approximately. More or less. A rough estimate, of course. Rather a—"

Ryan held up the SIG-Sauer to silence him. "Yeah, we got the picture, Doc."

"LOOKS CLEAR THAT THERE'S a single access down to the gateway part of the redoubt," the Armorer said after they'd been walking and climbing for close to half an hour. "Covered between two and three miles already."

Ryan nodded. He'd lost count of the side turns that had been locked and barred from them. There were discolored rectangular patches on the concrete walls where signs had been ripped down. They would probably have given them clues as to what the other sections of the complex had been.

Though, since access was impossible, it didn't make a whole lot of difference.

The worry was that they would eventually reach an end to the wide passage, an end that was staked off like a fox's den, giving them no choice but to return all the way to the gateway and try a jump out again.

"Is it my imagination, or is the air a tad fresher?" Ryan stopped and sniffed again.

After a few minutes of walking they'd dropped right down from triple-red to orange, which meant you could holster your blaster if you wanted, but you still kept well alert. It also meant that they'd stopped walking the extended skirmish line with Ryan at point and J.B. as rearguard.

"Could mean we're nearing the top. Close to the exit," J.B. guessed.

Ryan nodded. "Might be that. If the nuke power is drawing in any clean air from outside, it would be most obvious up here."

Doc leaned a hand against the wall, picking at the crusted blood around his nose and mouth. "I had rather hoped that there might be ablution facilities somewhere close by. A wash and brushup would be most welcome."

"Yeah. I stink of puke," Jak said sourly.

"Wash'd do us all good after that horrific jump." Mildred sniffed cautiously at herself. "Yeah. Can't say my armpits are charmpits."

They moved on.

THE EARTH WAS BARRED.

They stood in a huddle, dejected and downcast, looking at the single sec door that filled the end of the passage from side to side. It fitted flush all the way around the flanks, coming down to settle on the concrete floor without enough of a gap for an ant to crawl through.

"That's it," Krysty said. "Gaia! I really don't want to face another jump just yet."

"Nothing else to do." Ryan bit his lip, feeling a surge of anger. "Fireblast! Even if we could have gotten through to find somewhere to clean up, with drinking water and mebbe beds for a night, then I'd have felt ready to jump again. But this..." He glared at the blank wall of vanadium steel.

"I'll just punch in code and open door," Jak said, walking across with the lithe grace of the trained acrobat, light on the balls of his feet.

"Sure, and we'll just sit here and wait for three thousand years while you try all the possible combinations," Mildred said wearily.

The albino stood very close to the wall, peering short-sightedly from his pink eyes.

"What in the name of perdition is the young Ganymede doing?" Doc asked. "Does he seek the Holy Grail? The key to Rebecca? The Rosetta stone? The riddle of the Sphinx? The mystery of Kaspar Hauser?"

Ryan laughed, the sound startling and loud in the muffled stillness of the passage. "No. I know what it is he's looking for."

"Found it," Jak called. "Need some way blackening it." He smeared his hand over the film of dust on the sole of his combat boot, spitting in it and rubbing it into a gray paste. Carefully he wiped it on the wall beneath the code pad.

"You saw that they'd done this on other doors, didn't you?" Ryan called.

"Yeah. But scratched out. Guessed might leave main-door code. People always forget it. Seen that in other redoubts." He stared at the tiny incised markings, standing out dark against the cream concrete of the wall.

The others gathered around.

"Looks like a six, then two and nine," Ryan said, "followed by two letters. An *N* and a *W*, then another two and an eight to finish."

"Nine," Krysty said. "The last number is a nine not an eight, Ryan."

"Sure?"

"Sure."

The others agreed.

Krysty rattled it off. "Six, two, nine, *N, W,* two, nine. Well done, Jak."

"Enter it in, Jak," Ryan said. "Everyone back onto triple-red. Keep alert."

"I can't feel anyone near, lover."

He grinned at her. "Probably right, Krysty. Trader used to say that a man who rests his life on a *probably* doesn't get to be much older."

They stood off in a circle while the teenager took up his position by the control panel.

There didn't seem to be any manual override on the sec door, so it wasn't going to be possible to stop it after a few inches. It was all-or-nothing.

The buttons clicked in smoothly, and after a couple of seconds' hesitation, the green door began to rise ponderously into the air, leaving a film of fine dust hanging below it, finally settling silently into the recessed ceiling.

"Nothing," Ryan said.

There was a similar corridor beyond the door, but it was slightly less wide, and one or two of the ceiling lights had malfunctioned.

"Air's better," Mildred said, holstering her revolver.

"Reckon we could be close to ground level," Ryan guessed. "Passage is level."

"Plan over there that they haven't taken down," J.B. said, slinging the Uzi over his shoulder and balancing the scattergun on his other shoulder.

"Only shows this level." Krysty was trying to make sense out of the pattern of colored rectangles and circles on the schematic map, looking at the fluorescent yellow arrow with the words You Are Here.

"There appears to be some residential accommodation with washing-and-sleeping facilities," Doc said. "If they didn't strip it during the evacuation of the place."

"Sometimes they leave one small section for the final platoon or whatever was working here on the last cleansing." Ryan looked around. "That's up to the left."

"What was this?" The Armorer was stooped over the key, trying to read a small rectangle of white paper that had been stuck over one of the adjacent sections. "Says 'ART.' What does that stand for? Anyone come across it before?"

"Armament Retraining?" Krysty offered.

"Arizona Rangers' Tercentenary?" J.B. suggested.

"American Research and Technology?" Doc guessed.

"Must be something military." Ryan considered the acronym. "And it looks like it's something that they only came up with at the last moment. Stuck it on. Some kind of evacuation section." He shook his head. "No. Can't even guess."

"We can go look." Jak had holstered his blaster. "Can't we?"

"Sure. But that part with bathing facilities sounds like a number-one target for us. To the left and up a couple of levels. Hope there's no more locked sec doors."

RYAN FOUND HIS HOPE was fulfilled.

It was as if the big sec barrier had been a last resort, sealing off the lower part of the redoubt from above, locking it away for all time.

Before they moved on, J.B. took a stub of pencil from one of his capacious pockets and scrawled the code number of the door onto the wall by the control panel, ready if they needed it when they left the region.

Now there were more signs of human life, evidence of a hasty departure.

In a controlled and unchanging environment, the detritus of the evacuation had remained untouched. Soda cans lay crumpled in corners with gum wrappers. Wads of tissues were stained black with what could have been clotted blood, or might have been teriyaki sauce. After a hundred years there wasn't much way of knowing.

Clothes were piled everywhere, pants and shirts in olive green, some with badges of rank still shining dully on them.

"Looks like the end came fast." Ryan stirred a mound of scarlet berets that lay in a corner of one of the corridors.

"Wonder if they left any weapons." J.B. muttered to himself.

But Mildred heard him. "Damned if you don't have a one-track mind, John. "How about finding some worthwhile relics of the past? Books or movies or records. Pile of personal letters. Newspapers. Better than blasters."

"Depends on what you want them for. Book isn't much use against a gang of screaming stickies."

Doc coughed. "I once believed that the pen was mightier than the sword. Until I attempted to fight a duel with a feathery quill pen against a sturdy piratical cutlass. I must here admit that I was most damnably fortunate to escape with my life from that incident."

Everyone laughed, lightening the heavy, melancholy atmosphere of the redoubt.

"Let's head for the rest-and-washing section of the redoubt," Ryan said.

Now the corridors were more narrow, and a lot of the lights had gone out. A network of fine cracks ran along some of the walls and the ceiling, with deeper crevices here and there, looking like quake damage or possibly ancient nuke tremors.

Someone had painted a crude hammer and sickle on one of the locked doors to the right, with the warning Reds Out! You Want The Gain, Then Take The Pain.

"There was talk of invasion well before the actual time of skydark," Mildred said. "Rumors of millions of Russians and Chinese pouring across the Bering Strait into Alaska, marching down through San Francisco."

J.B. stopped a moment to adjust his weaponry, easing the straps. "Surprises me that we don't come across more boobies in these places. Way the world had war terror and total paranoia about the Russians beating us... When they left the redoubts, they must have had a genuine fear that the russkies would come strutting in and take them over." He pushed back his fedora. "Be easy enough to set some triggers."

"Guess they were frightened that any sort of booby trap might take out their own men once they came back after the war," Mildred commented.

"After the war," Doc said wonderingly. "Après la guerre. Where are the snows of yesteryear? Gone to graveyards every one. After the war, madam? Yes, verily I believe that was once what decent people hoped for. It would have been a brave land fit for heroes. Fit for muties and the rad sick. After the brief war was over, there was precious little left. Spoils to the victor. A spoiled world to the victor."

He had moved ahead as he spoke, his knees creaking softly, down a side corridor that the map had showed would soon lead them to the sleeping-and-washing quarters of the complex. A whole row of lights had gone down, and a stretch of forty or fifty paces was in total darkness.

Ryan was staring at the ceiling as the old man vanished into the blackness. "Funny," he said quietly.

"Back there the ceiling lights had simply gone out. Here they've been broken. The glass covers smashed. Deliberately broken. Now, why would anyone have done that?"

The answer came to him like a bolt of lightning from a clear summer sky.

"Doc!" He started after the vanished figure. "Don't move! Don't—"

But the cry of shock and pain told him that his warning had come too late.

Chapter Six

As Doc strode away, much of his mind was preoccupied with the thought of having some good hot water to luxuriate in and the possibility of a night's rest in a decent bed. Though his memory was erratic, he remembered all too vividly a redoubt, not all that long ago, when the comfort of hot water had been overlaid with instant horror.

Another part of his mind was flirting with a recollection of his dear wife, Emily. They had visited some caves down in the desert Southwest, with dark passages and the smell of dank air. The corridor with its broken lights brought back something of that time—his wife's small hand in his, and himself glimpsing out of the corner of his eye, the cameo locket she often wore around her throat as they stepped cautiously over the sandstone floor.

And another bit of his brain was considering what John Barrymore Dix had just been saying about the possibility of booby traps. How odd it was that they rarely encountered them in evacuated redoubts.

"Odd indeed," he mumbled as he stepped along in the gloom.

He felt the taut wire brush against his knees and

knew instantly what it was and reacted with, for him, astounding speed.

Doc dived sideways and down, hands stretched to break his fall, letting go of the ebony swordstick so that it clattered on the cold stone floor. As he went down, Doc was aware of a whispering noise just above his head and he felt something tug lightly at his silvery hair as it sliced by.

He landed awkwardly on his knees, yelling out in shock and pain, hearing Ryan's voice from behind him as he called out an urgent warning.

"Rather too little and rather too late, my dear old companion," he tried to say. But something seemed to have happened to his normally rich, deep voice, forcing it up a couple of squeaking octaves so he sounded like a rather irritable bat. So Doc contented himself with lying still on the concrete until his senses returned.

He could hear the others, shouting to him and to one another in a hubbub of confused noise, until Ryan's voice rose above the others, calling for silence.

"Doc?"

"Yes." He cleared his throat and tried again. "Yes, Ryan, my dear fellow. I am here."

"Stay dead still, Doc. Don't try and move at all until we know what the fuck's happened."

"I believe that John Barrymore's supposition has come true. I touched a wire and then, as I dived for safety, something swung by above my head."

"What?"

"I have no idea, my dear friend. But it felt like the pendulum in Mr. Poe's enchanting Gothic tale. Missed me by somewhat less than a whisker.'' He put his hand up and touched a loose hank of hair and a warm wetness that had to be blood. ''Indeed, it actually has scratched me but I am well enough.'' Still he felt very much like rolling on his hands and knees to be sick. His breath fluttered in his chest, and he could feel himself trembling from shock.

''Just stay still. I've got a self-light. I'll come slow and easy to try and find out what happened.''

''Be careful,'' Doc whispered.

He heard Krysty's voice, echoing his own warning to her lover.

''Be fine,'' Ryan said reassuringly. ''Rest of you stay back here.''

Doc found that his eyes were quickly becoming accustomed to the dark around him and he could see Ryan and the others silhouetted against the overhead lights farther back down the corridor.

He turned his head and stared directly above him, toward the invisible ceiling. He screwed up his eyes, calling to Ryan. ''I believe I can see the trap. My jest about the pendulum now seems less droll. There is some sort of ax suspended from wires that I triggered as I walked by.''

''Think I can see it, Doc. Wait a . . . There, that's better.'' He heard a scratching sound and saw the flare of gold from a self-light held in the one-eyed man's right hand.

''By the Three Kennedys!'' The tiny match gave enough light for Doc to be able to see clearly what hung above him, still swinging silently to and fro.

It was a large ax-blade, with a half-dozen needle-sharp bayonets strapped to it for extra weight and malice, strung onto a narrow leather strap that was fixed to a ringbolt in the ceiling. A thin length of wire glittered down the wall to where Doc had broken it as he walked past.

"I see it, Doc. Reckon it's safe enough for you to get up. Keep clear of the edge."

"A very sword of Damocles," Doc said, standing and steadying himself for a moment with a hand on the rough concrete wall. He stooped again to pick up his fallen swordstick, feeling oddly wobbly and dizzy.

"You all right, Doc? Got a little blood coming down the side of your head, above your left ear."

"A mere nick, Ryan." The self-light went out, and they were in darkness again. "A nick in time saved nine, as my dear old mother used to say."

THERE DIDN'T SEEM to be any further malevolent booby traps left behind by the fleeing occupants of the redoubt, but everyone moved more slowly and with more care.

The sec door into the section for living accommodations stood open.

"That bit with label for ART is close to us," Jak said. "Could go find out what is."

"Alternate Reality Technology," Mildred guessed.

"Hey, that sounds possible." Krysty glanced at Ryan. "What do you reckon, lover?"

"I think we put first things into first place. Let's sort out what we've got here."

It was a typical layout that they'd come across several times before, only on a slightly larger scale than usual.

There was a number of linked dormitories, each holding either six or twelve beds, each bed with its own plastic-covered mattress and pile of blankets. The material had become frail with age, but the temperature inside the complex was a steady sixty-eight degrees, so warmth wasn't a problem.

There were no external windows in any of the rooms, though the map had shown that they were now close to the surface levels.

This section was cleaner than some of the other passages had been, with no litter or discarded clothes.

"Bathrooms are here," Jak called.

The others followed him across a corridor into the vast washing facilities. They were divided into male and female, and both had toilet cubicles, as well as showers and bathtubs. There was also a long row in each bathroom of immaculate washers and dryers.

"Soap?" Mildred asked.

"There." Krysty pointed to an open-fronted set of shelves that carried sealed packs of hand soap, detergents, shampoos and gels.

"But is there any hot water?" Ryan answered his own question, walking to the nearest shower stall and turning the chrome handle from blue to red, from off to on.

"I fear that we are doomed to suffer a drought," Doc said as nothing happened. "If only I could recall the precise wording and steps of the Hopi rain dance that I was once privileged to learn. But that was in another country...."

There was a faint hissing sound, and Ryan took a few cautious steps backward.

The hissing stopped, and a few drops of sticky, rusty liquid seeped from the shower head.

"We're going to get real clean with that," Mildred said, shaking her head.

"Hasn't finished." Krysty stood closer, listening intently. "I can hear something."

The hissing resumed, accompanied by a metallic clunking sound, and water gushed from the shower. Ryan put his hand under it, wincing at the chill.

"Take it a little time to warm up after all these years," he commented.

But within moments there was a visible steam, wreathing from the faucet and condensing on the white tiles.

Doc beamed, showing his unusually excellent set of white teeth. "Upon my soul! I had never thought that hot water could have seemed so welcome. Manna from heaven does not get within a country mile of it."

Ryan turned the handle again, and the flood slowed to a trickle.

"I'll go close that sec door," he said. "Make sure we're secure. Mebbe I'll wait while you all have your baths and showers. Just in case."

"I'll take a bath-check too, lover," Krysty said. "That way we can all relax."

IT TOOK THE BETTER PART of an hour for J.B., Doc, Jak and Mildred to finish bathing themselves, then wash and dry their filthy, stained clothes.

Ryan and Krysty used the time to get beds ready. Mildred and the Armorer shared one room, while Doc and Jak had a small dormitory. The one-eyed man and his lover pushed two single beds together for themselves.

The air was filled with the scent of the soaps, carried on waves of warm steam, which triggered the air-conditioning into humming action.

"Looking forward to our turn with the baths, lover?" Krysty asked.

"Does a bear...? I just hope that they haven't taken all the hot water."

THEY HADN'T. He and Krysty took a bath together in the men's section, Krysty having slipped the sec bolt across to make sure they didn't get interrupted.

"Going to be that sort of a bath, lover?" Ryan grinned, sitting on the floor to kick off his combat boots.

"Long as you can rise to the occasion."

"Not normally a problem."

"Sure you aren't getting too old for it?" She was already down to her bra and silken bikini panties, her red hair tumbling free over her shoulders.

"You'll be the first to know," he grunted, struggling to slide his trousers over a tent-pole erection.

"Looking good, lover," she said, stepping through the tendrils of steam to turn off the taps in the bathtub, checking it with a toe. "Just right."

Ryan stood and stretched, smiling down at her, admiring her breasts, the nipples already hardening with her ready excitement. Krysty was sitting in the water, which reached her armpits, the rippling surface disguising the fiery splash of color at the junction of her thighs.

"Bring something to wash with, lover," she said.

"Sure." He walked to the shelves. "There's all flavors. More like cocktails than soaps. Mango and black currant. Kiwi and peppermint. Passion fruit and mandarin. Ylang-ylang and marjoram. Contents of a herbalist."

"Anything," she said, watching Ryan as he stood on the far side of the bathroom. Krysty felt a surge of love for the tall, lean figure, seeing again the countless scars that seamed his body, puckering the flesh across his chest and the small of his back. Knife and bullet. Once, in the early days of their relationship, Krysty had asked Ryan to tell her how he'd received all the wounds.

He'd shrugged. "Not enough time, and most of them I don't recall," had been his reply. "Things way past, not worth the forgetting."

His curly black hair was flattened by the damp atmosphere, and she was struck by a sudden resemblance between Ryan and his absent son, Dean.

Ryan's right eye, a chillingly pale blue, stared at her. "Like what you see?" he said quietly.

"Always have done," she replied. "Now I'd like to feel it, as well."

"First we wash. Then . . ."

SOMEHOW THE WASHING TURNED fluidly and effortlessly into lovemaking.

The bath was so big that they could both stretch out in it, taking turns soaping each other, rubbing the warm oils into responsive flesh, luxuriating in the rare pleasure.

Krysty waited until Ryan was half lying, half sitting, then moved to straddle him, lowering herself on top. She reached with cupped fingers to take his strength and guide it inside her, moaning softly at the sensation.

"Good . . ." she sighed.

"Yeah . . ." Ryan lowered his head to kiss her on the side of her throat, tasting the delicate oils, touching the tip of his tongue to Krysty's ear. He reached out and clasped her face between his strong hands, brushing his lips against hers, closing his eye as she responded, her tongue probing between his parted lips.

Now she was rising and falling, sending small waves lapping across the bubble-filled bath.

Once he nearly slipped out as the pace grew faster, feeling himself sliding with the smooth oils, but she felt the danger and responded in time, trapping him safely deep inside her. "Close one, lover," she panted.

"Your fault."

"How's that?" she asked in mock outrage.

"You keep giving two ups to my one down."

They had made love so often that they could sense each other's responses. Ryan knew that Krysty's breathing suddenly slowed as she began to concentrate on the speeding orgasm, and he became quieter, focusing on their joint needs.

The rush was as good as ever, leaving them both drained, clinging to each other, nuzzling while their pulses returned to normal.

"Nice," she whispered.

"Better than nice."

"How much better?"

He held his hands wide apart. "Least that much."

"Not that much?" She held her hands wider.

"Mebbe."

She reached under the floral-scented water and touched him, grinning at the instant response, holding her left hand in front of his face, finger and thumb a scant inch apart. "Feels like only that much, lover," she teased.

"Yeah, but I'm a growing boy."

THE PILED TOWELS had once been thick and fluffy, but time had taken its toll and what remained was thin and delicate, like antique lace, liable to disintegrate in your hands.

But there were enough of them to get Ryan and Krysty dry.

The washing machines did a fine job on their clothes, though Ryan contented himself with wiping the worst smears off his beloved coat.

In less than an hour both they and their garments were clean and crisp.

"All we got to do now is get some sleep," Ryan said, ducking his head to drink some cold water from the palms of his hands.

"And mebbe make some more love," she responded.

"No," Ryan said.

"Yes," Krysty stated, and eventually got her way.

Chapter Seven

Jak woke them next morning, knocking on the door. "Hungry. Go look food?"

Ryan squinted at his wrist chron. "Only six, Jak. Kind of early."

"Real hungry. Haven't eaten for whole day or more. Others are awake."

Ryan sat up. "All right, all right. Just give us a couple of minutes."

Krysty opened an emerald-bright eye. "Do this mean what I think it do?"

He laughed. "Yeah. It do."

THERE WAS NO FOOD in the redoubt.

At least there was nothing in the sections to which they had access. They could get into the kitchens that had prepared meals for the entire command of the fortress, probably two or three thousand strong at its height, but the kitchens were a melancholy fugue in dull, echoing chrome.

Row upon row of stoves, storage closets and garbage disposals stood silent and unused. Most were in amazingly good condition, with very little evidence of decay, looking as though they could be made operational again at a few minutes' notice if the call came.

"The call never came," J.B. said.

The main commissary section of the redoubt had also been stripped totally bare, emptiness wall to wall with scratches on the concrete where equipment had been moved.

"Soon as we get out of here we'd best get some hunting done. Or fishing." Ryan patted the walnut stock of the Steyr SSG-70 affectionately.

"Long as we don't walk out into some raging rad hot spot," Jak said.

"Think this is Tennessee?" Jak asked.

"No way of knowing." Ryan looked at the Armorer. "Any thoughts, J.B., on where we might be?"

The glasses glinted as he shook his head. "Jump code said Tennessee. Didn't say where. We've been around the state with Trader and the war wags."

Ryan grinned. "Good times and bad times, huh? There's some places around here where Trader's name's as fragrant as a straight-edge razor."

"Be good to see old Muddy again. Been awhile."

"I visited Memphis once," Mildred said. "Wanted to see Graceland."

"What's that?" Jak asked.

"Place where Elvis lived. And if you ask me who Elvis is, young Jak, then I shall be happy to kick you into the middle of next month."

"Some kinda singer?" the teenager asked innocently.

Mildred shook her fist at him. "Some kinda singer? Yeah, he was some kinda singer."

THEY HAD CHECKED OUT everywhere except the mysterious section labeled ART.

According to the master plan of the redoubt, this lay roughly between where they'd slept and the main entrance.

They were still coming up with fresh guesses as to the meaning of the letters.

Doc, not surprisingly, had gone way out on a limb with some of his more bizarre theories.

"A shrine dedicated to the goddess Artemis? Or some reference to a cult who tried to follow the spirit of King Arthur? Or, as we all obviously know, there was a son of Xerxes the First of Persia, whose name was Artaxerxes."

"I reckon it's short for Artillery," J.B. said. "Now, that would be something."

Ryan whistled softly between his teeth. "A whole segment of a redoubt dedicated just to artillery. Now, that would be something that most barons would give their right arms for. Never thought of that."

Krysty smiled at Mildred. "Want to leave the boys to play with their toys, honey?"

"Sure could do that, sweet thing. You and me can go down to the club and get in some serious dancing."

"I would not be averse to cutting a rug with a hot patootie myself," Doc said, twirling the ends of an imaginary mustache. "Big guns are not my idea of fun."

Ryan shrugged. "Fine, fine. Have your little jokes, friends. If it really is artillery, then we could mebbe make us some triple-serious jack out of it."

"Then let's go," Krysty said.

THE SEC DOOR HAD BEEN left shut on a manual override, like the entrance to the gateway units, a plain green lever that was lifted up to raise the door.

They found themselves in an open area, with three rooms opening off it.

"Entrance is along there," J.B. said, indicating the right-hand entrance.

"So the ART place must be through those two." Ryan had the SIG-Sauer unholstered.

There was a warning notice just inside the first doorway, explaining just what ART meant.

It wasn't artillery.

In fact it wasn't any of their guesses.

This section is closed to all personnel below B6 grading, and a special written pass is required at all times. No smoking and no food to be permitted in this section. Everything contained within this section is the property of the Tennessee Museum of Modern American Art and is not to be damaged, altered, moved or removed without proper cognitive authority.

"ART," Mildred said. "It means 'art.' Simple as that. Pictures and stuff."

J.B. tutted his disappointment. "Paintings! And I hoped for artillery."

DESPITE HIS REGRET, the Armorer was as enthusiastic as any of them once they entered the rooms and started to look at the pictures that hung there.

Each of the friends had his or her own particular favorites, but there was a general agreement that certain artists struck a common chord for all of them.

"Georgia O'Keefe," Krysty said. "The way she captures the light down in the Southwest is wonderful. And that early picture of the lights of old Newyork. Magical."

"She resided down in Abiquiu in New Mexico," Doc said. "Lived to a great age, but went blind toward the end of her life. Amazing, amazing woman. Look at the one called *Black Mesa*. Marvelous."

"I liked those sea pictures," Ryan commented. "Winslow Homer. Way he showed light on water. I've never ever seen real famous paintings like this. Thought they'd mostly been destroyed in the skydark times."

Doc was transfigured with ecstasy. "Happened in Europe during the big Second War. Hid treasures in mines and places like that. Good to see that someone here in Tennessee had enough sense to save these pictures. Miraculous."

Jak had paused a long time in front of a reproduction of a picture by Andrew Wyeth. "Named after my wife," he said. "Called *Christina's World*."

It showed a young disabled woman lying on a sloping field, staring away from the painter toward a group of buildings farther up the hill.

"Like a frozen moment," Mildred stated. "Bit like that other guy we all liked."

"Hoppy?" Ryan queried.

"Hopper. Edward Hopper." Mildred pulled at his sleeve to lead him back into the middle room, standing with him in front of a trio of Hopper pictures.

One showed a sunlit house with the draperies drawn across the second-floor windows. There was the feeling that someone was about to walk by or had just vanished from a window.

The second painting was of an office in a city, with a woman seated at a typewriter and another woman holding a mug of coffee, neither looking at the other.

The third Hopper featured an elderly man sitting in a canvas chair in the garden of a mansion overlooking a deep blue ocean. Once again there was that odd, timeless feeling of an event trapped forever in amber.

Single pictures had attracted each of them individually. Jak loved some capering little men in bright colors, but the label was missing from it; J.B. was taken by a print of an electric chair by Andy Warhol, though the others found it ghoulish; Krysty admired a geometric pattern by Frank Stella; and one of Mildred's favorites was of a stark industrial landscape, painted with great attention to detail by Charles Sheeler.

Doc was struck speechless by a magnificent Western painting by Frank Russell, depicting a man trapped on a ledge by a wounded cougar, high in the Sierras; Ryan was dazzled by the paintings, though they had obviously been hung in great haste, with no attempt to worry about alignment or lighting. One or two of the artists were people that he'd vaguely heard of, but he hadn't been prepared for the richness of color and texture. Even painters he didn't much care for had undeniable talent.

But his own personal favorite, which nobody else much cared for, was a gray picture of a misty sea with a bridge in the background, by John Sloan. It seemed to capture a feeling of isolation and loneliness that spoke directly to him.

"Shame we can't somehow take the pictures with us," Mildred said. "Still, just seeing them all like this has been truly fabulous."

"I had never imagined that such a collection of treasures still existed anywhere in this blighted Death-lands." Doc took a last look into the nearest room. "So rich."

J.B. cleared his throat. "Still would've preferred it to have been artillery. But the art was a good sur-prise."

"Hungry." Jak was surprised when the others laughed. "Am," he insisted. "Real hungry."

Ryan slapped the teenager on the shoulder. "You and me both, Jak."

"We going out the redoubt now?"

"Why not?"

THEY LEFT THE ART SECTION of the huge, rambling re-doubt behind them and moved toward the marked en-trance. Their route led them through an open set of double sec doors into a massive, vaulted hall, bigger than an aircraft hangar.

"Defensive positions all around here," J.B. ob-served. "Ready to repel the enemy."

Ryan nodded. "Only problem with that tactical planning was that all the enemy were dead, as well."

"What happened to all of the tens of millions of corpses?" Mildred asked. "I've always wondered that. Should be boneyards, shouldn't there?"

Doc answered her. "I also pondered that, madam. Indeed, I once was fortunate enough to visit the ruins at Mesa Verde and I asked the ranger on duty the same question. Where did all of the Anasazi bodies go?"

"And?"

"And, Dr. Wyeth, he pointed out that Nature is an excellent disposer of corpses. The weather combines with wild animals. It is close on one hundred years since the skies over the land of the free grew dark with nuclear warheads. Time enough for most bodies out in the open to have been absorbed back into the environment. Fortunately for all of us, mankind is intensely biodegradable."

THE MAIN DOORS to each redoubt had, up to then, shared a common three-digit code to open and close. Three, five and two was punched in to open the vanadium-steel door, then two, five and three to close it again.

This one was the same.

The code was printed on a white card, sealed in plastic under the control panel.

"Not all that secret, is it?" Ryan said. "Still, I suppose there were so many soldiers and whitecoats who needed to come in and out of all the redoubts, it was simpler to have the same entrance code for all of them."

"We using it?" Jak had moved to stand by the controls, his long white index finger poised over the buttons.

Ryan nodded. "Yeah. We're using it."

Chapter Eight

The air was fresh and clean with a hint of rain. The sky was overcast and dull, showing ten-tenths cloud cover, darkening toward the west. The door opened up on a dreary vista of what seemed like dozens of small lakes dotted with forested islands. There was no sign at all of human life.

J.B. had taken out his miniature sextant, using it to locate their position, checking with one of a number of tiny maps that he carried with him.

"Tennessee's right," he said. "Near as I can tell from this, we're close to the north of the state, but it looks like there's been some serious quake or fire damage up this way."

"Don't remember being around here with Trader," Ryan commented. "We went to Memphis a few times and we were going to that place with the country music."

"Nashville," Mildred said. "I was going to go there the time I wanted to visit Graceland, Elvis's home. I was real taken with country sounds. Willie and Waylon and Lyle and Dwight and Dolly and all. Wanted to go and see the Grand Ole Opry where they broadcast in the old days."

"Look at door," said Jak, who had lost interest in the conversation about predark times. Krysty had once pointed out this aspect of his character. It seemed as if the teenager wanted only to live in the present and the future. The past was an alien land to him.

They all turned away from the watery landscape and stared at the entrance to the redoubt, which was gaping like a gigantic maw.

"Looks like fire, sleet and candlelight," Doc said, runic as ever.

The metal frame was scarred and pitted, though it was made, like the door, of high-tempered vanadium steel. The concrete around the entrance was also scorched with the marks of some old fire that had broken chunks of it away, opening the stones to the elements.

"Skydark damage," Ryan commented, examining it more closely. "Must've been close to some serious nuking."

J.B. ran his fingers over the pocked concrete, shaking his head. "Amazing that the whole place didn't go. Look at the state of it." He stood back to try to take in the whole frontage of the redoubt. "Dark night, but it's well concealed. If you didn't know it was here, I reckon you could walk within a hundred yards and not spot what it was."

It was true.

The hillside above the hidden fortress was covered with trees, most of them looking about fifty or sixty years old. There was also the evidence of an earlier fire that had obviously raged with catastrophic force through the region, leaving a number of blackened, brittle corpses of pines to stand among the fresh, greener conifers.

"The whole land's changed a lot," J.B. said, peering at his map. "I think this was once close to what was called the Land between the Lakes and it was real near to the Tennessee River. But it wasn't like this then, with all these dozens of lakes and islands and stuff."

"Quakes?" Krysty suggested. "Not much of Deathlands is still like it was before skydark."

"Possible." Ryan felt an insect on his cheek and slapped at it before it could sting him. "Whatever it was changed the land. There's not much sign of anyone living here. No smoke. No buildings. Just a lot of nothing."

"Where do we go to get some food?" Mildred asked. "Don't see much wildlife, either."

"We'll find something," Ryan replied, sounding preoccupied. "Interesting that the redoubt hasn't been broken into. Specially as the entrance has been damaged."

"Still take a serious nuke to break it down." The Armorer sniffed. "Like I said. Probably can't see it unless you're on top of it. The trail that used to run from it vanished under water just down yonder."

They all looked to where he was pointing with the muzzle of the Uzi.

Ryan could follow the rough line of a two-lane blacktop road that sloped down from where they were standing, winding between a jagged bluff and a sheer drop, then disappearing under the limpid water of the nearest lake.

"Looks to me like this is an island."

Doc clenched his fist and placed it over his heart, as he did when he was about to declaim.

"No man is an island, dear friends. For we are all a part of a world of promontories, buttes, mesas, islets, archipelagoes and...and other geographical features far too numerous to mention here. Ask not for whom the bell tolls, my tried and trusted companions."

"Why not, Doc?"

"Why not what? What, what?"

Mildred tried again. "Why not ask you for whom the bell tolls? Doesn't it toll for thee?"

"For me?" asked Doc, looking increasingly harassed and puzzled.

"For thee," Mildred intoned solemnly.

Ryan kicked at some loose granite chippings, stained with yellow-green lichen. "When you two have finished your one-up brain games," he said, showing his irritation, "then we can all get moving and try and find something to eat."

THEY WALKED DOWN THE TRAIL in the dull midmorning light, winding between the trees. Ryan looked back once they'd gone a hundred paces and wasn't surprised to find that all trace of the huge, hidden redoubt had gone.

He had quietly checked the small rad counter that he wore in his lapel, finding that it was barely shaded out of the green toward the yellow, meaning that they were about as safe as they could be anywhere in Deathlands.

The labor that had gone into building the redoubt, and many others like it, was staggering, and the cost incalculable. All of them had been constructed in a hurry at the very end of the twentieth century, when the new cold war was raging with a particular threatening bitterness.

This one, built in a back-country area of rural Tennessee, was almost invisible. Much of it was below the surface of the land and, Ryan guessed, also below the levels of the surrounding lake, now blending perfectly into the much-changed landscape so that nobody had entered it for close to a hundred years.

"If it's an island, then how get off?" Jak asked, materializing at Ryan's elbow like a silver-haired ghost.

The one-eyed man had been wondering the same thing himself. Now he patted the teenager on the shoulder. "Like Trader used to say. There's always a way. Over, under, around or through. In this case it looks like it'll have to be over. Plenty of wood to make some kind of raft."

"You miss Trader?" the albino asked. "Lost track of how long since last saw him."

"Long enough and too long," Ryan replied, carefully stepping over a lightning-blasted branch that had fallen across the faint trail.

"Think he's still alive?"

Ryan thought back to the last glimpse of his old mentor and friend. Loyal little Abe was at his side, facing the forces of darkness, led by that swift and evil bastard, Straub. He could still see the man, with his shaved head and his silver-and-black hypnotic eyes.

"Heart says he's living. Brain tells me that he has to be chilled."

Jak shuddered and hunched his narrow shoulders. "Goose walked on grave," he said. "Thinking about Straub."

"Better not."

"He the worst?"

Ryan smiled at Jak's urgent, eager question. "The worst? You're asking someone who's lived all his time in Deathlands, much of it scraping scum off the wheel of life. Like asking someone what was the happiest moment of his life. Best meal he ever ate. Cleanest chilling."

"Straub worst of them?" Jak pressed. "Or was it Russkie? Was bad."

"Major-Commissar Gregori Zimyanin." Ryan sniffed. "Guess he would run Straub close as a powerful and dangerous man. But he wasn't somehow as wicked. Brutal and cruel. Not top-drawer evil like Straub."

Krysty had been walking close behind, listening to the conversation. "Cort Strasser?"

"Gets my unanimous vote for sicko bastard numero uno," J.B. said.

"At least most of these gibbering demons from the past are long dead," Doc stated. "And the earth a much cleaner place for their passing."

"And there's the legends you've talked about." Mildred swatted away a cloud of tiny iridescent flies from her face. "The Magus. The Warlock. The Sorcerer."

"Three names for a single man," Ryan said. "Steel eyes and half a face. First man to try and buy and sell stickies. Most decent folks would run a hundred miles before crossing up those muties. He used to sell them to Gert Wolfram. The ringmaster of the greatest traveling freak show in all of Deathlands history. Now, there's a truly evil couple."

Krysty heard the grating note in Ryan's voice, almost tasting the flatness of fear that overlaid his words. "But they're dead, aren't they, lover?"

"Nobody knows. Some folk say that the Magus was never really alive."

Now it was Krysty's turn to huddle up as though she were cold. "Ooooh, let's find something else to talk about. Just thinking of men like Straub and Strasser makes me feel sick to my stomach. Perversions of humanity."

"Moral muties," Mildred said.

They'd reached an open clearing that ran down toward a gently sloping beach, with open water beyond.

"Still hungry," Jak stated.

"You and your stomach!" Krysty chided.

"You one said change subject," the teenager protested. "Just done that."

FORTUNATELY RYAN'S supposition that the redoubt was now set in the heart of an island proved to be false. It was lucky because they found little or no fallen timber suitable for making a raft to get them off.

As they walked along the beach, Ryan in the lead and J.B. bringing up the rear, they found that their land mass was linked to another, larger body of land. A narrow causeway, less than six feet wide in parts, ran across, roughly southerly, with small waves lapping at it.

"Still no sign of wildlife," Jak said. "Mebbe fish? Could try?"

Ryan was walking cautiously along the path, constantly watching the water, aware of how vulnerable they were if any large mutie monster should attack them.

But the lake remained calm and placid, and they all made the crossing safely.

Only then did he answer Jak's question. "Fish? Didn't see sign of any."

"Could be good trout country," Doc said.

Ryan stooped and cupped his hand, bringing water to his mouth, tasting it and spitting it out hurriedly. "No fish in that. Nothing living in that."

Everyone followed his example, wanting to try it for himself or herself. All of them reacted the same way to the brackish bitterness.

"Polluted filth!" Doc gasped.

Mildred cautiously touched her tongue to the liquid, puckering her mouth. "Iron. Sulfur. Where there's pollution, there always seems to be sulfur. And some other metals. Lithium? Zinc. Just a hideous cocktail of poisons."

"Least we had plenty to drink in the redoubt," Ryan said, wiping his wet hands on his pants. "But the sooner we get right away from this ruined place the better."

"Trees look healthy." Krysty stared around. "But I can't feel any sort of life."

"No game. No fish. Not a bird in the sky." J.B. took off his fedora and fanned it in front of his face to shoo away more of the bothersome insects. "Just these bastard flies. And I don't fancy eating them." He flicked at his neck. "Though they don't seem to have any objection to eating me."

Ryan looked around, spotting what could have been the twisted wreckage of an old fire watchtower, jutting out several hundred feet above them.

"If I go up there, I should get a view all around. Mebbe find the best way out of this blighted maze of water and islands. Take me about a half hour there and back."

"Could we all come?" Krysty asked.

"No. We got no way of knowing how far we're going to have to walk to get something to eat. And drink. Best everyone conserve energy."

"I confess that I am already feeling just a trifle fatigued," Doc said. "I shall lay down beneath yonder ridgepole pine and await your return. All that I lack is a jug of wine and a slim volume of verse."

THE TRACK WAS DUSTY and narrow. Since there appeared to be nothing living in the region, Ryan wondered what kind of creature had made the trail.

As he climbed quickly upward, the sun broke through the sullen cloud cover, casting his shadow ahead of him, making him glad of the cover of the surrounding trees.

Ryan couldn't get a snatch of an old song out of his mind. He could remember only the first couplet, which was about the letter *T* standing for both Texas and Tennessee. It dogged him, so that he found himself walking in time to it.

The path wound clear around the peak, offering nim views in every direction, though the pines still prevented his seeing too far. Hopefully, by the time he reached the top, it might be possible to work out a route that would take them away from this timbered wilderness toward some sort of civilization.

A large dragonfly, nearly a foot long, hovered in front of him, the light catching its magnificent amethyst-and-onyx scales. Ryan watched it with some caution, knowing that some of these mutie insects could turn out triple-nasty.

But it flew away, wings shimmering like lightning gauze, vanishing among the trees.

Ryan finally reached the top, breathing hard from the tough climb, finding that he had been right. There were the four bent and broken legs of what had once been a fire tower, the cabin overgrown with long grass and fireweed, broken glass tinkling underfoot as he walked up to it.

The view was everything that he'd hoped.

Now that he was above the treeline, he had an uninterrupted vista for several miles in every direction.

The land that they were on at the moment was connected with the narrow causeway to the place that hid the redoubt. There was water nearly all around, but in the one direction, south, there was a stretch about a hundred yards wide that linked up with what looked like mainland.

Ryan shaded his eye, peering toward what seemed to be a thin column of gray smoke rising into the still air. Smoke almost always meant human habitation, and that would mean food. It might mean confrontation, but that was something to face when they needed to.

He didn't take a bearing on the smoke. There was no point. He had complete confidence in his own sense of direction and knew that he could lead the others toward the fire as soon as he had descended the mysterious little trail.

RYAN HAD BEEN WALKING down the track for only a couple of minutes when he had the odd but unmistakable sensation that someone, or something, was watching him.

There was the familiar prickling at the back of the neck, and his hand was reaching for the butt of the SIG-Sauer before he was fully aware what was happening.

The air seemed still and heavy, but a quick look all around showed him nothing.

He began to holster the blaster again when his acute hearing caught a strange, almost metallic clicking, like a safety being repeatedly snapped on and off.

And he finally saw the creature that had made the narrow, twisting path.

Chapter Nine

"Fireblast!"

There were two of them, straddling the trail, facing in his direction about a dozen paces away.

Ryan was able to spot a crumbling opening in the dirt to the side, which he imagined had to be their lair. Probably they had been sensitive to the vibrations of his feet as he passed by on his way to the observation tower and had come creeping out to discover what was happening.

They were insects.

But the larger of them was close to two feet in length, the other a couple of inches shorter. Ryan's first guess had them as some kind of centipede, as they were low to the ground and each had dozens of narrow legs that moved in a strange wavelike motion. Their skins were polished, like green brass, glittering brightly, the scales shifting as they moved nervously from side to side, long antennae quivering above razored jaws.

Ryan had seen similar mutated creatures elsewhere in Deathlands, often in regions that had suffered badly from intensive nuking.

Some of them sometimes squirted blinding or poisonous fluids from glands beneath the throat, and he backed away a few steps, looking for a possible way around them.

But as Ryan glanced sideways, he spotted four more of the hideous, scuttling insects as they emerged dustily from their concealed burrows. And he realized with a thrill of horror that the whole hillside was undermined by the mutie creatures. There could be dozens of them. Or hundreds.

KRYSTY WAS LYING near the water's edge, dozing in the sudden warm glow of sunshine. Doc was snoring softly to her right. J.B. and Mildred had gone off together about a quarter-hour earlier and vanished into the fringes of the forest. Jak was sitting down on the shingled beach, picking through the rocks until he found perfectly round and smooth stones, which he would flip with a sharp underarm whiplash at the still water, counting the bounces.

"Sixteen!" he said triumphantly.

Krysty sat up suddenly, her head turning toward the invisible top of the hill. "Ryan," she whispered, then stood and called to the others. "It's Ryan! He's in trouble."

RUN OR FIGHT. When it came down to it, as the Trader used to say, life in Deathlands often left you with a rapid choice of one of those two options.

The morning was flooded with a metallic chittering sound as the insects rubbed their antennae together and clacked their fearsome jaws. Now Ryan could count upward of fifty, creeping forward in their odd sidling motion, surrounding him, though none of them seemed to want to come too close.

He leveled the SIG-Sauer and shot the biggest one, carefully placing the 9 mm round an inch or so behind the turning head. It ripped through the carapace, nearly cutting the thing in two. But its legs continued to move, propelling it slowly toward Ryan.

The others had stopped for a moment at the thunder of the shot, their angular skulls swiveling toward the mortally wounded insect.

''Go get it,'' Ryan whispered encouragingly. ''Fresh meat for you all.''

A sticky turquoise liquid was seeping from the bullet wound. The powerful handblaster would have stopped a man dead in his tracks, but the insect still seemed to be functioning, ignoring the leaking hole in its body.

He fired quickly, two more shots, taking another couple of the mutie centipedes out of the game, blowing the head clean off the first of them, breaking the body of the second in two. This time some of the others scuttled sinuously toward their stricken comrades and began to devour the twitching, oozing corpses.

But the noise seemed to have stirred up the whole mountain, and Ryan was forced to move before he was trapped by a circle of eighty or more of the creatures.

The only way to move was back up the trail, toward the bare top of the hill. It would buy him a few minutes, but once he got to the wreckage of the watchtower there would be nowhere else to run.

MILDRED AND J.B. emerged from the undergrowth, looking slightly flustered, the woman tugging her jacket on, picking leaf mold from her plaited hair.

"What is it?" the Armorer asked. But a moment later his question was answered by the noise of a single shot, booming out over the lake. "Ryan's SIG-Sauer," he said. "Know that anywhere. Means trouble."

"Felt bad vibes," Krysty said, aware of a tightness in her throat.

As they waited, looking at one another, they heard two more shots.

"Let's go," J.B. said, turning on his heel and running for the trailhead.

RYAN WAS FORCED to jump over several of the insects, dodging them as they reared up to try to snap blindly at him. Once roused, they seemed able to move at surprising speed over the rough terrain, almost as fast as a running man.

At one point, jinking sideways off the trail to avoid one of the centipedes that was close to four feet in length, Ryan felt the earth crumbling beneath his feet, and he almost fell headlong into a burrow filled with writhing baby insects.

Excited by the hunt, the creatures were giving off a bitter, metallic odor that reminded Ryan of the unpleasant taste of the poisoned water.

The squat ruin of the watchtower was ahead of him now. The twisted girders formed a sort of nest, around a dozen feet from the ground. It was somewhere to make a stand against the mutie monsters.

But Ryan knew that the blaster wasn't going to save him. It was obvious that deaths among their number had no effect at all on the blood lust of the rest of the swarm. They would come, come and keep on coming after him.

The best he could hope for was to buy himself a little more time until the others could get to him.

That was as far as his plan went.

THERE HAD BEEN no more shooting.

"Figure he'd have found some way to tell us if things were all right up there," Krysty panted, leading the way up the oddly narrow trail.

The slope was steep and the footing treacherous, and already they were strung out. She and Jak were in front, with J.B. now about forty yards behind and below them. Mildred was fairly close on the heels of the Armorer, but Doc was already out of sight at the rear.

There was an odd, unidentifiable scent in the air, alien and unpleasant.

There had been no more noise from the top of the hillside, still out of sight, hidden by the dense trees.

RYAN CLUNG TO THE TOP of one of the girders, looking down at the seething mass of insects that shifted below him like a bright green ocean. The noise of the mutie creatures rubbing against one another was like a slipping fan belt on a war wag engine, loud and piercing.

Several of them had tried to climb the corroded metal, using their countless legs to grip their way up. But they had moved slowly and clumsily, and Ryan had been able to knock them off with the panga, pitching them down to be instantly devoured by their voracious comrades.

For the time being, Ryan was in no immediate danger. But there was no way that he could get down and try to run through that seething mass of mutated horror. One of the centipedes, largest of them all so far, was trying to lift itself, reaching almost five feet up the broken tower toward the man.

Ryan readied the panga. He knew that the others would have heard the sound of his three shots and would already be on their way toward him. He hoped that the lower part of the steep slope wasn't also infested with creatures—not that he could see how the others could help, short of finding a supply of gasoline from somewhere that would burn away the vicious horde.

"WHAT MADE PATH?" Jak asked, running fast enough to keep Krysty at full stretch, but not going on ahead of her.

"Don't know... Small rodents... No sign of anything living... Soon be there..."

She and the albino seemed alone on the slope. If she really concentrated, Krysty could hear J.B. and Mildred panting down below them. Doc was way out of sight.

"Something come out of burrows," the teenager observed, pointing to the right.

"Soon know what..."

FROM HIS ELEVATED POSITION, Ryan could see above the shimmering mass of insects to where the trail emerged onto the bare top of the hill.

There was so much noise from the besieging insects that he didn't hear the approach of the others. The first he knew was when he saw the two heads, one snow white, the other flaming crimson, appear out of the trees.

He instantly fired another shot into the creatures, backing it up with a warning yell.

"Look out! Killer bugs! Hundreds of them!"

KRYSTY AND JAK HAD BOTH stopped dead in their tracks at the fourth shot, spotting Ryan clinging perilously to the broken length of iron. Almost immediately they saw the peril, surging around beneath their trapped friend.

"Holy fuck!" Jak breathed. "Look at them."

"I'm looking, for Gaia's sake."

She called to Ryan. "Hang on there, lover."

"I'm hanging. Where are the others?"

The new voices had distracted the centipedes, and some of them on the fringes lifted the upper parts of their bodies from the ground. The sharp planes of their faces turned from side to side as they tried to locate the source of the fresh sounds, their antennae twitching.

Krysty looked around as she heard J.B. panting toward her, Mildred still a few yards behind him.

"Watch it," she warned. "There's an army of mutie insects got Ryan treed."

The Armorer took in the situation at a single, raking glance. "Be nice to have some gas or some grens. But we don't . . . so we gotta find another way out."

Mildred was painfully out of breath, doubled over with cramps, sweat dripping from her chin. She took one look at the glittering, poisonous horde and shook her head. "Jesus! How're we . . . ?"

Ryan swung the panga in a hissing arc, neatly beheading the huge insect that was climbing toward him, leaving its scaled corpse to scrabble down among the others, who, jaws clicking, promptly began to eat it.

Farther down the slope, they could all hear Doc lumbering toward them. "I can and I will. I can and I will. I can and I will." He repeated it like a mantra to draw him up to the top.

When he joined them he stared fuzzily at Ryan's predicament and promptly dropped to hands and knees, retching up yellow bile, his nose beginning to bleed with all the effort he'd put into the sharp climb.

"Any ideas, bro?" J.B. shouted to Ryan.

"Only one. Have to distract them enough for me to jump and run for it."

"They'll come after you. After us."

Ryan nodded. "Looks like Doc and Mildred aren't in great shape for another canter."

"Give me five," the woman said, standing up a little shakily.

Doc was also on his feet again, his face as pale as parchment, his swallow's-eye kerchief pressed to his nose. His voice was shaky and muffled. "If the choice is running or being engulfed and devoured by that hellish mass of metallic death, then I guess that my heels will sprout wings.''

Ryan felt the girder suddenly shift a little under his grip and peered down. He saw to his horror that some of the insects were busily burrowing into the dry earth, searching out the buried foundations of the old watchtower to undermine it and bring it toppling down.

And him with it.

''Better be quick,'' he yelled. ''Bastards are going to have this down in a minute or two.''

J.B. closed his eyes for a moment, concentrating all his attention on the military problem, opening them again. ''Doc, set off now, back down the hill. Dark night! Don't argue. Can't do anything here. Mildred. Go with him. Now.''

Without a word of argument, Mildred took the old man by the elbow and led him away, back over the brink of the hill, moving hastily to the right as half a dozen late-coming centipedes appeared on the trail.

Ryan felt the girder drop another couple of inches. ''Time's running,'' he called.

''Going to empty a clip from the Uzi. Spray it to try and lay down a narrow corridor of dead. Moment I finish shooting, you come a'running, Ryan. All right?''

''I don't have anything better. Let her go.''

On full-auto, twenty rounds of 9 mm ammo spit out of the Uzi machine pistol in a couple of heartbeats, with a noise like tearing silk.

Stinking ichor sprayed from the mangled bodies of the creatures as the bullets ripped into them, killing or wounding thirty or forty where they had been climbing over one another in their eagerness to reach the trapped man.

"Now!" J.B. shouted, slinging the empty blaster over his shoulder.

But Ryan didn't need the warning yell. The metal support was sliding gently sideways, and he jumped clear of it, landing foursquare in the corridor of dead and dying insects that J.B. had provided.

The scaly carapaces cracked and crunched under his combat boots, and he slipped and slithered, fighting for balance, knowing that to fall was to die.

Horribly.

It was a close-run thing.

The burst of fire from the Uzi had opened up enough of a passage through the shocked and disjointed insects to enable Ryan to sprint through. Several of the creatures struck at him, but he was moving too fast, using the long panga like an ax to clear a wider path, lashing out at any of the giant mutie centipedes that threatened him.

Once they saw he was going to make it, the other friends turned and started moving fast toward the top of the track, avoiding a few more of the insects that were wriggling from their sun-blind burrows.

One of the larger centipedes reared up in front of him, its head at the height of Ryan's chest, and he swung the panga at it without breaking stride, slicing through the armored body.

There was a strange noise from all around him, like the high-pitched mewing of drowning kittens, and the air was filled with the alien metallic stink.

Suddenly he was free of them, following the others helter-skelter down the slope. Ryan glanced a couple of times over his shoulder, but the mutie insects didn't try to pursue them.

They all arrived together down by the water, panting and exhausted. Doc's nosebleed had gotten worse, and Mildred had also been sick.

"All in good shape," Ryan said, grinning.

"Apart from your pants," Krysty observed. "Those little fuckers did a good job on them."

Ryan hadn't been aware in the headlong dash of just how close some of the clamping jaws had come to him. But when he sat on a rounded boulder by the brackish lake, he saw that the lower parts of his pants were cut and slashed in several places, as though a straight razor had been used on them.

"THERE'S THE SMOKE I saw," Ryan pointed with the SIG-Sauer toward the pallid column of gray that was twining into the overcast sky. It was the middle of the day, but the clouds had returned. Now it was warm and humid, with the threat of possible thunder in the air.

"Where there's smoke there's food," J.B. said.

"And where there's food, there's trouble," Ryan added. "Always the way."

Chapter Ten

They crossed over a ridge, leaving the poisoned water behind them, finding themselves in a cleaner and fresher part of the country.

There were sweeping banks of scented flowers, the blossoms drooping heavily toward the lush grass, and they forded three fast-running streams of good, sparkling water. All six of them drank deeply.

They could see the tall plume of smoke more clearly and could even catch the smell of it when the wind shifted a little. It carried the flavor of cooking meat, which made all of them salivate with hunger.

"Hope they're friendly to outlanders," Krysty said.

"Won't matter that much if they're not." Ryan's lean face was vulpine with the desire for something to eat and to put a lining on his groaning stomach.

They had seen tracks of deer at two of the crossings, and once a flock of doves circled noisily above them. Jak had drawn his Colt Python, holstering it at Ryan's snapped command.

"If we want everyone to know there's strangers in the woods, then we can yell out and tell them."

IT WAS A SMALL COMMUNITY.

They approached it with the greatest caution, in an extended double-red skirmish line. The streams had melted into a larger river, which flowed over bubbling shallows, running deeper a little farther beyond the village, through high cliffs.

About a dozen shacks, mostly thatched with reeds, stretched along a main street of trampled mud. The smoke that they'd seen from afar came from what looked to be a communal cooking fire, with two or three iron pots dangling over it. The smell of broiling meat drifting toward the invisible watchers, behind their wall of undergrowth.

Ryan counted seventeen people in the half hour they patiently watched and waited.

Nine were children below the age of adolescence. Five were women, one of them extremely old. Of the three men, only one looked to be under fifty, and he walked with a heavy limp, dragging a wasted right leg behind him as he moved, leaning heavily on a carved stick.

"Step in and take," Jak whispered.

"My guess is that the men are out hunting," Ryan replied. "Could come back any time. Don't want to get caught coldcocked and have to chill our way out."

"Not unless we have to," J.B. added.

"Yeah."

A couple of scrawny dogs sniffed around each other, occasionally snarling.

Mildred grinned at the sight. "I ever tell you the first time I saw two dogs making it? I was about six and I was out with my Uncle Josh. I asked him what the dogs were doing. 'Well, Millie,' he said. 'The poor animal in front has been struck sightless, and the one behind is helping to push it to the hospital for the blind.' Never forgot that.''

They all laughed quietly.

THE SCENT of the cooking stew was driving them all crazy.

''We been waiting here an hour or more, Ryan,'' Mildred complained.

''That food must be ready soon...'' Ryan explained. ''I want to see if the hunters come back to eat. Or whether it's just for the folks left here. Give it another half hour.''

''By then I fear that I shall have faded away utterly and be nothing but a handful of rags and a shred or two of skin and bone.'' Doc held up his hand. ''Look, my friends. It is more like the claw of an eagle.''

''I'd have said it was more like some old crow, Doc, but I guess you got the right on your side.'' Mildred sucked in her cheeks, miming starvation.

''Half an hour,'' Ryan insisted.

The friends were as close to open rebellion as he'd ever known them to be.

But Ryan was right.

Just when it looked as if Doc and Mildred were going to break ranks and go out alone into the village, they heard the sound of men's voices, coming toward them from the direction of the river. Everyone flattened, peering through the brush at a band of a dozen men, aged from midteens to midforties, walking by, carrying the carcass of a deer slung over a pole.

Most of them were hefting old single-shot, long-barreled muskets, while a couple had primitive cap-

and-ball pistols. Several had long, broad-bladed swords.

They wore mostly a collection of ragged clothes and patched furs.

"Double-poor," Krysty whispered to Ryan. "Kind that might turn on strangers like rabid dogs."

He nodded his agreement. "Could be. Pesthole like this won't welcome outlanders."

J.B. had the same thought. "Wish we had a war wag with us," he said quietly.

Mildred was puzzled. "They look decent, honest people. Why don't we just go and ask for food? Explain we gotten ourselves lost and we're hungry."

"Indeed." Doc licked his lips. "I find myself in agreement with my colleague. Surely they would not think to refuse poor travelers sustenance?"

"Would they not?" Ryan asked wryly. "I wouldn't want to stake my life on that, Doc. I've seen dozens— mebbe hundreds—of places like this. Tiny inbred communities, where everyone fucks everyone else and the only thing they unite on is a hatred of strangers. Get more kindness from mad dogs."

"So, what we do?" Jak asked.

"Talk loudly and carry a big stick," Doc suggested. "Is that not correct?"

Ryan smiled, standing cautiously and drawing the SIG-Sauer from its holster. "Put it your own way, Doc, but I guess the idea's right. Go in fast and heavy. Get out quick."

"Want me and Mildred to circle around and come in from the other side?" J.B. was peering past the dirt-poor houses. "Looks like a wider river through yonder. Could be boats. Take us away from here to do some exploring.''

''Right. Take four minutes from . . . now! Move in and try and keep them under control. Just tell them we only want to be fed and then we'll leave.''

''Chilling?''

''If we have to. Now go.''

J.B., carrying the reloaded Uzi ready at high port, vanished silently away to the right, followed by Mildred. Ryan stayed where he was with Krysty, Jak and Doc, checking his wrist chron, counting off the seconds.

''One minute to go. Remember that we have to make them think we'll blast them if they step out of line.''

Krysty looked at him, her face dappled in shadow. ''Well, we will, won't we?''

''Yeah. Yeah, we will.'' He looked again at the changing digital display. ''Ten seconds. Let's get moving, people.''

THE SUDDEN APPEARANCE of six heavily armed strangers, coming in from both ends of their tiny village, produced an instant panic. But to Ryan's great relief, the panic took the form of a passive defeatism.

The disabled man appeared to be the leader of the ragged community and he was the first to see them, spotting Ryan as the one-eyed man strode from cover toward the cooking fire. He immediately gave a great ululating cry of despair, falling awkwardly to his knees, hands clasped in front of him.

''Don't kill us, mister.''

"Everyone keep still and nobody do nothing foolish and nobody gets hurt." Ryan fired a single shot into the air to confirm the threat, the sound of the explosion echoing flatly around the small settlement.

"What do ye want, mister?" The whole village was on its knees, eyes rolling, mouths sagging in fear.

"Food is all. We got ourselves lost in that maze of lakes back there. Deeply hungered. Smelled your stew cooking and figured you wouldn't let honest folks starve."

The relief could almost be tasted. The man's face lost its pallor, and he kept looking back and forth from Ryan to J.B.

"Why, sure. Surely, neighbors. What we have is ye welcome to. Be ready to eat right soon."

"Ye can stay a night or more, neighbor," mumbled a toothless woman with a gaping sore that leaked a colorless liquid over her neck and stained her torn cotton dress. "Any of ye with no bed warmers'd be welcome to take ye pick."

Ryan nodded. "Thanks for that offer. But no thanks. A meal and on our way. What's the river yonder?" Now that he was in the center of the village he could see it more clearly, making out a ramshackle jetty with a couple of rafts moored there.

The man grinned, showing a mouth filled with rotting teeth that jostled and leaned against each other like a cemetery after a quake. "You don't know what the river is, neighbor. Where ye been all ye life?"

"Hither and yon," Ryan replied, falling into the same kind of drawling patois that he remembered from being in rural Tennessee with the Trader.

"That be Tennessee."

"The Tennessee River?"

"Surely be."

"Where does it run?" J.B. asked, standing with his finger on the trigger of the Uzi, watching warily.

"It runs to Canada and to the Gulf of Mexico," the disabled man replied. "So they says, as there ain't a man nor wench from these parts ever bin far enough to see. We travel a day or so to the north and south. No more. Not safe. Gangs of muties. Ye seen muties, neighbor?"

"Not lately. Plenty over the years. Ye be troubled by stickies?"

"And scabbies and swampies and ghoulies," cackled the toothless harridan, who seemed to be lacking several shingles from her roof. "Ye name them and we seen them."

Ryan looked around the circle of haunted, watchful faces, seeing the ingrained dirt and mistrust, the tiny red eyes like trapped rodents that flicked along the line of outlanders. His guess at inbreeding was obviously right. Hardly one in five looked normal, with every kind of mental and physical disease showing itself.

"Food," he said, "and we'll be gone."

THEY WERE GIVEN wooden bowls and spoons made from horn, taking the stew to sit on one side of the fire, blasters ready at hand while they ate. But the villagers didn't show any sign of rebellion, though resentment at giving away their precious food was etched clear on every ruined face.

"What is this place called?" Doc asked, trying to make conversation to fill the uncomfortable void.

"Ain't called nothin', neighbor. Don't give a name to a place you eat and sleep and shit. No point."

"No. No, I suppose there is some sort of logic behind that thinking."

The food was excellent, better than many a meal that Ryan had eaten in some of the wealthiest and most powerful villes in Deathlands.

It was a stew that seemed to consist mainly of roasted venison, though there was also some pork in it. There were chunks of potato, carrot and turnip, all spiced and flavored with an assortment of herbs.

Everyone went back for seconds, except Jak, who went back for thirds.

Ryan checked his chron, seeing that it was closing in on two in the afternoon.

"Where's the nearest ville to here?"

Hardly anyone had moved among the villagers. The disabled chief answered the question. "Be no ville. No baron rules hereabouts, neighbor. Nothin' to rule, if ye see what I means. Be villes to the south and west. Old Memphis has villes." He grinned without humor. "Not that any of us been there."

"Nashville?" Mildred asked.

He sniffed and spit in the mud. "Wouldn't know, girlie. Believe that Nashville was nuked out of the sight of God and man. So they says. Sodom and Gomorrah rolled together, it was. Worshipers at the shrine of Baal, they says."

Mildred opened her eyes wide, letting the "girlie" pass unchallenged. "And the ungodly were smitten and all their clothing rent and their dwellings cast down and the lord soweth their fields with salt and left not one stone upon another.''

Her words brought an unexpected and ragged chorus of ''Amens'' from the watching villagers.

''What book of the Bible did that come from?'' Doc whispered. ''I seem to almost recognize it.''

''The First Book of Mildred,'' she replied.

The old man gave a cackle of laughter and nearly choked on his last spoonful of stew. ''Upon my soul, madam, but you are a character, indeed you are. I tell you now that I am a person who likes to talk to a person who likes to talk.''

Ryan pointed at him. ''Can it, Doc. We're leaving.'' He kept his voice pitched low. ''This is where it could get warm.''

He addressed the villagers. ''Grateful for the meal, neighbors. Surely are.''

''Welcome, ye is.''

Now everyone was on their feet.

Ryan pointed toward the Tennessee River. ''One more favor. Like to borrow one of your rafts. Bring it back here to you in a day or two.''

''Ye askin' or ye telling'?''

Now the suppressed anger and hostility came seething out. Fists were shaken, daggers drawn, and fingers played with the hammers on flintlocks.

Ryan raised his voice. ''You got off light and easy, neighbors. No harm done. A little food is all. You can build another raft in a day or less.''

''Build one yeself.''

Ryan smiled and the shouting quieted. "God makes sheep and He makes wolves. That's His nature. You might not like it, specially as you're all the sheep and we're the wolves. But the best thing a sheep can do is keep its bastard head down and stay quiet. Wolves move on and not a hair harmed on a head. You all understand me?" Nobody spoke.

He addressed their chief. "You understand?"

"Yes." His sullen face was tight like a mask one size too small.

"Then that's good. J.B., you lead on and we'll follow you. Triple-red."

It looked as if it was going to work, but they still had to actually get away on the raft, and that would be the most vulnerable moment.

They skirted the fire, J.B. and Mildred going on ahead to check the raft and get it ready for a speedy embarkation. Ryan had the SIG-Sauer cocked in his right hand, walking slowly sideways, eyes never leaving the villagers, who had formed themselves into a half circle, moving parallel to the outlanders, toward the wide river. It was like a powder keg waiting for a spark.

"Shoot a few," Jak hissed. "Buy us time."

"No. Not unless we have to. They're still terrified of us. We can get away with no blood spilled on the ground."

J.B. and Mildred had loosened the mooring lines on the larger of the pair of crude rafts, checking there were long oars aboard to propel them along. They beckoned for Ryan and the others to come aboard.

The villagers were following them, like a pack of snarling curs, raging in anger, waving weapons at the outlanders. None of them dared to actually attack.

"We gave ye food and ye take our lives! We could've slain all of ye."

Ryan shook his head at the disabled chief. "Not true. We all know it. One wrong move and this stinkin' pesthole would cease to be."

The river was a hundred feet wide, flowing fast and clear. To the north were high cliffs and gorges, but the way south was between open bluffs, tree lined.

Ryan stepped aboard, followed by Krysty. Doc came next, stumbling and nearly losing his balance on the rocking logs. Jak hopped agilely on to help the old man. Mildred was already in the bow, J.B holding the single stern line.

"Let her go," Ryan said, watching the villagers.

Someone threw a jagged flint that hit Jak on the shoulder. He swung around and instinctively opened up with his Magnum, and the blood spilling began.

Chapter Eleven

The raft was about fifteen feet square with a crude cabin of logs, chinked with mud, at its center. There was a long steering oar fixed in a notch at the stern and four oars to help control and drive the vessel.

J.B. had jumped on, pushing the raft off from the muddy shore with his boots, grabbing for the steering oar as the current immediately picked at the bound logs, swinging them out into the main stream.

The thrown stone and Jak's instant retaliation took everyone, including Ryan, by surprise.

It had looked as though they were going to get away with it.

Now there was murderous mayhem.

On the slowly moving, rocking raft, Ryan and his companions were at a great disadvantage. The villagers, most of the men with firearms, were able to open fire at close to point-blank range, pouring lead at them.

Ryan saw Jak hit in the center of the stomach, folding over and writhing in pain, his legs kicking on the wet timbers, yelping in shock.

J.B. had let go of the steering oar and unslung the Uzi, readying it to retaliate, but he hadn't yet opened fire. Krysty and Mildred had both been heading for the small cabin and were unable to start shooting straightaway.

Ryan snapped off a couple of rounds before he felt a devastating blow in his right thigh and he went down, grabbing at the wound with his left hand, feeling the warmth of spilling blood against his fingers.

It was a bad moment, with musket and pistol balls slashing at the water, some of them thunking into the wood, tearing off strips of white timber.

Doc saved the day, turning as Jak opened fire, his Le Mat already unholstered. He braced himself against the movement of the raft while it gathered pace toward the center of the stream, leveling the hand cannon and firing the .65-caliber round at the enraged mob. The buckshot starred out and blasted a gap in the packed ranks of the villagers, leaving two dead and half a dozen down, screaming and bloodied, at the side of the water.

It gave J.B. and the women the few seconds' respite they needed to get their act together and open fire themselves. The single barking explosions of Mildred's ZKR 551 and Krysty's double-action Smith & Wesson were counterpointed by the Armorer's lethal 9 mm Uzi.

It was a lot easier to fire from land against a moving target than it was to fire at stationary targets from a moving raft. But Ryan's company had vastly superior weaponry and decimated the enemy while they were still struggling to reload their single-shot blasters.

Ryan himself was lying flat near the edge of the raft, ignoring the bullet wound in his leg, shooting from the prone position at the scattering villagers.

Jak was still hunched up and moaning with pain from what looked like a triple-serious wound. A musket ball in the belly could easily turn out to be enough to book him a place on the last train west.

"Hold fire," Ryan called. "They've broken. Use the oars and get the raft out into the current. On the far side. Then all take cover in case they start trying to snipe at us."

"You hit, lover?"

"Ball in the leg. See to Jak. Think he got shot in the guts. More serious."

While Doc worked the steering oar, J.B. took over Ryan's Steyr rifle and kept watch for any resumption of hostilities. But the villagers had taken at least a dozen fatalities and had lost all heart for the fight.

Krysty and Mildred dragged Ryan and Jak behind the cover of the cabin while the doctor checked their wounds.

She first examined Jak, who was still folded up, hands clasped over his midriff, moaning to himself.

"Move yourself, Jak, so I can see what the damage is."

Ryan had reloaded his SIG-Sauer, holstering it and sitting up to peer at his own wound. There was a ragged tear in his pant leg, halfway between the knee and hip. He touched himself gingerly on both sides of the thigh, whistling with relief as he felt both an entrance and an exit wound.

"Think I'm lucky," he said. "Think the ball went clean through near the outside. Doesn't feel like it hit anything too serious on the way. How's the kid?"

"Don't call me that, Ryan," Jak said through gritted teeth. "I'm all right. Sore."

"But I saw you go down, gut shot."

"Look," Mildred said, her voice high with relief. "Look at his belt."

Ryan rolled on his side and looked across the cramped little cabin, seeing that Jak's broad leather belt had a massive brass buckle. And there was the soft lead musket ball, splashed in a bright blur across the brass.

"Lucky," Ryan said.

"Feel like kicked by mule," the teenager complained. "Bastards!"

"We did take their food and their raft," Mildred stated gently.

"Still bastards. How're you, Ryan?"

Mildred left Jak and knelt by Ryan on the rocking, shifting logs.

After a few moments she agreed with his own diagnosis. "Need to look properly when we can get a chance. But I think you're right. Seems to have gone clear through and not even nipped the muscle. Pure flesh wound. I'll wash it out, then tie it up for you to ease the bleeding."

Outside there was the hollow sound of a smoothbore musket being fired, and a ball struck the outside of the cabin. But it sounded partly spent, with little menace. It was followed almost immediately by the full-throated crack of the powerful Steyr SSG-70, and a whoop of elation from the Armorer.

"Got that son of a bitch!" he whooped. "Don't think they'll bother us no more."

"Anymore," Krysty said from habit, though J.B. couldn't hear her.

"How is young Jak?" Doc called. "And what of our beloved leader?"

"Jak's got a nasty bruise around about his navel," Mildred shouted. "Lucky pup, I tell you."

"And Ryan?"

"I'll be fine in a while," Ryan yelled himself. "Got a musket ball went in and out. Have it bandaged and be righter than rain. How're we doing out there?"

"Making about eight or ten miles an hour," J.B. replied. "Think we're already clear from any more danger from the double-poor villagers."

Mildred had told Ryan to tug down his pants, and she examined the bleeding wound. "I think we should pull into the bank for a few minutes when it's safe," she said. "Like to do my medical work on dry land."

Jak was already on his feet, peering out of the cabin, wincing as he touched the deep purple bruise that had sprung up on his snow white stomach. "I'll help with oars. Steer us in."

"Me, too," Krysty said, stooping to kiss Ryan on the cheek. "Glad it's not too bad, lover. When you went down I thought . . . Well, I just thought. That's all."

Ryan lay back, feeling slightly sick, the pain beginning to swell in his leg, which throbbed with the pulse.

THEY HAD MOORED THE RAFT among a grove of tamarinds that grew close to the banks of the Tennessee River. J.B. went a little way upstream, and Jak picked his cautious path downstream to keep watch while Mildred operated on her patient.

Krysty stayed to watch and help, while Doc relaxed on the deck, enjoying a burst of bright, watery sunshine.

"A wound of honor, my dear fellow," he said.

"Honor!" Ryan bit his lip to avoid yelping as Mildred bathed the wound with cold river water, making sure there was no residue of cloth or dirt left by the ball's passage that might remain and putrefy.

"A strange thing, honor," the old man mused. "I do believe that it has caused almost as much sorrow, despair and death as religion."

"I have the feeling that you're building up to one of your interminable anecdotes, Doc," Mildred said, bending low over Ryan's thigh, examining her work with close attention. "Go ahead. Take his mind off the bandaging."

"I am minded of the time of the Crusades in Europe," Doc went on, as serene as ever.

"That the knights against the infidel?" Ryan asked. "Saw a bit of an old vid about that once. Years ago."

"Correct."

Doc watched the bandaging. "You have good hands, Dr. Wyeth."

"Thank you, Doc."

"The story about honor?" Ryan prompted, concentrating on not yelling at the pain from the wound. Despite all of Mildred's efforts, it was like having a red hot needle drawn through the tender flesh of his thigh. Krysty was holding his hand tightly.

"Ah, yes. During the Crusades an alarming number of young men of good families died. Some from the swords and arrows of the blaspheming Turks, far more from dysentery and typhoid. Back home in England, it was vital that the daughters of the wealthy and famous married well. It was a source of deep shame to the fathers if they did not. But there were no longer enough young men of standing to go around.''

''I thought they became nuns,'' Mildred interrupted.

''Some. But only a limited number. So some fathers came up with what were called 'marriages of honor' or 'marriages of heraldry.' Dreadful things.''

The afternoon was wearing on, and the Tennessee River flowed placidly toward the south.

''The father of a distinguished family would discover the name and rank of a young man who had died fighting for the true cross against the scimitar. Then he would announce that his daughter would wed him.''

''Though he was dead? How could they do that?'' Ryan was becoming intrigued by the bizarre tale.

Doc shook his head sadly. ''Of course they couldn't do it. But they did. The daughter and two or three of her attendants would be taken to an isolated part of the castle and there walled in together. The shield that bore that coat of arms of the dead 'husband' was placed against the barred door. A priest would recite the marriage ceremony, and then everyone went away.''

''Leaving them to starve?'' Krysty had become involved in listening to the story.''

''Indeed, yes. A bleak and miserable passing for the poor souls. After a sufficient time had passed, the father would come back with the same priest. This time it would be the funeral service. The daughter, legally wed, was removed and buried in the local church, with full honor and dignity. And everyone concerned was happy ever after.''

The tale was followed by a long silence, broken only by the river chuckling against the bound timbers of the raft.

''That is appalling, Doc.'' Mildred finished tying a knot in the length of torn material she'd used as a bandage. ''That is simply dreadful.''

''Is it true, Doc?'' Krysty asked.

The old man ran his fingers through the mane of silver gray hair. ''True? I believe so. But what is truth, my dear lady? Why, I am minded of an extraordinary tale set at the time that Kubla Khan had decreed his stately pleasure dome.''

''No, thanks, Doc,'' Ryan said, lying back with his eye closed, breathing deeply and slowly to overcome the belated shock that was seeping through his body.

''But it involves a sled carried by Custer on his expedition along the Rosebud.''

''No,'' Mildred said firmly. ''Now, Ryan needs some quality rest. Everyone off the raft for an hour or so. Maybe find some fruit if we all look around.''

''Careful,'' Ryan stated, puzzled that his voice was barely a whisper.

''Sure thing,'' Krysty said, finally letting go of his fingers. ''You just sleep. Everything'll be fine, lover.''

He felt the clumsy raft rock as everyone stepped off onto the lush grass on the shore.

His leg felt comfortable, tightly bound, and he flexed it experimentally, wincing at the stab of fresh pain. But he'd been shot and stabbed often enough to know that this wasn't too bad a wound. He began to think back to other times when he'd suffered from a bout of lead poisoning and quickly drifted off into a warm and comfortable darkness.

WHEN HE WOKE UP, starting from sleep with a momentary anxiety that he didn't know where he was, Ryan realized quickly that the raft was moving again. He was alone in the cabin, though he could hear the murmur of conversation from outside on the deck. When he checked his wrist chron, he found that it was eighteen minutes after four in the afternoon.

His leg felt less painful, and the shock of the shooting was already fading away.

"Where we going?" he called, his voice much stronger.

Krysty ducked in out of bright sunshine, blinking in the gloom. "You feeling better, lover?"

"Some. Where we going?"

"Where the river takes us. South. Just south."

Chapter Twelve

He slept again, not waking until the sun was setting away to the west, beyond some high, wooded bluffs that lined the Tennessee River.

Ryan could hear the creak of the steering oar and the rippling of the fast-flowing water.

"How're we doing?" he croaked. "Anyone got any good drinkin' water out there?"

Jak appeared in the doorway, moving stiffly, carrying a battered metal cup filled with fresh water and a handful of mixed berries, which he offered to Ryan.

"Rich land," he said. "Plenty of game if we need it. Saw deer and pigs."

Ryan sat up, wincing as the healing wound pulled. "Thanks," he said. "How're you feeling, Jak?"

"Sore. Got bruise like stormy Colorado sunset." He knelt slowly. "You?"

"Better than I was. Anything happened on the run south? Seen anyone?"

"Old man fishing with no line on rod. No ears, neither. Called out 'hello' to us, real cheerful."

"No danger?"

The albino shook his head slowly, the tumbling veil of long snowy hair seeming to fill the gloomy cabin with its brightness.

"Nothing."

"We mooring up soon?"

"Probably."

Conversation had never really been one of Jak's strong points.

"Thanks for water and fruit." The berries had been delicious, tangy and sharp, taking away the furry taste from his mouth and tongue.

"Welcome."

The teenager crept out, leaving Ryan alone again. But a few moments later Krysty came in.

"How's the wounded hero? Been snoring like Doc while we sailed along."

"Doesn't feel bad. Wouldn't back me to run against a hungry stickie."

"It's been a beautiful afternoon." She squatted at his side. "Jak bring you some fruit?"

"Handful of berries. Good. And some water. I needed that. Felt thirsty."

"J.B. reckon we should be tying up for the night real soon, before it gets dark."

Ryan nodded. "Sounds right to me. If you give me a hand, I'd like to see some sun before it all goes."

He shuffled out on his ass, helped by Krysty, moving backward and dragging his wounded leg behind him. He felt a numb pain as it knocked against the rough timbers, but nothing that he couldn't cope with.

The light from the setting sun was a bright reddish orange, casting long shadows across the river. The waterway was nearly a quarter-mile wide, still flowing clean and free.

"How is it?" Mildred asked, sitting near the stern of the raft, close to J.B., who was steering.

"Not so bad. We mooring soon?"

The Armorer nodded, his eyes invisible behind the burning light reflected off his glasses. "Real soon."

"Know where we are?"

Krysty pointed ahead, where there were the remains of what had once been a major highway bridge across the Tennessee, its supports shattered and distorted either by the nuking or by quakes. "Mildred thinks that could be old I-40," she said.

"Running east-west," he said, steadying himself and looking all around.

Doc was dozing near the bow, while Jak was on watch for any sign of life.

"Been a good afternoon," Krysty commented. "Makes me think that there could be worse ways of passing your life than on a boat on a good, safe river."

"Thought you wanted a small farm with fresh grass and a spring and a few cattle." Ryan reached and squeezed her hand. "We'll get what we want one of these days, lover."

She stared at him, her emerald eyes intent on his face, looking as if she was about to say something, then Jak called out from the bow.

"Good mooring place to left."

Ryan was still holding Krysty's hand. "You going to say something, lover?"

"I was, but let it pass. Nothing we haven't both heard plenty of times before."

J.B. threw his weight against the steering oar, bringing the clumsy craft toward the riverbank. "Best get into the cabin for a while, bro," he said to Ryan. "In case there's any trouble."

But there wasn't.

It was an idyllic scene, with an inlet where they could moor the raft to a tall, solitary live oak. A fast-flowing stream bubbled into the main river with the freshest, coolest water, and there were bushes of all kinds of berries, along with the overgrown remnants of an ancient orchard, the bent trees still bearing succulent pears and apples.

Jak borrowed Ryan's panga and vanished into the surrounding countryside, returning a half hour later with a brilliantly whittled walking stick.

"Thanks a lot. Make me mobile." Ryan took the stick and walked up and down the sloping shore, limping heavily and finding it hard going on the soft earth. But gradually it became easier, until Mildred made him stop.

"Look, you stupe! You've started to bleed again. Got to rest it as much as you can. Or I'll take your nice new stick and break it over my knee."

"Oh, I love it when you get angry," Doc teased with a faked shudder of excitement.

"Maybe I'll break it over your bony ass instead."

"Promises, promises."

J.B. HAD GONE HUNTING with the Steyr, and they heard the booming sound of the powerful rifle, sending a flight of wood pigeons susurrating into the evening stillness.

By the time the Armorer returned with a dead hare slung over his shoulder, Krysty had a fire going and a pot of water bubbling over it.

Mildred had gone scouting for herbs and vegetables, returning with a large handful of mixed greens that she now tossed into the steaming stew.

"I feel sure that I could set my mind to some verses about the pleasures of life on the open highway," Doc said, seeing the looks on everyone's faces. "But perhaps it can wait for a subsequent occasion."

The sun had set by the time the hare was cooked. Krysty pulled it out and dismembered the carcass, laying it on a large leaf for everyone to help themselves, digging into the pile of boiled greens, as well.

"Good," J.B. said, licking his fingers. The steam had condensed on his glasses, and he took them off, putting them safely into one of the deep pockets of his coat.

"Only good, John?" Mildred queried.

"Better than good. Delicious."

"See any other game?" asked Ryan, who had found that a half sitting, half lying position was least uncomfortable for his wounded leg.

"Deer, but I couldn't carry a body back on my own. And it would have taken longer to cook. There's tracks all over the place. Horses, unshod. Some cattle. Wild pigs. Man could live here for a long time and not go hungered."

Everyone lay back, relaxing in the warm gloaming, feeling the deep satisfaction of having shared a good meal among the best of friends.

"Get some more wood for fire," Jak offered, getting up and walking away into the quiet darkness surrounding the camp, his magnesium hair visible a long while after the rest of him had completely vanished.

"No sign of men or muties?" Ryan asked.

J.B. had his head in Mildred's lap, his glasses perched again on the bridge of his narrow nose. "Nothing. Apart from that solitary crazie we saw fishing, we haven't seen a soul. No smoke. No buildings." He hesitated. "Though it looks like this might once have been part of a large estate. The orchard and the stuff that Mildred found could've come from a kitchen garden."

Ryan was feeling tired, his eyelids drooping. "Best decide just where we're going and what we're doing."

"A time out of war," Doc pronounced. "A time to rest and a time to take it easy. A time for eating and sleeping. A time without fighting. Ah, me! But it has been a perniciously long time since we spent any time together without death and destruction dogging our steps."

"True enough," Ryan agreed. "I guess there's no reason why we shouldn't just cruise down for a day or so. Where would we end up, J.B.? Memphis?"

"Hell, no. Memphis is a ways west of here."

"How far?"

"Hundred miles. One-twenty."

"What's the biggest old ville we come to if we carry on down the Tennessee?" Krysty asked.

Jak returned with a pile of dry wood, dropping it with a clatter by the side of the fire, putting a few branches on to keep the flames burning brightly.

"What talking about?"

"Where we get to if we keep going south along the river," Ryan said.

"Savannah," J.B. offered.

"That's in Georgia," Mildred corrected. "That's not what you mean, is it, John?"

Doc interrupted. "John Barrymore is right as ever, Dr. Wyeth. Where are all your memories of the great War Between the States? Your historical education was obviously somewhat lacking in this area."

"Gone to flowers, every one," she replied. "What happened at Savannah, Tennessee, then?"

J.B. spoke again. "Shiloh. Bloody Shiloh. Only about ten miles away from Savannah." His eyes sparkled behind his glasses. "Dark night! We went close there with Trader, but I never visited the battlefield. If it still exists. That would be a wonderful thing to do."

"How far from here?" Ryan asked.

The Armorer shook his head. "Depends on the goosenecks of the river. Twists and turns. I'd hazard a guess it'll be around eighty to a hundred miles. Speed the water's flowing, that wouldn't take us more than a day's plain sailing."

"I would be interested to see Shiloh," Doc admitted. "This is such fun, my friends. My good, good friends. A boating holiday. Hurrah!"

SINCE THERE DIDN'T SEEM to be any threat, Ryan agreed that it wasn't necessary to post a guard. He believed Trader's theory that everyone needed sleep and to suffer deprivation was like having a battery depleted. The more you could store away, the better it was for any bad days that might be around the corner. So an early night sounded like a good idea for all of them.

His own wound was pulling painfully, and Mildred confirmed that he was running a slight fever.

"Maybe I should've stitched it for you," she said doubtfully. "But both entrance and exit wounds were nice and neat. No deformation of the ball."

Ryan shuddered. "Being stitched is high on the list of things I fucking hate, Mildred."

"Then you shouldn't go around getting yourself knifed and shot, should you?"

He grinned. "Guess not." He paused for a moment. "And I appreciate what you've done for me. Cleaning it and bandaging it and all."

"Part of the job." She laughed. "How pompous and stupe that sounds. Sort of thing I'd probably have said when I was in my late twenties. Before the operation and the... the freezing. Part of the job... I'll be telling you all about my Hippocratic oath next."

A white egret, with a wingspread of at least a dozen feet, flapped low over the moored raft, diverting its course slightly at the sight of the fire, floating elegantly above them like a snowy ghost.

"I think I'm ready for bed," Ryan said.

"On land or on the raft, lover?"

"Land's a sight softer. Those logs have already worn some bare patches off of my skin."

"Keep the fire going?" Jak asked. "Can go get some more wood." The teenager stood, gasping and pressing both hands to his midriff at the sudden pain.

"You all right, Jak?" Mildred moved J.B. off her lap and went toward the albino.

"Yeah. Just sharp."

"I checked and I'm fairly certain that there's no fractures to the ribs. Might easily have damaged the intercostal cartilage, I suppose."

"Be fine," he insisted.

"Pile the wood on the fire and then let it go down," Ryan said. "Seems a safe enough campsite to me."

Chapter Thirteen

The night passed uneventfully.

Ryan was awakened once by a hunting owl, circling around the smoldering remnants of the camp fire, its mournful hooting echoing across the silent river.

There was also some pain from his wound, stabbing and making him gasp when he tried to get up for a piss around four in the morning.

The whole leg had tightened, and there was enough moonlight for him to see that the bruising had come, purpling the swollen skin around both entrance and exit wounds. It had stiffened while he'd been sleeping, and to move away from the others, propping himself against the live oak, hurt Ryan.

Krysty had awakened as he moved, but he'd whispered for her to go back to sleep.

The night was still, with just a faint breeze flowing south with the Tennessee, carrying the scent of magnolias, sweet and fresh. A silver segment of moon sailed bright and serene between ragged shreds of high cloud. Away to the east, inland from their camp, Ryan caught the infinitely distant rumble of thunder and saw the silver lace of a chem storm. But it was all far enough away to give no cause for concern.

Doc's phrase about it being a time out of war struck at him as he finished relieving himself. After the brief firefight at the dirt-poor frontier pesthole, the day had been calm and gentle. No threat from the elements or from any living creatures.

And the coming day promised to be similar, cruising quietly along, carried safely on the bosom of the mighty river, south through the green fields of Tennessee. It was so rare for any of them for even a day to pass without some sort of threat of violence or, so often, actual violence.

Once dawn came up they would set off toward Savannah and Shiloh. Ryan had read a little about the Civil War, and he knew that Shiloh had been the bloodiest of battles, with close to twenty-five thousand men killed or missing or wounded, unimaginably huge losses in those days.

He picked his way around the glowing embers of the fire and laid down again at Krysty's side.

She stirred and opened her eyes. "All right, lover?" she muttered.

"Fine. Just fine."

"No trouble?"

He patted her hand. "None."

RYAN SLEPT SOUNDLY, waking only when Jak began breaking up some dry wood to rekindle the fire, whistling to himself, his breath pluming out in the dawn chill.

"Coffee, toast, ham, eggs over-easy, fresh orange juice, grits, pancakes, maple syrup, fries and then some

more coffee.'' Ryan grinned at the white-haired teenager. ''You got all of that?''

''We got berries fresh and berries medium-rare and
berries well-done, Ryan.'' He brushed back his hair
from his ruby eyes. ''Oh, and we also got berries.''

''Serve me up a steaming platter of those elusive
berries, myrmidon,'' Doc called.

''Should we do some hunting?'' the Armorer asked,
stretching his arms wide and adjusting his fedora.

''Might not be a bad idea.'' Ryan yawned. ''No
hurry to leave this place. Who knows what the food
situation'll be like farther south? Could run into an old
hot spot or find ourselves in some mutie paradise.''

''Get us a deer,'' Jak suggested.

''Pig might be better. If it wasn't for my leg, I'd
come with you. Even with my stick, I figure I'd get in
the way.''

''I'll go with John,'' Mildred offered. ''If game's
that plentiful, I can certainly bring something down
with my revolver. Could do with some practice.''

Ryan nodded. ''Fine. Rest of us'll stay around here.
Collect some more dry wood. Scavenge around for
vegetables to go with the meat.''

''I believe that I saw some sweet potatoes last night,''
Doc said. ''Should I go and dig some up?''

''Yeah. And if there's any old buckets or pots to
cook in . . . If there's this orchard, then the remains of
an old house can't be all that far away.''

''We could go look,'' Krysty said eagerly. ''Don't
have to make it all the way south to Shiloh today. Just
for once we got this quiet time. Let's make the best of
it.''

JAK AND DOC STAYED to gather wood and to get vegetables and more fruit for the meal, while J.B. borrowed the Steyr rifle again. "Just in case you miss,
Mildred."

"That's about as likely as Joe Montana missing a
fourth-and-inches," she said, seeing bewilderment.
"Greatest quarterback ever lived. Played mainly for
the Niners during the eighties. I mean, the greatest."

"Young deer or a tender little piggy," Ryan said.
"Leave it to you."

He and Krysty struck inland, following J.B. and
Mildred until their greater speed took them ahead, out
of sight.

"How's the leg, lover?" Krysty asked once they were
alone in the lush green wilderness.

"Had worse. Had better. From my experience of
getting myself shot, the second day's often the worst.
Bleeding's stopped and the bruise's coming out. Got to
stop the muscles all stiffening up. Bit of exercise like
this is about the best thing I could do." He grimaced as
his stick slipped in some muddy grass and he stumbled. "Anyway, Mildred said she thought that it likely
wouldn't do me no harm."

"Any harm."

"What I said." He grinned at her.

"Sure." She took his arm over a rough patch of
ground. "Looks like this might have been steps once.
Part of a formal garden, mebbe?"

He gazed around where they stood. They were
among some delicate flowering shrubs with pink-and-
silver-fronded flowers. Ryan didn't know the names of
many ornamental plants. Trader often used to say that

there wasn't much point in knowing the names of something you couldn't eat.

"Suppose there could be a garden somewhere under all this. A house even?"

She closed her eyes and drew in a deep breath. "The scent of those flowers is wonderful, lover. If there *is* the ruins of a house, it could be buried in among those trees yonder." She pointed to the northeast, where the tops of a grove of sturdy sycamores waved in the freshening morning breeze.

He hobbled after her, the end of the makeshift stick clicking off stone flags that lay just below a layer of grass. Doc had offered him the swordstick, but Ryan had refused it, worried that his weight might splinter the delicate ebony casing if he should suddenly need to throw his weight on it.

"Steps," Krysty warned. "With sort of carved faces on the rocks over that little pool."

The pool was dried up, long ago, maybe due to leaking conduits, but its green stained sides showed where it had stood. As they looked, a pair of tiny frogs, glittering like golden jewels, hopped across the path in front of them.

"This must've been a hell of a beautiful place once," Ryan said, steadying himself for a moment on an ornamental balustrade. "Serious jack involved."

"Unless it was some sort of a public park," Krysty suggested. "Mebbe a museum or a gallery."

"More paintings like in the redoubt? That I wouldn't mind seeing."

"All right to go a little farther?"

"Sure thing." He looked around to the right at the sound of a gunshot, a flat, muffled echo. "Mildred's target revolver. One bullet. Should mean we'll be having some good eating when we get back to the raft."

"You don't mind us not moving south straight-away?"

"'Course not. Why?"

"You're a walking dude, Ryan Cawdor. Man who moves and wants to keep moving. Staying still in one place, even for a few hours, isn't hardly in your nature."

"Thing doesn't move, then it rots."

"Thing doesn't put down roots and it'll die," she replied. "Mother Sonja warned me about marrying a gambling man or a traveling man. She would have liked you, Ryan."

"Think so?"

"Know so."

"Would I have liked her?" He answered his own question. "Yeah, I know I would. Sorry that I'll never get the chance."

"They didn't say she was dead. Just up and vanished." Krysty turned away, but Ryan caught the glint of sudden tears. "Mebbe one day..."

"Why not? Look at Trader. Thought the old dog bought the farm years ago. Then there he was. Large as life and twice as bastard unpleasant."

"Mother Sonja could be alive, couldn't she?"

Ryan nodded slowly. "I don't lie to you, love. Odds are she's long dead. Way it is in Deathlands. But there's a chance. Sort of woman who was your mother has to have something special going for her. Why not?"

Krysty sniffed and wiped her eyes on her sleeve. "Stupe to get upset on such a lovely morning in such a lovely place. Should be enjoying living, not getting maudlin and sad about the...about those who've gone."

"Right. Shall we go on up these steps and see what we find?" He peered at the soft ground. "Can't see any tracks of any kind around here."

The stairs were wide enough for a good-size wag to drive down them, lined with creepers that hung their purple flowers to the ground.

They opened onto a long terrace, edged with ornamental shrubs and drooping willows, growing alongside a narrow stream that flowed slowly through the garden, its limpid surface covered in waxen pink lilies.

"There," Krysty said. "That looks like a building, covered with ivy."

"Could be. Looks more like a church."

"Yeah, it does."

Now they could see it more clearly. It consisted of a single story, a kind of stubby tower at one end, with a crenellated top to it and a large clock face, handless, the gilt Roman numerals faded and worn.

There were windows all along the side of the building and a door, iron-studded, protected by a large porch.

"It's definitely a kind of church," Krysty said. "Looks real old. Lovely honey-colored stones."

"Doesn't seem much damaged."

"There's a track leading to it from the opposite direction. Mebbe there's a highway out that way."

Ryan nodded. "Could be. Don't want to go too far and attract attention to us. Take a quick look, then I think we should get back to the raft. See what kind of food Mildred shot for us. I'm already feeling hungry again."

"Me, too." Krysty sniffed again at the scented air. "Beautiful flowers. Make you feel almost dizzy with their smell. All right, lover, let's go take a look."

THE SMALL BUILDING WAS in an amazingly good state of preservation. On one side there was a range of stained-glass windows, but from the exterior it wasn't possible to see what they portrayed. On the other, northern flank, the glass was crazed and clear, as if the color had been leached from it.

"Could have been some kind of radiation from a skyburst," Ryan suggested, leaning on the stick and staring at the windows. "Likely a neutron nuke."

"Path's been kept trimmed back, and someone's mown the grass at the side by the porch." Krysty beckoned him to her. "Let's look inside."

Ryan wasn't comfortable. The short hairs at his nape were prickling, often a sign of some sort of impending threat. "You feel anything?" he asked.

She stopped, her hand reaching for the twisted iron handle of the arched double door. "Yes... Could be someone's not too far away. Feeling's sort of blurred."

"Bad?"

"No. Not bad. Not anything. You know it's often sort of confused. Might be someone good at veiling their true feelings. Come on, let's look inside."

Inside the porch was a wooden notice, painted black, neatly lettered in gothic gold printing: The Shrine Of The Blessed Antoninus Of Padua. Founded 1889. Come In To Worship.

Ryan ran his fingers over the lettering, looking at them. "Clean," he said, speaking quietly. "Been wiped free from dust in the last day or so."

"Must be a priest."

"We should get back to the raft." He had an urgent feeling that wouldn't translate into words.

"In a minute. Door's open, look."

Krysty pushed it silently back, walking away from Ryan into the cool interior. He followed her, combat boots ringing on smooth gray stone, catching the strong smell of incense, a scent that seemed to overlay another, more familiar odor that made him hesitate. But he couldn't quite identify the elusive smell.

There were a dozen pews ranged down each side, and a stone altar sat at the far end of the nave. Now in the gloomy interior, with the bright sun outside, it was possible to appreciate the delicate stained glass.

Five separate windows ran down one side. The other side still had the lead patterning, but all color was gone and the glass was starred and fractured.

Ryan looked behind him for a moment, sensing the door closing of its own accord. He saw that it hung on drop hinges and relaxed a little. Walking down the aisle, they admired the workmanship of the pictures.

They all, oddly, showed scenes of violence but done in a Victorian classic way, strangely devoid of emotion. Despite the horror show, nobody seemed to be actually suffering any real pain or emotion.

A man in a white sheet was being stabbed to death by a dozen others, similarly clothed. A tall, powerful black man was strangling a slender young woman across a wide bed. A grizzled man in armor knelt on the floor, arms held tightly, while a shadowy figure was plucking his eyes from their sockets. A blond woman held out stumps of arms, mouth wide open to show the bloodied rags of her tongue. And in the last picture a wretched man was being drowned in what looked like a barrel of beer.

Krysty had also been looking at the stained glass, turning away from it with an expression of disgust. "Brilliantly done, but horrible," she said. "Why put something like that in a church? Hideous."

"Concentrate the mind on death," Ryan said.

"I remember reading some plays by an old-time predark writer called Shakespeare, back in Harmony. I think these... some of them, anyway, are from his plays, Mebbe the other side was the same before it got nuked."

A large Bible stood open on a lectern in the shape of a brass eagle. Ryan walked to it, stopping by a carved plaque set in the wall.

This is a shrine to the blessed memory of Saint Antoninus of Padua and all penitents, remembering the legendary visit to this spot of Josephus of Arimathea, where it was once stated that this site on the Tennessee River was, perhaps, a hiding place of the Holy Grail.

"Holy Grail," Ryan said. "I didn't know that any of the old gospelers ever got this far west."

Krysty had walked to the bottom of the tower, craning her head back, staring up at a single bronze bell, with a long red-and-white plaited rope dangling from it.

Ryan looked at the book on the lectern, realizing that it wasn't actually like any Bible that he'd ever seen. It was open to the second chapter of the Dissertation of the Blessed Alphonse Donatien.

Only through pain and suffering shall there be redemption and an end to mortal weakness. Agony is seemly. There shalt be those who endure and tolerate the rending of their flesh and the splintering of their bones, and there shalt also be those that shall carry out such punishments in the name of all the holy ones.

"Sick stuff," Ryan said, turning away.

Krysty had been unable to resist the temptation and had loosened the rope from its cleat, tugging gently at it.

The bell tolled immediately, sending out a booming note across the summer morning.

"Leave it," Ryan snapped. "Want to rouse the whole bastard country against us?"

"Nobody here but us chickens, boss," she said, her teeth flashing in the gloom of the belfry. "Take it easy, lover. I always wanted to do this."

Ryan noticed that there was something lying on top of the altar. It was a multithonged whip, with tiny metal barbs knotted into each lash. All of them were stiff and stained black with what looked unmistakably like old, dried blood.

Suddenly the feeling of a threatening danger became much stronger. "Come on," he called. "Something's not straight about this place. Not a proper church."

Krysty let go of the rope, letting it dangle loose, the bell carrying on ringing, quieter and quieter, until its whispering sound faded away.

"Probably be able to hear that down by the river," she said. "Unless the noise of the water drowns it. Still, Mildred and J.B. would be close enough."

Ryan joined her, peering up in the darkness at a narrow metal ladder that climbed into the tower, seeing the softly swinging, silent bell.

"Out of here," he said urgently. "Before someone comes and brings trouble."

Neither of them heard the door whisper open, but they both recognized the audible click of the twin hammers being drawn back on a scattergun.

"Welcome, pilgrims," said a jolly voice.

Chapter Fourteen

In a wrecked vacation cottage somewhere up near what remained of the Great Lakes, Ryan had once found a stash of children's books. Included was a beautifully illustrated copy of the adventures of Robin Hood, who had been an English outlaw in the Middle Ages who'd allegedly robbed the rich and given the proceeds to the poor. It was a way of life that had been a source of endless raucous amusement to the crew of War Wag One.

Robin had some friends, one or two of which had stuck in Ryan's memory, a giant called Little John and a fat priest who had been named Friar Tuck.

Now, as Ryan turned slowly to stare down the yawning railroad tunnels of a Winchester Model 24, 20-gauge, he gaped at the figure holding the lethal blaster.

He wore a long brown gown, like a woman's dress, that fell to sandaled feet, tied at the waist with a length of knotted cord. A whip, twin to the one on the altar, was stuffed into the makeshift belt.

Ryan's initial guess put him at close to six feet, but he was so fat it was hard to judge. Really big men often looked shorter than they were. He looked around three hundred pounds, but it was easy to see that a lot of that was hard muscle.

His face was round, with several wobbling chins, clean shaved. The top of his head had also been shaved in a kind of circle, exactly like the picture of the legendary Friar Tuck. The eyes were difficult to judge in the gloom of the church, but they were so dark they could have passed for black, almost buried behind layers of fat, looking like little currants that had been thrown hard into a vat of white dough.

And he was smiling.

"Welcome, dear pilgrims. Such a pleasant surprise to find a pair of worshipers waiting for my services so early on such a fine morning."

"Not exactly worshipers, Father," said Krysty, whose face had gone pale. Ryan also noticed that her sentient hair had responded to the alarming apparition by curling in on itself, tight on her skull.

He beamed at her. "What a deeply ecumenical comment, my dear child. For surely all of us are 'not exactly worshipers.' How aptly spoken."

Ryan allowed his right hand to drop casually toward the butt of the holstered SIG-Sauer, on the blind side to the monk. But the man spotted the movement and gestured toward him with the barrels of the Winchester.

"No, no, no," he tutted. "We have only just met and you are trying to force me to speed you to your own personal Gehennah. Pray make no hasty moves."

"Gehennah? That near Savannah?" Krysty asked. "That's where we're bound when we spotted your church and we were just so taken with it."

"Filthy whoring harlot," he said, the broad smile untouched by the anger in his voice. "An untruth in the mouth of a strumpet is like unto worms in the brain of a camel."

Ryan guessed that the man was crazier than a shit-house rat, but he was also as dangerous as a cornered rodent. The chubby finger was tight on the triggers of the scattergun, the mean little eyes not flickering from them.

"You live here?" Ryan asked, trying to turn the conversation into safer waters.

"I have a small home close by. But I am remiss. I am called Father Sandor by my poor flock."

"There's a ville nearby?" Krysty probed.

"Oh, indeed, yes. Praise the gods."

Ryan was vaguely bothered by the strange smell that lurked underneath the reek of incense, a smell that also clung to the body and clothes of the fat monk.

"You don't need the blaster, Father," Krysty said, taking a casual step across to her left, trying to cover Ryan from the man's vision.

But Father Sandor was alert, gesturing with the shotgun for her to move back again. "Stupidity'll get you very dead, my child. Before your time. And who knows when the hour cometh? Be prepared, foolish harlot."

"Interesting stained glass," Ryan said, gesturing toward the windows, but the monk's attention never wavered for a moment. "Unusual."

Father Sandor stopped smiling, so suddenly that it was like a scream. "Enough talk."

"You aiming to keep us here?" Ryan asked. "Won't your flock get suspicious?"

The smile came back, frosty and bleak as pack ice. "My dear one-eyed dead man, my 'flock'—as you call them—shit themselves if I even glance in their direction. They know that this is not as other churches, and this is what the dirt-poor triple-dumb bastards secretly need. Not to be loved. To be cursed and whipped and tortured and sometimes chilled. That is a form of religion that makes sense in their brutish lives."

Ryan thought about the whip with its blood-clogged barbs lying on the altar, and he knew that life for both of them was hanging here by a hair. If there was a glimmer of a quarter chance, then to miss it would be to die. He'd known plenty of cold-heart killers in his lifetime in Deathlands, and Father Sandor was right up there with the best of them.

Or the worst of them.

"We'll go down into the crypt, pilgrims on the highway to celestial suffering."

He gestured with the scattergun, pointing them toward the front of the church, by the altar.

"Behind the pulpit, outlanders."

As they moved slowly forward, Ryan noticed that the figure of the crucified Christ that hung at the farther end of the church was sheathed in coils of razored barbed wire.

Father Sandor stayed a safe six paces behind them, not giving them a ghost of a chance to jump him.

"Ring in the floor. Lifts easily with the aid of the gods and a good counterbalance. Find a lamp and some self-lights just inside it and some steps down. Get the lamp going and walk down the steps. Go straight to the far wall and wait there for me. Don't thee move or speak.''

Ryan stooped and tugged on a wrought-iron ring set in the stone floor close by the altar. He heaved on it, surprised at how easily it swung open.

''Gaia!'' Krysty gasped in horror at the noxious miasma that floated up from the black hole.

And Ryan knew instantly what the smell had been that he'd first noticed in the church, clinging to the person of gross Father Sandor.

It was death, spilled blood, fresh and old, putrefaction of human flesh, ancient and modern. The vault below the aisle was nothing more or less than a charnel house.

Ryan hesitated at entering the pit, and the priest grew angry.

''Now or later. Matters not a jot to me, outlander. But most of my parish find breath oddly attractive and cling to it. Longer than one would have thought possible.''

''I'm going.'' Ryan lighted the oil lamp and adjusted the wick to give a steady, golden light that showed him a narrow flight of steps that wound down into a deep cellar.

''I think the time has come for thee to lay aside the weapons of unrighteousness, brother and sister. The two blasters can go down on the floor, at the top of the stairs. Perhaps that crooked stick, as well.''

''Can't walk without it. Got a bullet in my leg. Can't even stand.''

There was a long, menacing stillness, and Ryan knew that the monk was considering the option of blasting him in the spine. But the first option of having them both untouched in his crypt finally won out.

"Very well. But thy automatic and thy double-action Smith & Wesson, daughter of ungodliness. Very slow and very careful. Lay them down, pilgrims."

Ryan and Krysty obeyed the soft, oily voice, gently putting down their handblasters.

"Now thee may creep into my crypt."

THE CELLAR WAS unbearably hot, with two coal fires burning in iron braziers, one at each end, casting a fiery, crimson glow across the space that heightened the images of Hell.

Rows of torture instruments were hung on strong metal hooks: probes, files, hammers and pokers; whips in all shapes and sizes; knives, razors and cleavers; a rack and thumbscrews; chains and loops of thin wire, manacles and iron collars with padlocks.

It was a fully equipped torture chamber, like an engraving from an ancient tome about the horrors of the Spanish Inquisition.

And it was occupied.

Ryan and Krysty immediately saw the body of a young person, hung from one of the hooks like a rejected side of meat, so mangled that it was impossible to tell its sex or its age.

The corpse had been torn and battered in a hideous manner that screamed of endless hours of unimaginable pain and suffering.

Father Sandor was all too obviously a man who enjoyed his own skills.

"Ah, that," he said, beaming again in the light of the oil lamp, the fires casting a sweating sheen over his jowls. "A local youth who helped me with a service for good crops for the ville. A successful operation, but the patient, sadly, died." He laughed at his own humor.

He gestured for Ryan and Krysty to stand against the far wall of the cellar while he laid several probes and pokers in the braziers to grow hot.

"Suffering is pleasure and pleasure is suffering," the fat monk muttered, still keeping the Winchester scattergun aimed at his two prisoners.

It was obvious to Ryan that the priest intended to chain them, then torture them both to death. This was as inexorable as the sun rising in the east and setting in the far west. It meant that the moment was coming like a runaway train when some sort of move would have to be made, go up against the menace of the shotgun, whatever the outcome.

It was the most slender of chances, but it was a whole lot better than no chance at all.

He knew that Krysty would be thinking exactly the same, but there was no way of communicating with each other, no plan to be hatched.

At the back of his mind was the desperate idea of making a suicidal attack and hope that Sandor fired both of the barrels, giving Krysty a good chance of making a break for safety, then bringing J.B., Jak and the others back with her to avenge his own death.

Even at that dark moment, Ryan grinned wolfishly to himself, amused by his own shadowed plan of dying.

If the monk had been holding a handblaster, there would have been a goodish chance that he might miss. Ryan remembered seeing a nervous bounty hunter in a clothing store in a nameless ville in Pennsylvania fire eight shots from a Ruger P-85 at a dodging killer. All of them were at a range of less than ten feet, and every single bullet missed the target.

That wasn't going to happen at that range with a 20-gauge scattergun.

Father Sandor was breathing heavily with his own bustling exertion, readying himself for hours of sheer delight. His voice had become high and thin, like a eunuch's, with his own sick arousal.

"Now," he said, "thee can strip thy bubonic bodies naked and then chain thyselves to the walls. And we shall commence the service."

The instruments of torture in the hot coals were already beginning to glow cherry red.

"The scum of my parish will be so happy when they hear that I have consecrated a pair of strangers in the church. They will be happy because they will know that they will be spared for a short while." Sandor giggled. "But it will be a *very* short while."

Ryan hadn't moved, leaning on his clumsy walking stick, clinging to each passing second. Mildred and the Armorer hadn't been all that far away from the little church, and there was always a remote chance that they might come along and save the day. It was a small hope.

"Clothes off," Sandor snapped.

"Please," Krysty said.

"The time for begging will come later," he replied. "When the blood flows and salt fills your eyes and mouth, and your flesh is scorched and you crave butter for the smarting. But there is no butter here in Hell!"

"Just let her go and keep me," Ryan said, going along with time-buying.

Sandor grinned so widely his whole face became a huge creased smile. "I have two pets for my collection. Why, outlander filth, should I give either of you up?"

The shotgun barrels were about eight feet away from the two prisoners.

Too far.

Krysty took a step toward the priest, her hands spread for mercy. "Please," she said again.

Instinctively Sandor took a similar step back from her, gesturing with the big shotgun for her to stay where she was. But his movement had made him bump into the dangling corpse. The chains rattled noisily, and the eyeless skull slumped suddenly down onto the burned chest with a strange clicking sound.

In the atmosphere of bizarrely heightened tension, the monk jumped with shock, head turning to stare at the bobbing body, the Winchester scattergun swinging away from Ryan and Krysty for a moment.

How do you measure a moment when your entire life hangs in the balance?

Half a second?

A single beat of the human heart?

An indrawn breath?

All of Ryan's combat reflexes had been stretched to the limit, since the first appearance of the malevolent priest, ready to take instant advantage of any chance that appeared.

Sandor had a deep and ingrained sense of primitive evil on his side, combined with a total and brutish disregard for the sanctity of human life.

There was flurry of movement, a yell of surprise and the boom of the shotgun being fired, the charge shattering the oil lamp, plunging the cellar into almost total darkness.

Chapter Fifteen

"Go low!"

Trader's familiar and well-remembered instruction when tackling someone with a scattergun was still so potent that Ryan actually heard the voice of his old chief ringing in his ears as he made his move against Father Sandor.

He dropped his stick, powering himself off his good leg, face contorted with pain at the enormous effort it took, diving across the eight feet or so of the cellar that separated him from the fat, brown-robed figure.

He heard Krysty start to scream out, and thought he heard the monk blaspheming at the attack.

There was the shattering boom of one of the 20-gauge barrels firing, and the scorching breath from the explosion that burned his hair, the immense force of the shot raking across his shoulders.

Then he collided with the enemy, shoulder striking Sandor just below the knees. Despite the man's considerable bulk, the power of Ryan's attack sent him staggering backward, off balance. The broken lamp was rolling around on the stone floor, at the center of a small pool of spilled, burning oil, casting a purplish glow across the crypt.

Just because the first stage of his plan had been successful, Ryan knew that the secret of winning a hand-to-hand combat was continuity. You attacked with all of your force, and you kept on attacking and attacking until your opponent was down and done.

Sandor kicked out at Ryan, but the one-eyed man had a good grip on his right leg, just above the ankle. He levered up with all of his strength, trying to ignore the stabbing pain from his wounded thigh. He hefted the huge figure backward, keeping himself tucked under the man's belly, so that the monk couldn't reach him with the scattergun.

"Fuck you!" the murderous priest yelled, swinging down the barrels, catching Ryan a glancing blow on the shoulder, but doing nothing to loosen his hold.

Krysty had screamed only once, then came quickly in to help Ryan, launching herself feetfirst at Sandor, the heels of her Western boots catching him waist high.

The man grunted in pain and shock, swaying backward, giving Ryan the chance to try a second heave on his leg, toppling him right off balance.

"Get blaster," he panted, crawling up the sweating body, wincing as Sandor clubbed him across the temple with a massive forearm.

Krysty had rolled on hands and knees, moving with the agile grace of a big cat. She grabbed desperately at the barrels of the Winchester, keeping them steered away from Ryan as Sandor fought to fire the second 20-gauge round at his attackers.

Apart from Sandor's brief curse and the heavy breathing, the fight was carried on in almost total silence.

The priest was rolled on his back, close now to the larger of the braziers, one chubby hand gripping the stock of the Winchester, the other scrabbling down at Ryan, trying to beat him away from his face.

The man was extraordinarily powerful, preventing Ryan from getting a good stranglehold on him, while also hanging on to the shotgun.

''Bastard shitters . . .''

''Love you, too,'' Ryan panted, finally managing to snatch the monk's left hand, twisting and snapping the thumb out of its socket, eliciting a scream of pain.

Sandor's robe had ridden up over his knees, and he kicked out at Krysty, catching her in the ribs, the air whooshing from her lungs. She flew sideways, still holding desperately to the semibeavertail forearm. Her weight pulled on the shotgun, and the second trigger was released.

Ryan heard the thunderous boom, filling the cellar with noise, and was aware of Krysty's body flying to one side, landing in a heap against the wall near the dangling corpse.

And the killing rage overwhelmed him.

He batted aside the flailing shotgun, sending it spinning into the shadows, where it clattered against a crudely built rack. He brought his elbow around in a cracking blow against the side of Sandor's face, making the fat man gasp.

''You're fuckin' dead,'' he panted, straddling the monk, raining blows on the upturned face, breaking the nose into a bloodied pulp, closing both eyes. The priest coughed and spluttered, spitting out shards of broken teeth through his cut lip, mouth sagging open as he fought for breath.

Ryan's sole desire was to end it and end it quickly and brutally.

Sandor was semiconscious, breathing noisily, blood bubbling from his shattered mouth. Ryan glanced quickly around, seeing that Krysty was struggling to sit up, rubbing the side of her head.

He was aware of the scorching heat from the iron brazier at his side, with the wooden handles of the torture instruments, mostly wrapped in steaming wet rags.

Ryan grabbed at the nearest, seeing that it was a straight iron poker with a twisted end, like a corkscrew. The tip glowed almost white hot. The handle, despite the protective rags, was almost too hot to hold.

Sandor blinked open his puffed eyes, shaking his shaved head as if he couldn't recognize what was happening, or couldn't quite believe it.

"What?" he said quietly, pink blood frothing over his layers of chins.

"So long," Ryan panted. "Enjoy Hell!" He carefully placed the almost molten iron tip over Sandor's mouth, then thrust with all of his weight behind it.

The hissing of steam and the stench of blistering flesh flooded Ryan's nostrils, almost making him puke into the priest's upturned face. The doomed Father Sandor thrashed and kicked like a blubbery landed whale, a muffled, choking scream of living horror erupting from him.

But Ryan was inexorable and as cold as granite, pushing the probe down to the back of the monk's mouth, over the burned tongue, into the top of his throat, filling the dying man's lungs with the stink of his own body burning. He drove the poker deeper and deeper, until it was nearly two feet deep inside the murderous priest's chest.

The body shuddered, and tears flooded from the bruised eyes. There was a trickle of bright arterial blood from the open mouth, hissing on the hot iron.

And then stillness.

KRYSTY HAD A DARK BRUISE flowering on the side of her forehead, close to the hairline, and she was still trembling from the horror of the experience. But apart from the residual shock, she was in good shape.

Ryan had retrieved his stick, limping heavily and biting his lip in the fresh pain from getting a kick on the bullet wound from Father Sandor.

But at least they were both still alive and relatively unharmed, and hadn't joined the poor maimed corpse that still hung reproachfully in the chains from the wall of the noisesome crypt.

Krysty had found a large barrel of lamp oil among the shadows of the cellar.

"Be good to clean out this nest once and for all," she said. "Cremate that vile piece of human shit at the same time." She kicked the corpse of the fat monk with the chiseled toe of her dark blue boots.

"Sounds good. Let's do it."

They managed to heave the barrel halfway up the steps from the crypt before knocking out the bung, letting the liquid gush down onto the stone flags.

"Heat from the braziers won't ignite it, will it?" Krysty asked.

"No. Not like gasoline. Chuck a couple of the pews down into it to feed the flames once they start."

Safely out in the body of the picturesque church, they each picked up and reholstered their blasters. Ryan took the blasphemous Bible from the lectern and pitched it down into the crypt, having torn out a handful of pages first, twisting them into a makeshift torch.

"Ready?"

She nodded, handing him a self-light. "Sure. Let's do it and get out of here."

He flicked the match, applying it to the bundle, watching the flare of flame, bright in the dim interior of the church. He tossed it down the flagged steps, pulling back at the whoosh of flame from below. They moved toward the door as black smoke wreathed out into the chancel.

On an impulse, Ryan hobbled to the altar and picked up the bloodied whip, heaving that into the sea of flames that surged up the stairs.

"More pews?" Krysty asked.

"Why not?"

THE WHOLE BUILDING was ablaze.

As Ryan and Krysty looked behind them, there was a huge pillar of smoke, dark at its base, lighter as it rose into the blue sky, billowing through the shingled roof, which was blazing fiercely. More smoke came through the open door, and tendrils crept from the slitted gaps in the tower.

"Won't be working any more evil," Ryan said.

"And it was such a pretty building." Krysty shook her head, her dazzling red hair gradually easing out across her shoulders as the tension relaxed.

"I'm sure that Doc would have some neat little saying about there being a worm at the heart of the red apple," Ryan told her. "Something like that."

He winced and shifted his balance again, aware of the warm stickiness of fresh blood trickling down the back of his wounded thigh.

"Hurting?"

"Some."

"Get Mildred to take a good look at it when we get back to the raft."

He nodded. "Sure will."

They were out in the beautiful gardens, still staring back at the flaming church.

There was a great crash that made them duck, and the exquisite stained-glass windows on the one flank of the doomed building exploded in a shower of multi-colored splinters, bright orange, purple, crimson, emerald, turquoise, gules and argent.

"Gaia! It's like a fountain of glass. Lovely."

The rope had to have burned through at the bottom of the belfry, as the bell began to toll, slowly at first, then faster.

Its sonorous tones echoed out across the fertile land of the old gardens, as though calling the news of the death of the wicked Father Sandor.

"Leaves the place a mite cleaner than when we arrived here," Ryan said thoughtfully.

"Generally do, lover. We generally do."

THEY MADE THEIR SLOW WAY back toward the clean-running river, where the others were waiting for them. The column of smoke had been spotted, and J.B. had been preparing to lead a recce party to find out what had happened.

The corpse of a large wild pig, shot neatly behind the right ear, lay on the ground, being butchered by Jak, ready for cooking on their own bright fire.

"Have any adventures out there?" Mildred asked. "You both look like shit."

Krysty began to laugh and Ryan joined her.

Chapter Sixteen

After the horrors of the morning, the rest of the day drifted by in a haze of sunshine and overeating.

The roast pig was absolutely delicious, the crackling thick and crunchy, the meat pink and tender, flavored with the wood smoke. Mildred had found a tall tree in the old orchard with some ripe pears and another that dripped peaches. She sliced them all together and boiled them for a few minutes until they simmered down into a kind of fruit stew.

It was the middle of the afternoon before everyone had recovered enough from the enormous meal and was ready to embark once more on the raft, pushing off back into the fast-flowing stream of the Tennessee.

They took a pile of sliced and hacked pork with them, ready to eat when they camped for the night. They could wash it down with the clean water from the river.

Mildred had checked out Ryan's wound, whistling between her teeth at the amount of fresh blood and the deep bruising around it. She warned him that he couldn't afford to keep aggravating it, pointing out there was a serious risk of poisoning if he didn't take proper care.

"Don't tell me," he replied. "Tell that crazed son of a bitching priest!" He grinned up at the woman. "If you can find him."

"MAKE SHILOH AROUND NOON tomorrow," J.B. said, lying back alongside their fire as the sun sank to the west and a cloud of midges buzzed over the inlet of the river. "Long as we don't laze around stuffing our faces with roast pork all morning or set fire to some churches."

"That's if Shiloh's still there," Ryan stated.

"Not many people around. Only seen a few today." Jak had peeled off his shirt and was gingerly massaging the spectacular bruise that lay below his belt buckle.

Doc had been teasing him about the injury, comparing it to something in an old song about a tattooed lady. "Looks like a still life of plums on a golden blanket," he said. "Are you sure you don't have the guards in line, all along your spine, or a fleet of battleships all around your hips?" He cackled with laughter at the expression on Jak's pale face.

They had moored among the ruins of what had been a small village of riverside cottages, most of them very close to the water. It was, as Jak had noted, a strangely deserted region of Deathlands.

They had seen a total of five people all day, since leaving their overnight mooring.

There had been a pair of whiskered old men in a tiny rowboat, battling their way upriver against the current. They sat side by side, each with an oar, backs straining, hardly looking across at the clumsy raft as it rolled past them in the opposite direction, panting out a "Good day," watching them vanish south while they labored to gain a few precious yards.

A woman and child had been sitting on a shallow bank on the eastern shore of the Tennessee. She was blind, with smooth flesh covering where her eye sockets should have been. The child that played by her feet, picking up tiny pebbles and laying them in a mazelike pattern, had a look of blank idiocy on its face, not showing the least interest in the strangers that drifted by a few yards away from them.

Krysty had called to them, but neither the woman nor the child reacted in any way.

The last of the people they saw was a young man with delicate features and a halo of thick golden hair. He had been walking along a path that ran by the river, in the same direction as they were sailing.

Jak had called out to him, making him jump, oblivious to their silent approach.

"Good afternoon to you," he'd replied with a cheerful wave of the hand.

"We far from Shiloh?" shouted J.B. who was at the steering oar.

"Wouldn't know, friend. I have to get to market. Carrying a flock of sheep hidden up my ass."

The reply was so absurd and unexpected that everyone on the raft stared at him in silence.

He smiled and nodded merrily, keeping pace with the raft for about a quarter mile, with no more exchange of conversation, until the Tennessee bent away to the right and the path carried straight on.

Ryan had been lying on the deck, near the bow of the rudimentary boat, and he watched with the others as the cheerful young man vanished with a last, friendly wave of the hand.

"Few rounds short of a full mag," he'd said.

"STRANGE SORT OF REGION we've come through," J.B. said as they lay around their bright fire, with the shades of evening drawing down.

"I don't recall being anyplace along the Tennessee with Trader." Ryan yawned, reaching out and taking another slice of cold meat.

The Armorer nodded. "Me, neither. Rad count's safe in the green, but we haven't encountered anyone yet that you could call a norm. Not since leaving the redoubt."

"Least there haven't been any out-and-out muties. Just a few triple-strange." Krysty folded her hands behind her head and stared up at the velvet sky, watching the myriad stars winking into life. "Good air and grass and water."

"And tomorrow, Shiloh," Doc added. "A cousin of my father gave his life there." He blew his nose on his blue kerchief. "Fought in the Fifth Division of the Army of Tennessee, under William Tecumseh Sherman. Under Grant himself. You know that Sherman had a kind of breakdown in 1861, and Grant liked the bottle too well."

"I know the story," J.B. said. "Sherman said that Grant stood by him when he was crazy and that he stood by Grant when he was drunk."

"That is correct," replied Doc. "That is absolutely correct. I heard it from Cousin Wilfred himself, so it must certainly be true."

RYAN WAS AWAKENED a couple of times during the night by the dull pain of his wound, getting up once to piss among the stunted rosebushes that ranged around some of the silent, derelict cottages.

In the stillness he suddenly realized that he could hear J.B. and Mildred making love, a little way along the bank of the river.

Embarrassed, Ryan limped farther alongside the Tennessee to relieve himself, moving as silently as he could through the dew-damp grass, leaning heavily on his makeshift crutch. He spent a little time sitting on the bank, back against a beech tree, watching the river flow. He thought about the crazed priest that he'd sent off to knock on heaven's door and about the serene beauty of the countryside around them.

To his surprise, he actually dropped off to sleep, waking with a start, shivering and cold. He glanced down at his chron, but it gave him no clue as to how long he'd been dozing. It was an indication to him of the way a wound could weaken a man, far more than he might expect.

He levered himself upright again, with the help of his stick, drawing in a whistling breath at yet another stab of pain burning through his leg.

An owl swooped out of the starry darkness, wings spread, eyes like saucers, veering away at the last moment as its keen sight picked up the motionless human.

Ryan watched it go, floating low over the calm surface of the river. There was a sudden ripple, and he spotted something lithe and silver leap clear out of the water, hanging for a moment, the patchy moonlight gleaming off the scales.

The owl had seen it and veered sideways, jinking like a running back heading for the end zone, but it was a heartbeat too late and the fish disappeared in a burst of foam.

Ryan grinned at the closeness of the escape and hobbled back to sleep again alongside Krysty.

DURING THE LATTER PART of the night, the sky became cloudy and the dawning was gray and overcast. Ryan sniffed the air, tasting a fine drizzle on his breath.

"Might as well get moving early," he said. "No point in sitting around if there's rain on the way."

There was a brief shower as they were launching their raft, pitting the surface of the Tennessee, the rising wind ruffling the branches of the trees around.

AROUND TEN O'CLOCK the river narrowed dramatically, steep bluffs rising on both sides, raising the pace of the current to something close to twenty miles per hour.

Jak joined J.B. on the steering oar, while Doc and the women also took an oar each, ready to aid in the struggle if the raft got out of control. Unable to do much by way of steering, Ryan propped himself up at the front of the craft, struggling to balance on the spray-soaked logs, keeping a watch out for any dangers in the rapids ahead.

''Bridge!'' he shouted, spotting a spidery edifice of strung ropes that dangled low over the foaming surface of the Tennessee, around six hundred yards in front of them.

''And people!'' the Armorer yelled, pointing with his right hand to movement at the top of the cliffs.

Ryan stared up, seeing about a dozen men, all of them gesticulating and running, moving fast toward the narrow bridge. Peering through the spray, he made out that some of them were carrying coils of rope with what looked like long hooks attached to their ends.

''Aiming to catch us!'' he yelled.

''Off the bridge,'' Krysty said. ''They'll try and snag us from the bridge.''

Ryan dropped to hands and knees and crawled back into the cabin, emerging with the Steyr. The raft was pitching so much that it would take an amazingly lucky shot to hit anyone until they got real close. But a few rounds buzzing around their ears might make them cautious.

''Steer to the right, away from them!'' he shouted, pointing with the muzzle of the bolt-action SSG-70.

''Can't!'' Jak replied, his wet hair matting around his long, narrow skull. ''Too fast!''

They were closing on the bridge at an amazing rate, rocking from side to side. Ryan steadied himself against the roof of the makeshift cabin, trying to draw a bead through the scope on the scampering men.

But it was impossible.

The roaring of the torrent made conversation hopeless. All of them could see the danger as the group ahead was already moving out onto the swinging bridge, allowing the iron hooks to dangle below them off the looping ropes. A couple of them had long guns strapped across their shoulders, but most seemed to be armed with daggers, swords and axes.

But the pitching of the raft totally negated the value of the blasters.

They had closed to less than two hundred yards and they could see the faces of the men who hung to the bridge, agile as monkeys, gesturing toward their prey.

There were eleven of them altogether, mostly bearded, with thick, shaggy hair, swinging hand over hand, mouths open as they yelled their hatred at the oncoming outlanders.

Ryan tried with the Steyr, squeezing off a couple of shots. But they had no visible effect, beyond seeming to anger the men on the bridge.

"Try to cut ropes if we get hooked!" Ryan shouted to the others.

The raft seemed to be moving faster and faster, and the noise of the pounding waters in the gorge was deafening. Ryan tried another snap shot, snarling with delight as he saw one of the waiting men lose his grip and fall lifelessly into the Tennessee, fifty yards or so ahead of them, a crimson rose blossoming on the front of his white shirt.

The closer they drew, the more Ryan realized that the weight of the locals on the bridge had dragged it down until it was barely a dozen feet above the foaming breakers of the river. It was going to be more than possible for some of them to jump onto the raft, easier if they could snag it with their hooks and hold it for a few moments against the ferocious tug of the current.

Ryan heard the pop of Mildred's Czech revolver, the sound of the shots almost drowned by the river. He counted three rounds, seeing another of the waiting men throw his arms wide and fall from the bridge, dropping his hook and coil of rope as he slumped to his death.

The one-eyed man turned and gave the woman the thumbs-up, getting a grin in return.

But there were still nine of them, several already lowering their iron grapnels, swinging them to the surface of the river, ready to try to hook onto the raft.

Ryan threw the rifle inside the cabin and drew the SIG-Sauer. The pain in his leg seemed to have disappeared into the background, and all his combat reflexes were tight and ready.

"Here they come!" he yelled.

Chapter Seventeen

One vital factor became instantly obvious as the first of the hooks rattled against the spray-slick timbers. The force of the Tennessee River and the weight of the raft were both far greater than the attackers on the flimsy bridge had realized.

Four or five hooks made good, solid contact, but the rushing motion of the heavy craft was hardly checked. Three of the men jumped as the bridge was pulled even lower, one of them landing off balance on the side of the raft, slipping and tumbling helplessly over the edge. He vanished into the tumbling foam with a muffled scream of despair.

The other two landed safely on the raft, one on top of the cabin, the other near the front, where Ryan was standing and waiting.

He leveled the SIG-Sauer and shot him at point-blank range through the upper chest, the force of the 9mm full-metal-jacket slug kicking him off his feet, where he also slipped over the side into the river.

Krysty shot the man off the cabin roof, putting two bullets into him from her Smith & Wesson, the heavy .38-caliber rounds rolling him onto the deck, where he lay screaming, both hands clutched at the double wound in his stomach. Krysty and Mildred heaved him off into the racing stream.

Ryan looked away, seeing no further threat from any of the three attempted boarders.

There were six men still hanging on to the bridge, four with their barbed grapnels dug into the raft, finally slowing its racing progress. But they had looped their ropes around the spidery bridge, which was now dipping perilously low, the cords that built it strained like banjo strings, singing above the deep thunder of the river.

''Gaia, it's coming down!'' Krysty screamed at the top of her voice.

Jak had moved from the steering oar and was busily crabbing around the raft, trying to cut through the cords that snared them. But they had become wet and taut, like bars of iron, almost impossible to slice.

Another of the men jumped from above, landing awkwardly, close to Doc. He turned his ankle as he fell, with a dry crack, audible above the bedlam. He shrieked once, showing a completely toothless mouth. Doc was holding the Le Mat in his right hand, but he hesitated to waste a valuable shotgun round. Quickly holstering the commemorative cannon, he drew the trusty swordstick.

The attacker reached up and grabbed at the honed rapier blade, but Doc tugged it away from him, cutting the man's palm clear to the bone. Blood spouted over the wet timbers.

''Chill him!'' Ryan called.

Doc stumbled, steadying himself for a moment against the low roof of the cabin, and two more men dropped onto the raft, one of them slashing at the old man with a billhook with a vicious beaked blade.

There was a high twanging sound, and the bridge suddenly collapsed into a tangle of broken ropes and splintered wood, tearing away from both sides of the gorge. It fell into the Tennessee just astern of the raft, dumping the last of the doomed men into the river.

Released from the restraint, the raft shuddered like a hound dog ridding itself of fleas and began to race downstream once more, slowed only by the snarled weight of the wrecked bridge.

Three of the enemy were aboard, one with the broken ankle and horribly cut hand, and two others, one attacking Doc who was parrying for his life, the slender Toledo steel ringing against the clumsy cleaver.

The last of the locals had dropped to hands and knees, a slender dagger gripped in each hand, and was crawling toward J.B., who was still wrestling at the back with the long, clumsy oar.

Ryan was vaguely aware that there was white water ahead, with jagged boulders sticking above the roiling surface of the river, threatening further disasters.

Doc finally slip-parried a powerful thrust from the billhook, and turned quickly to thrust the needle-tipped blade of his sword between his opponent's third and fourth ribs, slicing through heart and lungs as he twisted his wrist before withdrawing the blood-slick steel.

Mildred had managed to find her balance long enough to put a bullet through the forehead of the man with the wounded hand, blowing away half the back of his skull, emptying a grue of brains and blood into the waiting river.

Which left the man with the pair of knives, making his way toward the rear of the raft and the helpless Armorer, unable to let go of the steering oar as they plunged into the raging rapids at the heart of the shadowed gorge.

Ryan snapped a shot at the man, but the craft was tilting and rocking and he was forced to throw himself down onto the bloodied logs and hang on for dear life.

Jak saved J.B.'s life.

Not trusting to his own lack of skill with his big Colt Python, the albino went for his beloved throwing knives, drawing one of the leaf-bladed, weighted weapons from its hiding place in the small of his back, gripping it by the taped hilt and throwing it in a snapping underarm motion.

Despite the shifting platform, the teenager's aim was as accurate as ever.

The knife hit the crawling man on the side of his throat, clinging there like a glittering insect that suddenly spouted bright crimson from the severed artery. The doomed attacker pulled it out with his right hand and threw it down with a curse, not realizing that he was already dying.

He spotted Jak and threw one of his own knives at the red-eyed youth, who ducked away at the moment that the raft, despite all of the Armorer's efforts, struck the fanged spur of a submerged rock and tipped savagely to starboard.

Jak was thrown into the icy water of the Tennessee River.

Mildred and Ryan both saw the accident, the woman scuttling to the rear of the raft, ready to try to help the teenager if he surfaced from the churning maelstrom.

Ryan faced the last of the surviving attackers, who was standing in a stooped crouch, arterial blood gushing from his throat, glaring from side to side like a stubborn beast trapped in the shambles.

It was only a matter of time, but Ryan wanted him down and out. He crawled on hands and knees toward him, gasping at the pain from his thigh, the SIG-Sauer held out toward the dying man like a crucifix toward a vampire.

"Cut head off, you shitter outlander!" the attacker grunted, waving his dagger.

"No," Ryan said, shooting him carefully through the center of the chest, seeing a chunk of flesh burst from the exit wound between the shoulders, flecked with the white splinters of ribs and spine.

The turbulence was growing worse, and only the dragging wreckage of the ruined bridge was helping to hold the raft on course in the main current, stopping it from swinging completely around, out of control.

There was a loud crack as the main steering oar snapped in two, leaving J.B. holding a useless stump of wood barely four feet in length.

"Where's Jak?" Ryan yelled, trying to make his way toward the stern, kicking one of the flailing corpses out of his way, clinging onto the pitching, sodden timbers.

"In among the cordage," Mildred replied, pointing with the barrel of her own blaster. "One of the bastards is caught in there with him."

Ryan saw Jak's flaring white hair, like a beacon among the frothing dark green water. He was hanging on to the mass of tangled ropes and planks that had been the bridge, waving with his free hand to show that he was alive and well.

"Gets quieter ahead," Krysty shouted, her mouth close to Ryan's ear. "Should survive."

But Ryan had also seen the man that Mildred had spotted, only a few feet behind the teenager, working his way toward Jak with a rusty cutlass gripped in his rotting teeth.

The raft was shuddering, and Ryan noticed that several of the main bindings had come apart, loosening the timbers so that they moved against one another, rubbing and chafing. If they didn't get into calm water soon, Ryan guessed that the whole thing was about to fall apart.

"Jak hasn't seen the other bastard," J.B. shouted, still holding the stump of the oar.

Though Jak was a couple of yards nearer than the enemy, they were almost in line with each other, making a shot far too risky to attempt.

The Armorer managed to balance for a moment and pitched the remains of the oar over the stern, aiming at Jak's attacker.

But the hunk of wood overshot by a dozen feet.

Krysty was gesturing to the albino, pointing behind him, giving the traditional signal for danger.

At last Jak realized, shaking hair from his eyes, glancing over his shoulder. The attacker was now close enough to him to take the sword from his teeth, clinging to the knotted wreckage with his left hand, trying a violent slash at the teenager, missing him by scant inches.

The others could only watch helplessly as the deathly struggle began less than twenty feet away, yet it might as well have been on the dark side of the moon.

The man was stout, in his forties, with thinning hair and a red complexion. In among the dashing spray, Ryan noticed that the enemy's ears were on backward.

Jak had drawn another of his knives, using it to peck at his attacker, but it seemed like a child using a toy blade against a grown man with his powerful cutlass.

"Gaia, help him," Krysty muttered, barely audible above the roar of the Tennessee through the steep gorge.

But Jak didn't need any help when it came to hand-to-hand fighting.

The other man was slow and clumsy, terrified of losing his grip on the tangled wreckage of the fallen bridge, aware of the corpses of several of his colleagues that were being dashed on the rocks around him or sucked under in whirlpools.

Jak was constantly on the move, always hanging on by one hand, once vanishing below the surface of the river, emerging directly beneath his opponent, cutting up at him, severing the tendons in the man's right wrist. The old sword vanished into the water, leaving him one-handed and weaponless.

"Now," Ryan said, holstering the SIG-Sauer, seeing that it was all done.

The man was trying to back away from his fate, but it was impossible to move safely with only one functioning hand and he was almost paralyzed with terror.

The watchers on the raft could see his mouth opening and closing as he begged for mercy from the red-eyed teenager.

But *mercy* wasn't a word that featured large in the vocabulary of Jak Lauren.

"Rain on him boy," J.B. said.

Jak feinted with his left hand, but the blade had switched to the right. It thrust out like a tongue of a snake, faster than anyone could see, burying itself in the socket of the man's left eye, hilt deep. For a moment there was a splash of pink among the foam from the river.

The teenager pulled the knife free, watching as his opponent writhed for a few moments in his death agony, finally letting go of the ropes, slipping away into the hungry waters.

"Haul him in," Ryan called.

The cliffs were becoming lower, the river widening, slowing its churning passage as they began to leave the gorge.

It was easy to pull the teenager in off the snarled, twisted cords and shattered wood, back to the relative safety of the damaged raft.

"Need to get to shore and do some repairs," Ryan said, aware as the tension passed away that his injured leg was hurting him like fire.

FORTUNATELY THEY HAD plenty of spare ropes to make the raft secure again, using the mass of cordage hooked on from the ruined bridge.

But it was a long process.

By the time they had finished and were ready to push off again, the sun was way past the middle of the day, just visible through ragged cloud, and they were all thoroughly tired.

"That last meat?" asked Jak, who had been sitting by the river's edge, using a stone to renew the honed edge on his throwing knives.

"Yeah." Ryan had finished reloading the automatic and the rifle. J.B. was still fieldstripping his own blasters, though he hadn't fired either of them, making sure they were dry and clean and oiled.

"We look for food now?"

"Mebbe. Haven't thought much about that."

"Or wait until we stop?"

"Could do that also."

"How far Shiloh?"

Ryan looked across the clearing at J.B. to answer Jak's question.

"Not sure. That gorge wasn't on any map. Must've been some big earth movements."

"No bridges," Mildred said, rubbing her hands together. "No towns. No cities. Not even a dirt-poor frontier pesthole to give us some clue where we're all at."

"My guess is not far from Savannah," the Armorer said. "But that could be another forty or fifty miles. And Shiloh's a little way past that."

"Not far. Forty or fifty miles." Mildred stood and looked at him, hands on hips. "Jesus, John! The river's slowed right down again. Four or five miles an hour, I'd guess. So it could be way late this evening."

The Armorer smiled, the watery sun reflecting off his glasses. "True enough, Millie. All we can do is launch her and see where we end up by evening."

"Will that oar do duty as a replacement rudder?" Doc asked from the shade of a bushy eucalyptus. "I assume it will."

Ryan had tested it, throwing his weight against the makeshift binding. "Should do fine."

"Want me to take another look at your leg?" Mildred asked. "Took a pounding during that fight."

Ryan shook his head, trying not to lean too heavily on his stick. "Caught it a couple times. But it feels like it's getting better."

Krysty narrowed her eyes. "When it comes to lying, lover, you're strictly little league."

He hobbled quickly to the raft, ignoring her, stooping to loosen the mooring line. "Less talk and more sailing, friends. Let's do it."

Chapter Eighteen

Savannah had been used as a military base for some of the top-secret, silo-based ICBMs that had dominated American military policy for much of the latter part of the previous century. It had brought wealth to the city, and extra prosperity to the merchants, builders, tavern owners and storekeepers.

It had also brought the wrath of the Russkies, raining molten fire from the heavens, wiping the town and the surrounding region to the northwest away into an arid wasteland of black glass and rolling sand. It was a dangerous hot-spot that, nearly a hundred years after skydark, still sent the rad counters off the orange section of the scale way across into the red.

The raft drifted on south, carried by the gentle stream of the Tennessee.

The clouds had vanished, and the afternoon saw temperatures rising well into the upper nineties.

Everyone except Ryan took turns steering the raft, following the center of the river as it wound its way between the deserted land. There was nearly half a mile between the banks, and they saw nobody to threaten them.

At the place where the rad count was highest, they saw a number of small, capering creatures that hopped and skipped, throwing stones in their general direction. They were less than three feet in height, and several of the vaguely humanoid muties seemed to have extra limbs, with one or two having secondary skulls. But there was a heat haze lying over the river, and it was difficult to be absolutely certain.

At the most blighted part of the terrain, Jak had been dabbling his hand in the river to cool off, when he jumped. "What fuck that!" he exclaimed, looking at a bead of blood that clung to the tip of his white finger.

They all looked over the side of their craft, trying to see beneath the sun-dappled surface, shading their eyes against the bright sunlight.

"Eels," Mildred said, leaning so far over that her beaded plaits nearly dangled in the water.

There was a sudden explosion from the deeps of the river, and several tiny eels erupted and clung to the plaits. They were no more than four or five inches long, thick as a man's finger, and had a dozen protruding eyes and staggeringly ferocious triple sets of needle teeth.

The woman screamed in shock, pulling back, while J.B. and Jak tugged the vicious little creatures off her, throwing them back into the sullen water.

After that, everyone kept clear of the edges of the raft, avoiding the places where the logs didn't fit well, with gaps straight down into the river.

JUST PAST SAVANNAH the Tennessee forked, split down the middle by a gigantic spit of muddy yellow sand.

Doc was at the helm, and he called out for instructions.

"Right or left? Should I sail for port or for starboard? Starboard or larboard? Red light or green? Keep off the lee shore, Mr. Hornblower! Pass the starboard.... I mean, pass the port, if you please." He was grinning broadly, the light breeze tugging at his silvery mane of hair. "Clockwise or counterclockwise or widdershins about?"

Ryan had been sitting on the roof of the cabin, and he stood, balancing with care, trying to see which of the channels seemed the better option.

"Try left, I think," he called, then hesitated. "No, make that right. Seem to be shallows to the left. Yeah, steer her to the right, Doc."

The makeshift steering oar creaked as Doc heaved at it, sending the lumbering craft crabbing its way to the side, passing the soft shallows on the left.

"Boat ahead," Krysty called.

Everyone looked down the Tennessee, where it bent to the right. Just on the crown of the bend was a small rowboat, with a pair of oars rising and falling in perfect rhythm.

It was coming upriver toward them, making fine progress against the sluggish current. Because of the way that they were facing, the oarsmen had no idea that they were closing fast with the raft.

Ryan waited until they were fifty yards ahead and then hailed them.

"Yo the boat!"

If he'd launched a frag gren at them, it would hardly have had more effect.

The man on the left caught a crab, his oar digging in deep, the loom rising and hitting him under the chin, sending him sprawling flat on his back in the bottom of the little boat. His companion tried to look around while carrying on rowing, which meant that his oar completely missed the water, flailing around in the air like a demented windmill.

"What the fuck is this?" yelled the man lying sprawled on his back, kicking his little legs in the air, his arms whirling as he tried desperately to recover his balance and regain his seat on the thwart.

"Sorry to startle you," Ryan called. "But you were going fair to hit us."

The rowboat had gone around in two tight, complete circles, but the occupants finally managed to get her under their control again.

"Tarry-hootin' Yankee bastards!" Both men were now revealed as elderly, with identical white beards. "Sneaking up on a couple about their lawful fucking business and trying to run them down and fucking sink them."

"Hey!" Krysty shouted. "Watch your language. There's ladies on board here. And you would have run straight into us if we hadn't warned you."

Now that they'd turned their skiff around and had it gentled down, the two old-timers also calmed themselves. One of them wore a battered Stetson, and he raised it to Krysty.

"My 'pologies, ma'am. My tongue sort of ran away with me. Guess we owe you thanks for saving us from getting plowed three fathoms deep."

"Eel-bait is what me an' Jericho would've been," the other old man shouted.

"We seen the eels," J.B. said as the two crafts came almost alongside each other. "Vicious little bastards. Figure that it would be triple-bad news if you went over the side with them anywhere around."

"Many a good man been lost to them," said the one called Jericho.

"You live nearby?" Ryan asked.

"Little ville off a side stream of the Tenner. Called Down the Line. Sixty-four Christian souls. My name's Daniel, and this is my wife's brother, Jericho. Hardly ever see anyone comin' south on the water. Not out of the dark lands."

The raft continued to drift with the current, the little boat keeping station with it.

Ryan didn't feel like going into a lot of detail about who they were and where they'd come from. "Traders," he said. "From up yonder." He pointed vaguely past where Savannah had once stood, toward the north.

"Where ye headin'?" Daniel asked.

Ryan jerked his thumb in the opposite direction, still keeping a tight grip on his stick, balancing against the gentle pitching of the craft.

"Y'all visiting Shiloh battlefield?" Jericho asked. Their boat was drifting away from the raft as they worked at the oars to try to hold it on station.

"Thought we might. How far is it from here? Can't be a great distance."

The two oldsters cackled with laughter. "You northerners sure speak kind of strange. Can't hardly understand it. Strangle the words in your throat."

"How far?" Ryan repeated.

The two old men looked at each other, simultaneously putting their heads on one side, like a couple of world-weary crows on a fence watching an unwary frog. Ryan caught Krysty's eye and grinned at her.

"Clumsy old raft like that should get you to the landing by Shiloh around dusk," said Jericho.

"Want the tour of the battleground?" Daniel asked.

"Be interesting," Ryan admitted. "You know someone does that down there?"

"My brother's cousin's your man," Jericho said. "Name's Judas Portillo."

"Judas!" Doc exclaimed. "Does that mean we shall have to pay him thirty pieces of silver for his guiding? Or he might hang himself?"

The two old men looked at him with total bewilderment. "Why'd you do that?" Daniel asked. "Handful of jack or some chawin' tobacco or a couple rounds of .38s'll do him fine. Silver wouldn't be no good, no how."

"Let it pass, let it pass," Doc said.

"We gotta go," Jericho called. "Losing all the good ground we sorely won against the Tenner. Good luck to ye."

"Judas Portillo? We'll be sure to look out for him," Ryan said.

"Tell him he owes me for a faucet in his shack," Jericho said as he and his partner began to pull away together in fine style, propelling the little boat over the water, swiftly widening the gap between them and the raft.

Ryan waved to them, watching as they moved off, shrinking until they were only a tiny blur on the surface of the meandering Tennessee.

THERE WAS A SUDDEN FLURRY of light rain as the sun set on their starboard quarter.

J.B. stayed at the steering oar while the others crowded into the cramped little cabin.

"Won't last," Jak said, peering out of the rough-hewn window at the leaden sky. "Shower."

"Sure?"

"Yeah, Ryan. Blue sky coming this way from south. Get here soon."

"Look for a good place to moor us up for the night," J.B. called.

Jak had been correct. The rain quickly stopped, the sky clearing, bringing the promise of a fine evening and night. Once more they all went out onto the wet timbers, watching the wooded banks of the mighty river drifting by.

"Some sort of sign there," Mildred said, looking ahead and to the north bank.

"Who's got the best sight?" Ryan shaded his eye, seeing the black lettering on a white board but unable to make out what it said.

"Not I," Doc replied. "I can see a blob of white that could be this sign you speak of. But I fear that I can see no detail upon it."

Krysty was concentrating on it. "Something Landing," she said hesitantly.

"Shiloh?" the Armorer suggested eagerly, working the makeshift sweep oar to bring them closer to the right bank of the river.

"No. Begins with a letter *P,* I think. Yeah." The sun lanced through from behind a low bank of cloud, illuminating the sign more clearly. "Pittsburg," she said. "Pittsburg Landing. And it says to alight here for the Shiloh battlefield experience and tour. Spelling's kind of rough. This is the place."

A SMALL COLLECTION of ragged tar-paper shotgun shacks lined a narrow trail that ran westward from the banks of the river.

Rat-eyed, dirt-poor men and women came out of shadowy doorways to peer suspiciously at the outlanders, some of them making no effort to hide crude cap-and-ball pistols, or shouldering smoothbore muskets.

Ryan had called out, asking if it was all right to moor the raft at the primitive landing stage, but at first nobody would give him a reply. Then a large woman wearing a dress torn across her pendulous breasts, smoking a corncob pipe, came swaggering out of a building that called itself The Stor.

"Moorings cost good jack, outlander. You want free, then go back a spell up Snake Creek. Or farther down the Tenner you'll find an inlet called Dill's Branch. Mile or so downstream's Lick Creek. Free there."

"How much to moor here?"

She sniffed, wiping her running nose on her sleeve, leaving a slimy trail like a snail. "Depends on what you got. You want it looked after safe?"

Ryan's patience was never all that high, and he had never responded well to threats.

"We got enough blasters and plas-ex to blow every building in this ragged shit hole to the other side of Memphis," he snapped. "And to chill anyone tries to make out they can threaten us with their cheap trade blasters."

"Whoa back there, buck," she said, holding her hands out, palms spread. "No need to get your balls in a twist, mister. Just tryin' to be friendly."

"So, we can tie up here for the night free? That what you're telling me?"

"I guess so. Sure, I guess so. You come for the tour of the battleground?"

"Mebbe."

"Then you'll likely want Judas Portillo. Kin of mine, young Judas is."

"Heard word of him on the river. Couple called Jericho and Daniel. Said that Portillo owed him for a faucet. Put in his new shack."

The woman slapped her thigh, beating out a cloud of dust and fleas. "Damned old goats! Reckon if there's any owin' then the foot's in the other boot."

Ryan nodded. "Thanks for your kindness, lady. Your store carry food?"

"Trade it for a handful of them bullets you got for those pretty blasters."

"If the food's any good, you got a deal."

"And I'll send word along to Judas to come see you all while you eat?"

Ryan shook his head. "No. Been a long time traveling downriver. We'll take some supper and then sleep some. See Portillo at breakfast."

She nodded. "I'm Ma Jode."

"Still trampling out the grapes of wrath?" Doc asked, beaming broadly at the puzzled woman.

"You a few buckets short of a full flood, mister?"

"Just a small jest, ma'am."

"Very fuckin' small."

"That's what they all say," Mildred said with a grin.

Ryan turned away from the settlement. "We'll tie up safe and snug and come along for some eats."

Ma Jode pinched her nose between her fingers and blew a spray of yellowish snot into the dust by her broken-down boots. "Be welcome," she said.

Krysty looked at Ryan. "Can't wait, lover. Just can't wait."

Chapter Nineteen

Nobody had very high expectations of the food offered in the Stor. But Ma Jode surpassed all their hopes and set aside all their worries, though, as Krysty remarked, it was probably just as well that they never got to take a look in the kitchen. The big woman didn't look as if she placed hygiene high on the list of culinary essentials.

She served them a fish soup to start with, snapper flavored with red and green peppers. Several of the little eels had been cooked until they were more like dry husks, added to the dish for extra flavor.

The main course was pork, stewed long and slow with sharp apples and a spiced gravy, with sweet potatoes and thin-sliced carrots and turnip greens, fresh corn bread on the side with salted butter.

There was cider to drink, chilled and dry on the palate, to wash down the good food.

Everyone except Jak refused the steaming platter of cherry cobbler, though the teenager easily stuffed down two brimming helpings.

Ma Jode appeared from the scented kitchen to offer some coffee sub. "I'm all a muck-sweat," she announced. "Runnin' down cross my tits and soakin' over my belly. Hotter than the ovens of Satan out there."

She opened the door and spit out into the darkness. Cicadas were chirping in the velvety night, and there was a faint breeze off the river.

"That was real good," Ryan said. "Want to settle up now with us?"

"Sure, outlander. Full meal for six of you. It's .38s that we need best. Those outland foreign 9 mill shitters aren't much use round here."

"Six rounds," Ryan suggested.

"Each?" The woman grinned.

"Call it twelve between us."

"Call it four rounds each, and you got the best deal this side of Old Miss."

Ryan pushed back his chair, hearing it scrape on the boards. "You got a problem, Ma Jode."

"How's that?"

"Push your luck. You were doin' it out there about mooring the raft. Now you're doing it again."

She laughed, slapping him so hard on the shoulder she nearly knocked him off balance. "Think I don't know it, stranger? 'Course I do. Twelve rounds of .38s and you also get a real good breakfast in the morning. And I'll make sure Judas Portillo's here to show you around Shiloh."

"Deal," Ryan said.

The woman held out her hand, horny and callused, the size of a small ham. "Take 'em now," she said.

Ryan shook his head. "After breakfast."

"You might just up stakes and sail away in the night. That wouldn't be neighborly." There was an edge to her voice, and Ryan realized that Ma Jode wouldn't be a person to cross. Not unless you had a lot more firepower.

"We'll be here. Around eight."

She nodded slowly, her small, hooded eyes staring at him. "Be there or be hung out for the gulls."

RYAN AND J.B. AGREED that it would be a good idea to keep a watch for their night at Pittsburg Landing.

It wasn't all that likely that any of the locals would risk taking them on, but you didn't get old in Deathlands by placing your stakes in the square marked Likely.

Jak, still complaining about the deep bruising behind his belt buckle, took first watch, from eight through to eleven, then came Doc until one in the morning.

Mildred and J.B. agreed that they'd share a double watch, from one until four, and Ryan and Krysty would be together until the dawn.

The weather was calm, with just a few high clouds blown in tatters across the face of the moon.

THERE WAS NO THREAT during the night.

Ryan slept badly, still plagued by the healing of the double wound in his thigh. It prickled as if someone had rubbed chilies into it, and the skin felt hot to the touch. But eventually the gentle lapping of the river against the huge logs lulled him to sleep, and he woke when J.B. touched him on the shoulder.

"Time."

"No trouble?"

"Nothing."

"Weather?"

"Dry. Light northerly. Nobody moving around the ville that we've seen."

Ryan slept fully clothed. He pulled on the combat boots and slid the SIG-Sauer into its holster. Krysty was at his side, doing the same, settling the short-barreled Smith & Wesson .38 on her hip.

He limped out of the little cabin, taking a deep breath of the fresh, cool air, using the stick to steady himself. The moon was sailing low, and there was already the faint lightening of the sky, heralding the arrival of the false dawn.

HE AND KRYSTY WATCHED Pittsburg Landing coming to early-morning life, the dawning sun reflected off the rolling waters of the wide Tennessee.

There was a faint haze hanging above the surface of the water, and clouds of tiny gnats darted and danced, occasionally falling victim to the silvery leap of a large trout.

They saw Ma Jode opening up the Stor, pausing to give them a wave, hawking up a ball of phlegm that she spit at a lean mongrel that was slinking by.

"All's right with the world," Krysty stated.

"Wonder how Dean's getting along," Ryan said, leaned on his stick, experimentally moving the wounded leg. It certainly seemed easier this morning.

"Knowing the kid, he's probably taken over the running of the school by now."

THEY WERE JUST FINISHING an excellent breakfast when Judas Portillo made his appearance.

The local guide to Shiloh battlefield saw himself as something of a fop and dandy. He was a little below average height, slim, with long hair greased back with a heavily scented pomade. His face was fleshy with the beginnings of a third chin, the lips thick and fleshy, his eyes dark and liquid with unusually heavy lids.

His clothes had a faded grandeur to them. He wore a frock coat, not unlike Doc's, but without the macabre patina of great age, and two mother-of-pearl buttons were missing. His pants were tapered, dark blue, with a strip of black satin down the outside of each leg. Portillo's ankle boots looked as if they had been polished early that morning in a room with inadequate light. Parts of them were still smeared with river mud, and other parts gleamed like a mirror. He had an elegant jabot of slightly stained lace at his throat, which he tugged at constantly.

As always in Deathlands, when he met a stranger for the first time, Ryan weighed him up for weaponry.

There was a small-caliber revolver of indeterminate make with pearl grips on his right hip, and an enormous bowie knife balanced on the left. Ryan also had a shrewd suspicion that there was a derringer, probably in a spring release, tucked away up the right sleeve.

His hat was a cream-colored Stetson decorated with turkey feathers. As he arrived at their table, he took it off with a sweeping gesture and bowed to Ryan. "I am Judas Portillo," he said, in a surprisingly broad Southern cracker accent. "Have I the honor of addressing *the* Ryan Cawdor?"

"You're addressing *a* Ryan Cawdor," the one-eyed man replied with a grim smile.

Portillo forced a smile in return, which flickered for a moment across his well-shaved jowls and then disappeared. "You wish to be shown around the battlefield?"

"Yeah. How much?"

Portillo shrugged his shoulders. "Just a small handful of jack if you're pleased."

"I got a very small handful of jack," J.B. said. "Very small."

The smile hesitated again. "I am sure that you outlanders won't disappoint me."

"I'm sure," said Ryan. "Just so long as you don't disappoint us, Judas."

They settled their account with Ma Jode, who insisted on hugging them all and wishing them well in their journeying, assuring them that their raft would be safe and snug at the landing when they returned.

IT WAS SURPRISINGLY CLOSE to the river, an easy walk that took only a short time. Even Ryan, with his healing wound, enjoyed the morning stroll.

They had passed through rolling fields of wheat and barley, along narrow, high-walled lanes and lines of trim picket fences that divided meadows where horse-drawn plows went about their placid business.

Doc stopped, waving away some persistent flies. "By the Three Kennedys! But this is truly a pastoral idyll. It quite takes me back to my days of yore when I would lend a hand with the harvest."

"Good land," Portillo said quietly.

"This the scene of the battle?" Krysty asked as they paused on a crest of land, looking toward the northwest. The light mist had burned off, and it promised to be a fine day.

"Road passing left to right is the old River Road. Also called the Hamburg Road. Look way over yonder and see the little spire. That's a church stands on the same spot as the meeting house of Shiloh."

"The heart of the fight was ahead, wasn't it?" J.B. asked eagerly. "I recall places called the Peach Orchard and the Hornet's Nest."

Portillo scowled. "Want me to tell you or not? I'd just as like go sit on the porch and sip moonshine."

The Armorer sniffed. "You go right ahead. Tell us like it was."

The guide adopted a strange singsong recitation as he began to tell the bloody saga of Shiloh.

"April 6 and 7 of 1862 saw the first major battle of the western campaign of the series of fights called either the Civil War or the War between the States, depending on where you come from. During the Battle of Shiloh, the Northerners lost over thirteen thousand men, while we only lost a tad over ten thousand good old boys."

"So the Confederacy won?" Krysty asked.

Portillo hesitated, his love of the South fighting with his desire for truth. "Well . . . the South failed to push home and beat the Yankees, and that opened up the trouble at Vicksburg. Guess the fact is that Shiloh was like a poisoned arrow straight in the heart of the Stars and Bars. But Grant took the losses hard, and it kind of slowed down the war for a while."

Ryan shifted position, trying to take a little weight off the injured thigh. The good news was that it definitely felt a lot better than it had the previous day. He looked across the green, undulating fields, trying to imagine them scattered with lines of weary men in blue and gray.

"I got here a plan," Portillo said, reaching into his pocket and pulling out a tattered piece of paper that he unfolded and laid carefully on the ground, smoothing it.

There were rectangles and arrows in different colors, mainly either blue or red.

"Yankees is blue," Portillo said, pointing with a long twig he'd picked up. "South's red."

"Not gray?" Doc asked. "Why red?"

"Gray faded and got kind of dirty," their guide replied, pulling a sullen face. "So's I had to go to red. Look here. Reading from the north, the Army of Tennessee, as they called themselves—I says the bluebellies—was commanded by Sherman here, with McLernand, Prentiss, Wallace and Stuart. On the other side we got Hardee in the middle with Number Three Corps of the Confederate Army of the Mississippi. Bragg with Two Corps is here, just behind him. Major-General Leonidas Polk with One Corps is in the third rank, and Brigadier-General Breckenridge at the rear with the gallant lads of the reserve."

Ryan looked at the fields, with their gentle curves. The coppices of young trees, leaves bright green, turning and shifting in the light breeze. And he tried to imagine the battle unfolding in front of him as Judas Portillo droned on: the damp, muddy ground, churned by hooves and boots and the wheels of the heavy artillery; the swirling masses of men, their uniforms streaked with dirt, wreathed in huge, blinding clouds of black powder smoke, many of them terrified and utterly, hopelessly confused, praying for the noise and the slaughter to stop so they could go home to their farms and families.

Ryan knew enough of military history to be aware that muskets collected after the fighting would often carry multiple charges. A soldier, mind blanked in panic, would ram home minié ball after ball, until the blaster was totally blocked with up to a dozen unfired rounds.

Or they might use their ramrod to force down powder, shot and wadding, then let panic win the day, squeeze the trigger and shoot off their ramrod, as well, leaving themselves with a totally useless weapon.

"To put it simply, the battle of Shiloh was a battle of six big mistakes. Huge, triple-stupe ones. Some on one side and some on the other."

He led them away, his folded map tucked under his arm, taking them across the scene of the great fight, stopping here and there, in the Hornet's Nest and the setting of the old Peach Orchard, unrolling his plan again, using his long willow twig to point out the salient details of the field.

"Basically you got Grant and the Army of the Tennessee, settled around the church."

"How many men would Grant have had under his command?" Mildred asked.

"Forty thousand, blue-bellies. Thicker'n ticks on a hog's belly."

"And the Rebs?" J.B. asked.

"Rebs? The gallant boys in gray had around the same number."

"What were these mistakes? I recall someone mentioning plucking defeat from the jaws of victory," Doc said, beaming at Portillo and showing his fine, strong teeth.

"Don't know nothin' about that. First mistake was Johnston's. Knew that Buell was moving north with reinforcements and decided to get in his blow first. But the roads was bad and his maps poor and his whole army a shambles of confusion. Took a day to sort it out, so he delayed the fight until dawn on Sunday, April 6. Should've been three in the morning the day before."

The sun was rising steadily in a cloudless sky, and the temperature was rising with it. Ryan's guess put it somewhere in the mideighties.

"Second and third mistakes both came from the North." Portillo paused, fishing out a filthy kerchief and blowing his nose noisily on it, peering at the contents as though he expected to find traces of gold in it. Then he folded it up and put it away. "Grant was drunk in Savannah and never expected an attack. Mistake two. Following on this was the fact that the bluebellies never bothered to put out proper patrols around Shiloh. Fact is that most of the men were still asleep when we hit them. Number three."

"Wasn't Lew Wallace at Shiloh?" Doc asked. "Man who wrote *Ben Hur?*"

Portillo pasted on a sneering grin. "Sure was. Gotten himself chilled in leading a breakout a mite later.

And he came up with mistake four. Soon as Grant heard firing, he sailed up to the landing here. Brigadier-General Wallace had the Second Division of the Army of Tennessee and he was moving with a long column of men down that narrow road yonder. Away from where the battle had started. Instead of turning the whole column ass-about so the rear became the front, he ordered the men out front to turn and march back through the column. Kind of reversed it, making it march through itself. Total shambles like a dozen drunk men changing their clothes in a small closet.''

They moved across the battlefield while the man's monotonous singsong voice painted a picture of the way the fight swayed back and forth, with a general movement toward the east of the area.

They spent some time in what had been called the Hornet's Nest, where the land was completely sodden with blood and you could walk from one side to the other stepping only on the corpses from both armies.

''This more or less like it was?'' J.B. asked. ''Hasn't it changed over the years?''

Portillo shook his head. ''It was kept as a kind of monument. National Military Park. Right up to skydark. Visitor center got blasted by a stray nuke.''

''Fifth mistake?'' Krysty asked.

''Supreme commander of the Confederate boys was General Albert Sidney Johnston. In the big charge he'd had a couple of small wounds and had the heel ripped from his boot by a ball. Bit later he got hit in the bend of the knee by a stray round. That was about half after one. Johnston didn't know it was serious and ignored it. That was number five. Hour or so later he nearly fell from the saddle. An aide, Governor Isham Harris of Tennessee, asked if he was wounded. Johnston replied, 'Yes, and I fear seriously.' Bullet severed an artery and his boot filled with his lifeblood. Had a tourniquet in his field pack that would easy have saved him. Died around half after two.''

Doc swatted away another cluster of the importunate flies. ''If my memory is not too ailing, I believe that General Johnston was the most senior officer to die in battle during the entire war.''

Portillo shook his head. ''Wouldn't know that. All I know is what happened here.''

Ryan heard the saga of Shiloh winding toward its end, saw in his imagination the scattered bodies of three and a half thousand inexperienced young soldiers, thinking about the horrors of the field hospitals of the day with the blunted saws and no anesthetic. Sixteen thousand had been wounded, three thousand taken prisoner or simply missing in action.

''Buell's on his way north with reinforcements, but Grant's men are being pushed back toward the Tennessee. Dusk was falling, Beauregard took over on Johnston's shocking death and here came the sixth and biggest mistake.''

''Defeat from the jaws of victory,'' Doc muttered with a smug smile.

Portillo nodded, licking his thick lips, hooded eyes glaring at the old man. ''Right. He held off, and the gutless blue-bellies escaped and everyone went home.''

They stood in silence in the broiling heat of the late morning, everyone locked into his or her own thoughts.

Far above their heads a white-ruffed kestrel was riding a thermal, eyes scanning the verdant fields below it.

"That wasn't bad," Ryan said, finally breaking the silence. "Not bad, Judas."

"Thank you, sir."

J.B. fished in one of his bottomless pockets and pulled out a jingling handful of small jack, counting it with his eyes and then handing most of it over to the guide, who fingered it suspiciously, then nodded and smiled.

"It'll do," he said grudgingly. "Yeah, it'll do."

Chapter Twenty

Both Ma Jode and Judas Portillo, accompanied by eight snot-nosed, ragged urchins and three mongrel dogs, came to see them leave the landing.

The raft drifted slowly off into the current, steered by Krysty, with Doc and J.B. working the sweeps, letting the Tennessee take them away south.

"We going far?" Mildred asked. "I was sort of surprised you told them we planned to stick with the river. Way that old woman kept eyeing our blasters, I wouldn't be surprised if we didn't find we had some company downstream."

Ryan was sitting on the roof of the makeshift shelter, enjoying the early-afternoon weather. "What I tell them and what we're doing is two different things, Mildred. And you're right. I saw some skulking and whispering going on, and half a dozen men with muskets left just after we went to visit the battle site."

"So we leaving the water?"

He nodded. "Sure are. Get us around the corner, then we'll break away from it and strike off west."

"I'm sure there used to be a big dam to the south," Mildred said.

"River's changed its course." Ryan squinted behind

them. "Ma Jode told me that. Said the actual battle was nearer the Tennessee than it used to be."

"Whole damned country's changed its shape," Doc said sadly. "Sea to shining sea. California to Newyork. State slid into the Pacific, most of it, and Newyork had been transmogrified into the ruined haunt of ghouls and ghosts."

They floated south, the settlement vanishing behind them into the shimmering heat haze. The sides of the river were lined with luxuriant bushes and a row of aspens that trembled in the faint northerly that rode at their shoulders.

"Man could get used to this," J.B. said, pushing back his fedora and taking off his glasses, polishing them furiously on his sleeve.

"You're quiet, Jak," Ryan commented. The albino was lying on the front of the boat, chin in his hands, watching the water as it bubbled under the rough bow.

"Nothing to say. Battlefield depressed me. Didn't want talk. Now out in open again, feel better." He grinned suddenly. "Still got nothing to say."

"That bruise better?" Mildred asked.

The teenager nodded. "Some."

THEY'D TRAVELED ABOUT A MILE when Ryan pointed to the western bank and they steered into a narrow inlet.

It was lined with wild rosebushes, unusually scented, that filled the air with their fragrance. Ryan waited, the SIG-Sauer cocked in his right hand, while Jak leaped ashore with the line, tethering the raft to a sturdy dogwood.

As they started to get off, Krysty pointed behind them, across the river and a little way downstream. "Looks like we just missed the reception committee."

A group of raggedy men had emerged from behind a raised shoal at the top of the far bank. All of them held long muskets, and they were waving their arms and shouting. But the Tennessee carried any words away.

"Bastards!" Mildred exclaimed angrily.

"Not surprised," Ryan said. "Best surprise is no surprise, like Trader used to say."

The woman stared across at the men. A couple had raised their blasters, and they saw the puffs of black-powder smoke. One ball hit the surface of the water about fifty yards short of the raft, and the other simply disappeared.

"Way out of range," J.B. said. "Still, just a slight chance getting a hit from a spent ball. Best get out of sight of the sons of bitches."

Doc favored the friends with a wide grin. "That puts me in mind of the famous last words of...I disremember, but I believe he was a ranking officer in the Civil War."

"Make it fast, Doc," Ryan urged as they saw another mute burst of fire from the men on the far bank, none of the balls coming anywhere near them.

"His last recorded words were, 'Stand fast, my gallant lads. They could not hit an elephant at this range. Aaaargh!'" Doc clutched melodramatically at his breast.

They all laughed—all except Mildred. She glowered across the steady current of the river at the small group of men still firing at them. Finally she drew her Czech target revolver.

"No way, Millie," J.B. said, shaking his head at the ZKR 551. "Not even you."

"Want a bet, love?"

"No. Man bets against you over a shooting stands to lose his jack."

"That's a good range, even for you and even for that blaster," Ryan said doubtfully.

"Go for it," Krysty urged. "Teach that murdering scum a sharp lesson."

Another cloud of powder smoke rose into the air from the far side of the river and, just as J.B. had predicted, one of the spent balls ricocheted off the water, like a wrist-skimmed stone in a child's game of ducks and drakes, and thudded into the sodden timbers of their raft.

Mildred immediately took up the classic shooter's standing pose, feet slightly apart, right arm holding the blaster outstretched, left arm at her side. She looked along the sighted barrel with both eyes wide open, slowing her breathing. "Trick's to squeeze the trigger real gentle between beats of your heart," she said softly.

It was a goodish range for a hunting rifle, but for a handblaster it would be a phenomenal shot.

The men opposite saw what she was doing, and their dancing and jeering intensified, rising this time above the ageless whispering of the Tennessee.

There was a long pause, and Ryan found that he was holding his breath along with Mildred, peering out through the haze at their would-be killers.

"Fireblast!" Ryan whispered, awed beyond belief as he saw one of the capering rednecks throw up his arms, then fall motionless to the dirt, life quitting him on the instant, leaving him a bundle of sprawled flesh and rags alongside the silent-flowing river. His comrades immediately fell silent, one stooping over the corpse.

"Best move," J.B. said. "Get them fired up, and they might find a way across and come after us. Leave while we're ahead of the game."

"Amazing shot," Jak said. "Good as any I ever seen you do."

"Didn't allow enough for windage and thermal off the water," the woman said, calmly reloading the spent round. "Aimed at his chest and took him through the mouth."

Ryan was grinning as he limped toward the west, ignoring the impotent spluttering of muskets from the far side of the Tennessee.

THEY MADE STEADY PROGRESS through a roasting afternoon, finding the ruler-straight remnants of an old farm road that ran from horizon to horizon across the baked land. It had obviously once been good wheat country, but it had long reverted to nature, with patches of dense scrub and mesquite and occasional stands of oaks and beeches and the shadowy deeps of a large forest hovering at the northern horizon.

Jak found a pile of tangled string and amused himself by making a slingshot, picking up small rounded pebbles and winging them at old rusted cans and rotted tree stumps.

To nobody's surprise, the albino teenager immediately showed phenomenal skill with his new weapon, eventually bringing down a rabbit on the full run at all of fifty yards, the stone cracking its fragile skull open just behind the limp, trembling ears, bowling it over in a dusty flurry of kicking paws.

"Supper," Jak said, consistent in his habit of using the absolute minimum of words.

"OUGHT TO HAVE KEPT that sling," Ryan said as they sat around a small, bright, smokeless fire that evening, savoring the rabbit on spits of green wood over the dry branches of apple from an ancient predark orchard. "You had a real skill with it."

Jak hadn't bothered to keep it, chucking away the cunning construction of knotted cords shortly after his spectacular success with the rabbit.

"Bored." He leaned back, shirt pulled up over his flat, muscular stomach, studying the shrinking yellow-purple bruise, touching it gently with his long pale fingertips. "Anyway, easy make another if want to."

"Bruise better?" Mildred asked.

"Sure. Still slows me some around edges."

"I reckon you might have broken a rib," she said. "Not that there's much we can do if you have."

"Not much use for all your medical skills out in the untamed wilderness of Deathlands, is there, Dr. Wyeth?" Doc teased, belching his pleasure at the meal. "By the Three Kennedys, but that coney was damnably as good at the second tasting."

Mildred was lying on her back, her head in J.B.'s lap, while his nimble hands worked at some of the beads that had come loose from her braids. "One day, Doc, you old goat, you'll have something bad wrong with you and you'll come yelping for a doctor. And I'll be the only one for ten thousand miles and a hundred long years. And don't you forget it."

AFTER THE MEAL Ryan stood and stretched. "Think I'll go check out the neighborhood."

"If you meet any nice couples, then invite them back for cocktails and a late-night coffee," Krysty said, smiling up at him. Her brilliantly red hair reflected the golden highlights of the flames, spread out on either side of her narrow face like a bridal veil of living fire. Its relaxed condition was a true indicator that she didn't sense any immediate danger close to them. Her eyes glittered at Ryan like burning emeralds.

"I'll do that." He paused, trying to remember details from some of the old mags, vids and books of what else neighbors used to do before the missiles rained down. "They can watch our vacation movies."

Mildred laughed delightedly, clapping her hands. "Brilliant, Ryan. If all else fails, ask them if you can borrow a cup of sugar."

"I'll take a couple of canteens and see if I can come across some good water. Last lot's already turning brackish in this heat."

He patted the butt of the SIG-Sauer in an automatic reflex before stepping off into the darkness, choosing to move north through the dry land, moonlight throwing weak shadows across a narrow, winding game trail.

THE MOON HAD SNEAKED from behind a bank of low cloud that rested on higher ground to the far north, and the land darkened for a few minutes.

Ryan kept going, his excellent night vision, even with only one good eye, carrying him safely and silently along. He paused in midstride, hearing what might have been the echoing cry of a coyote.

Might have been.

"Wolf?" he whispered to himself, the blaster suddenly cocked and ready in his fingers.

Another animal answered the first one as the moon broke through again. They were close together and not all that far ahead of him. Ryan spotted the glint of water just to his right, where there was a clearing in the brush.

He moved with extra care, sensing a change in the night. There was a new stillness, and even the light southerly breeze seemed to have dropped away. Not a leaf was moving on any of the bushes around him.

The double howl and response was repeated once, and then there was a deep, brooding silence. The cicadas had stopped their ceaseless cheeping, and it felt to Ryan as if the world around him were holding its breath.

He stooped by the edge of the water, cupping his left hand and dipping into the cool fringe of the small pond. He brought it to his lips, his head turning constantly, sniffing at the air like one of the feral creatures of the night. The water was cold and fresh. It lay in a shallow saucer of cropped grass and was obviously a drinking hole for deer and all kinds of small predators. Ryan checked carefully up and down the rutted strip of dried mud and found no human tracks nor the spoor of any larger beasts.

The moon had brought back the noises, and the insects began to buzz again. Ryan slowly filled the two canteens, hearing the water gurgle into them, swishing it around and rinsing it out before repeating the process and capping them off. He hung them on his shoulder. He'd left the Steyr back at the camp. The hunting rifle carried a Starlight nightscope, but it wasn't the kind of weapon for a casual evening recce. The SIG-Sauer was snug in its holster.

He decided to walk a little farther, hoping the exercise would help to stretch and strengthen the muscles around the fast-healing wound in his right thigh.

The land was fairly flat, and he strolled toward the fringe of the forest, pausing yet again when the veering breeze brought the smell of smoke—a cooking fire, with meat on it, meat that smelled like it was burning.

"Burned?" Ryan said to himself.

At least wolves and coyotes didn't light themselves fires in the evening, unless they were some kind of new mutie that Ryan had never heard of.

Which was always a possibility in Deathlands.

The smell grew stronger with every step, and he crouched, squinting above the tops of the dark chestnuts, spotting the coil of smoke, pale against the moonlit sky.

He drew the blaster once more, making sure that the canteens didn't chink against each other, catfooting between the spaced trunks, seeing that the fire was in a clearing less than a hundred yards into the woods.

As Ryan moved closer, constantly stopping to check that nobody was going to coldcock him on his blind side, he could make out two ragged figures hunched over the fire. Both had long hair, and they were talking to each other in a conversation that seemed to be mainly unintelligible grunting accompanied by violent gestures.

Only when he was very near could he be certain that they were male and female.

Ryan waited a couple of minutes, checking that the couple carried no blasters, seeing the glint of metal at both waists that told of hunting knives. When he felt safe, he walked out into the circle of the fire, blaster steady.

"Come to borrow a cup of sugar," he said.

Chapter Twenty-One

The man and woman leaped to their feet with a strange, clumsy agility, both drawing their short-bladed pecking knives. The man spit out a coughing expletive, falling instinctively into a fighter's crouch while the woman remained more upright.

In the cold moonlight, Ryan could see them both with a new clarity.

The man was around five-six, squat, about one-fifty pounds. His arms seemed too long for his body, the knuckles of the left hand almost trailing in the leaf mold. A mane of the filthiest hair that Ryan had ever seen partly masked the brutish face.

"No danger," Ryan said, holding out his hands, but keeping the blaster focused. "Just passing by. Keep it quiet and nobody gets to be hurt."

He was fascinated by the state of the man's hair. It was matted and tangled, and seemed to contain a day's supply of food. There was a piece of green, rotting cheese as large as a thumb, stuck above the right ear. As Ryan stared at it, he was horrified to see an opalescent cockroach, scales glittering in the silver moon, crawl apparently from the man's ear and make its way toward the cheese.

The woman was shorter and skinnier, her withered, naked body visible through a twisting shroud of rags.

A small rodent's carcass was stuck on a spit above the fire, the outside black, charred and smoldering. Ryan pointed at it. "Meat's done."

"Not for us not. Only like it burned," the man muttered, not letting go of the knife. "Scared us, jumpin' like a bandersnatch out the dark."

"Sorry. Didn't mean to. You live these parts?"

"Yeah," the woman replied, sheathing her blade and squatting by the fire, thighs apart, seeming to deliberately expose her sex to him. Ryan swallowed hard and looked away, wishing he'd kept on moving. Apart from his disgust, there was something else that was keeping the short hairs prickling at his nape.

"Lived here forever. Was more us." The man reached down and squeezed something in his crotch that made a popping sound. He examined it and slipped it into his mouth. Ryan managed to avoid throwing up.

"A ville?"

The woman shook her head, and bits of bark and dried dirt flew from it. "Not ville. Small. But him and me's all left. And we don't walk good."

The couple looked in the last stages of some gross degenerative disease, hollow eyed, with dried and weeping scabs around their crusted mouths.

Ryan simply wanted to make his excuses and leave the clearing. He was unconsciously trying to breathe fast and shallow through his mouth to minimize the risk of breathing in some foul taint of corruption.

"Got jack, mister?" the woman asked, holding out a clawed right hand, showing that most of the nails were missing. "Help us out, it would."

Ryan shook his head. "Jack I got's the jack I keep," he replied. He was aware of the canteens, swinging heavy on his shoulder. It would be easy enough to fill them up again on the way back. "You got a container, I'll give you good water." He unslung them and opened one so that the fresh gurgling sound filled the clearing.

The reaction was startling and scary, similar to his first demon-king appearance in the firelight.

The woman threw back her head and screamed, the sinews in her scrawny throat as taut as bowstrings, eyes rolled back in the sockets so that only the bloodshot whites showed.

The man dropped to his haunches, suddenly bringing to mind Ryan's fancy of shape-changing, wolflike muties. His head settled in his shoulders, and for a moment he resembled a crouching predator, eyes gleaming yellow under the mane of hair. He was snarling deep in his throat, and flecks of reddened foam dripped from his peeled-back lips.

"Fireblast!" Ryan backed off a couple of paces, index finger on the trigger of the SIG-Sauer.

"Water chills!" The man's voice cracked, sliding up the scale until it became a lupine howl of mindless rage and fear. "You chill us!"

Then the round slipped into the chamber, and Ryan guessed what he'd encountered.

"Rabies," he said. "You both got rabies. Wiped out your whole community. Now you're the last."

"Blood saves," the woman whispered, eyeing him hungrily, sliding toward him. The knife was back in her hand.

Ryan fired two shots, the 9 mm rounds booming out, the sounds muffled by the surrounding trees.

The first one took the female through the upper part of the right cheek as she turned her head away from the threat of the blaster. It bowled her over on her back, legs kicking, fingers scrabbling while blood poured from the massive exit wound at the back of her angular skull.

The second round caught the man in midleap. He had powered himself up in a vaunting spring toward Ryan's throat, knife in his outstretched hand, open jaws showing the foam-smeared fangs, curved and yellow.

Ryan shot him in the chest, going for the safe option, despite the close range and good light.

By one of the freaks of combat, the full-metal-jacket round went clean through and out the back without striking anything vital, missing heart, lungs, ribs, spine and scapula, barely slowing the leap.

Ryan was taken by surprise, unable to get off a third shot before the howling creature was on top of him. There was just time to use the snub barrel of the SIG-Sauer to deflect the knife from his throat, then he was down in the dirt, rolling and wrestling with the rabid man.

He was incredibly strong, fueled by the ravening sickness that was sliding fire through his veins. Ryan got a grip on the right wrist, which held the knife, dropping the now useless blaster, managing to keep his thighs pressed together to stop the intruding knee. He jabbed a couple of short, chopping, savage punches into the man's lower abdomen, but they hardly checked the ferocious attack.

The man tried to bite his face, and Ryan barely pulled away in time, knowing that if blood was drawn by the infected creature, then the odds were that he, too, would be contaminated and confront the same brutish passing.

There was a vital pressure point beneath the breastbone that Jak had taught Ryan, and the one-eyed man went for it, feeling his fingers beginning to slip in the sweat on his enemy's wrist. It was only a matter of moments before the knife hand was free again. The stink of death from the gaping jaws was overwhelming, and Ryan kept his own face turned away, fingers groping, feeling for the point, hard under the upper ribs, aware of the jerk of shock and pain from the man on top of him as he finally located it and pressed with all his strength.

The howling shifted gear, downward, into a roar of agony. The man kicked clear, rolling in the dirt, right across the fire, scattering ashes, flame and burned meat everywhere. The knife dropped from the pain-racked fingers, and the man came up in a crouch.

Ryan didn't hesitate. Following up the advantage, he was already back on his feet. For a moment his hand went to the taped hilt of the eighteen-inch steel panga. But he winced from the thought of the rabid blood smearing the clean blade, and he left it sheathed on his hip.

Stepping in, perfectly balanced, he kicked out with the steel-tipped combat boot, the point of the toe catching the kneeling man at the angle of the jaw on the left side. There was a snap like a dry branch under the heel, and the head slumped loose on the broken neck. After a moment's pause the dying man went down and rolled on his side, lying still.

"Son of a bitch," Ryan said, backing away, picking up the fallen blaster, automatically reloading before checking himself to make sure he hadn't taken any unnoticed scratches or wounds in the tussle.

But he was clean. Shaken and bruised, but unharmed. It had been a lucky break.

The canteens had tangled themselves around his upper arm and one had emptied itself in the dry dirt, leaving a black patch in the moonlight.

Some of the embers from the fire were smoldering in the fringes of stubbly grass under the trees, setting them smoking. Ryan trod them out carefully before leaving the scene of death, his nostrils filled with the stink of the blackened meat and the two corpses.

HE WAS KNEELING by the pool, the background noises of the woods returning again after the mortal fight, when he caught a sound just behind him.

"It's me, Ryan," he whispered.

"J.B., Jak and Krysty," came the reply. "Heard the shots. All right?"

"Sure. Met those neighbors we talked about, and they turned out hostile."

"They still hostile?" the Armorer asked.

"No," said Ryan. "Not anymore."

The others filled their canteens at the sweet pool and when they were all back at their own campsite, he gave them a brief account of the encounter with the rabid couple.

"Sure you didn't get even a scratch, Ryan?" Mildred asked worriedly. "Not really a good enough light now to check you over. Best do it first thing in the morning."

"I'm fine."

Krysty squeezed his hand. "In any case, Mildred, nothing you could do for him if they'd wounded him. Just a matter of waiting and seeing."

"Guess so. Least we can clean it thoroughly. Cuts down on the odds."

"Think we should post a watch?"

Ryan shook his head at J.B. "No."

"Sure? There might easy be other sicko freaks around in the woods."

"Before they died, they said that they were the last survivors of a small community of dirt-poor folk. Something brought in rabies. Bats, mebbe? There were some in the trees. All of the others had died."

The Armorer nodded. "Sure. Night's passing. Best try and catch up on some more sleep."

"We go on to Memphis?" Jak asked.

"Tomorrow. Don't know how far." Ryan looked again at his oldest friend. "Couple hundred?"

J.B. thought about it, pushing back the fedora from his high forehead. "Easy. Long way. Sure we want to take the trouble to go there?"

Mildred slapped him on the arm. "You know I want to see if Graceland is still standing, John. You promised. We can find a highway and pick a lift."

"All right, all right. I don't recall ever hitting old Memphis, Ryan."

They'd been so many places over the riding years with the Trader, that names and villes all blurred, like the faces of the dead, mostly forgotten.

"Can't recall it, J.B., must admit. Anyway, let's all go get us some sleep and start fresh in the morning."

Doc put on a saccharine-sweet Southern voice. "Why not? Then tomorrow can be another day, and I shall still be relyin' on the kindness of strangers." He looked at the blank faces around him, only Mildred grinning knowingly. "But let it pass, my trusty companions. Let it pass."

Chapter Twenty-Two

An hour into a muggy, humid morning, they picked up on the ribboned remains of what rusting green signs told them had once been old I-64. Now it was a faded patchwork of broken slabs and undulating sections of concrete, overgrown with full trees a hundred feet high in places. But there were weaving tracks along it, showing that motorized transport still used the highway.

And it showed them the way west to Memphis.

In several places there was stark evidence that this region of Deathlands had been badly hit by the earthquakes and major geographical changes that had altered the face of the United States of America and turned it into the new world of Deathlands. The road disappeared under rolling hillsides and lakes spread across its original route. Twice the highway vanished completely in a clean, savage cut and suddenly reappeared up to half a mile away in either direction.

In each case a rutted trail showed that the wags had carried on around all of the skydark obstacles.

"GUESS OLD-TIMERS WOULDN'T be able to recognize very much of this," Ryan said as they paused by a stream to refresh themselves.

They'd been walking steadily for about three hours and covered, at Ryan's guestimate, close to thirteen miles, and they hadn't seen a living soul.

Doc lay back and fanned himself with his swallow's-eye kerchief, wafting away a cloud of tiny midges that seemed attracted to the rivulets of sweat that settled in the crevices of his cheeks. "I don't believe that there's much in this tired land that 'old-timers' would recognize, young fellow," he agreed. "Mighty little."

"Where's this lift that you said we were going to pick up, Mildred?" Krysty asked. "I'm kind of interested in Elvis's home, but to walk two hundred miles through this heat and damp... I'm getting less keen."

Mildred stood and stretched, looking around at the yellow fields around them and the strip of tarmac that wobbled away to east and west. "Well, now, like my pa said, you have to pray before you can get your prayers answered. Maybe he was right."

She was pointing to the east, behind them, where they could all now see a faint smudge of dust on the horizon.

Ryan uncoiled with the grace of a sidewinder, unslinging the Steyr. "Anyone make it out?"

Krysty had about the best day sight, and she stood frozen for several seconds. "Five or six wags. Trucks. Some kind of convoy, coming slow and easy this way."

"Could be what we want. Or it could be some serious firefight material. Everyone take cover, condition triple-red, and we'll see what we see. Move it."

Everyone hustled away from the center of the highway, looking for concealment among the ridges and rises.

Ryan was last to move, staring at the cloud of dust, the rifle cradled at his hip, finger through the guard, wondering what the next half hour would bring.

Good or bad?

THE WAG JOLTED AND ROLLED as though the suspension had last been checked a couple of weeks into the long winters. The engine labored, often missing and choking.

Mike Sullivan was a jovial, sweating, red-faced man, head of the convoy of five trucks that was shipping grain from a large farm in eastern Kentucky, heading southwest all the way to what remained of the metropolis of Memphis.

He'd been more than happy to pick up the six heavily armed strangers, spreading them in pairs among his vehicles.

"Nobody robs grain wags," he said in a high-pitched giggle. "We got us blasters, as well, and I reckon there'd be more blood spilled than profit made."

"You going all the way into town?" Ryan asked.

"Nope. Do business with the countess, little way this side of the big ville."

"Countess?" Krysty clung to the edge of the seat, balancing against the reeling movement of the wag.

"Sure. Countess Katya. Runs her own ville tight as a tick's ass. Mighty powerful, handsome woman. Got herself through at least three husbands and the Lord knows how many 'friends.' Each time she walks away stronger than ever, and they mostly end up buying themselves a six-foot plot."

''Never heard of her.'' Ryan glanced behind, making sure the others were still following in line. He could see Mildred and J.B. perched on the high front of a nameless rebuilt wag just a dozen yards back, its rear brimming with golden grain. And there was the shock of Jak's white hair, with Doc alongside him on the third vehicle in line.

''You'll get to meet her. Everyone passes through Memphis gets to meet the countess. She got some triple-odd people around her. Not a woman to cross, if you take my meaning.''

THEY STOPPED for the evening by a looping waterway. Sullivan told them that it was called the New River, since it had appeared out from nowhere some time after the ending of the long winters.

''Good drinking,'' he said. ''One thing you can rely on.'' He slapped the side of his engine, ticking as it cooled. ''Like a John Deere engine.''

''How do you do for gas?''

The farmer looked at Ryan. ''I do what I can. Quality gets worse as the processing plants fall apart. But there's still places. Long as you know where to look for it and you got the pocketful of jack to pay them for it. We tow it in the pair of bowsers at the back of the last two wags in line. That's more of a risk from cold-hearts than the grain.''

SULLIVAN HAD TWENTY good men working with him, with a couple of hard-faced women to do the cooking and washing. Everyone was related to everyone else and all came from the same farming ville, speaking rarely in the soft Kentucky twang.

Sentries were posted for the night camp, and the offer from Ryan to let them share the guard was gently but firmly refused. It was done with a generous good nature, but Ryan would have done the same thing if he'd been in the farmer's place. You didn't just up and trust armed outlanders to the extent of letting them watch over you while you slept.

It was a good night, and Ryan slept dreamlessly, waking with the freshness of dawn dew on his sleeping bag, lying alongside Krysty, appreciating a magnificent golden sunrise that spilled all across Tennessee.

"We reach Memphis today?" he asked, seeing Sullivan toweling water from his gingery hair as he walked by toward one of the cooking fires.

"No. Some rough track to come, where the land shift was worse. Stop off at Country Row for the night. Make the ville by noon tomorrow."

"What's that?"

"Oddball little ville. Tell you about it over bacon and biscuits. Time you folks was up and doing. We'll be hitting the highway within the hour."

THE FARMER ELABORATED as they sat around snatching the relics of breakfast, while the taciturn women waited to clear away their plates and get them washed and stacked. Engines were coughing into life on the grain carriers, turning the air blue-gray with their thick fumes.

"Country Row's one of them places that got born and popular just because it was there. Nukes didn't leave much of Nashville, and what was left kind of fell apart. But in these parts everyone still loves country music, so folks wanted a focus. A place to hear the beating heart. Touch the soul of old America. About ten years ago a guy called Wolfram came and opened up Country Row. Filled it with costumes and guitars and all kinds of stuff he swore was genuine. Waxworks. Records. Memorabilia..."

"Wolfram?" Ryan said. "There's a name you keep stumbling across. He still there? Be good to finally catch up with him after all we've been hearing over the years."

"Long gone. But place is thriving. It's kind of become its own myth."

"Sounds fun," Mildred said.

Sullivan looked sideways at her, hesitating. "Fact is, ma'am, and I don't want you to think we're prejudiced..."

"But?"

He caught the note of instant anger in her voice and held up his work-hard hands. "Not me, lady. I don't give a flyin' fuck what color a person is or how they choose to worship their own gods. But that don't apply everywhere and for everyone around this neck of the woods."

"I've been dealing with redneck peckers ever since I was knee-high to a possum hound, Sullivan," Mildred snapped, lips a thin line of bitterness. "Few more won't make any odds."

"Country Row's a kind of redneck heaven, ma'am," one of the younger, freckled drivers said hesitantly. "Black folks keep clear and—" he turned toward Jak, who was brushing out his long mane of snow-stark hair "—long hair doesn't go well with them good old boys, neither. My advice might be for you to stay with the rigs for the night. We can put a real good watch on you so there's no trouble."

"That your advice, too, Mike?" Ryan asked. "Stand aside from the racists?"

"Easy and safe," the farmer mumbled, shuffling his scuffed boots in the roadside gravel.

Doc rapped the ferrule of the swordstick on the highway. "All it takes is for the decent people to stand aside when evil passes by."

J.B. had been polishing his glasses furiously, a sure sign that he was thinking deeply about a problem. "Let's lay this on the back burner," he said quietly. "Something we can tackle when we have to. Meanwhile, time's passing...."

THEY SAW MORE SIGNS of civilization as they made their slow way west, along the break-back remains of the highway, stopping twice to refuel from the bowsers.

There were little hamlets and isolated sodbusters' homes, shacks and shanties surrounded by a few miserable acres of windswept crops, dark-skinned faces peering from curtained doorways. Broken-down wags looked as if they'd been settled there on their broken axles since before skydark, and instant suspicion darkened every eye.

"Friendly," Jak said to their driver.

"You live close to the edge and you get friendly to strangers," he replied.

"If you only got a little, then you don't take to anyone got even the smallest tad more," added the shotgun guard, a one-armed, grizzled man riding on a high shelf seat behind Doc and the albino teenager.

"Truest words I ever heard," Doc said, nodding wisely. "That lies at the root of most of the world's evils over the last millennium."

A GAWKY BOY in faded coveralls, looking about eighteen with a melon-shaped head that lolled on narrow shoulders, came running from a ditch and threw a stone at Mike Sullivan, missing by inches. Ryan drew the SIG-Sauer and would have blasted the kid off the broken highway, but the farmer laid a hand on his arm.

"Thanks, but no thanks," he said, raising his voice above the crackling rumble of the powerful old engine. "Won't make the world a better place, Ryan."

The blaster was holstered and Ryan felt the sting of the reproach, aware how easy it was to live by your own set of rules, forgetting that some people operated differently.

Chilling wasn't always the only answer.

AN INDICATION of the appalling way that the total nuking of a century earlier had altered the land was the bizarre sight of a series of five small volcanoes, ranged to the north of the highway. None was more than a thousand feet high, but all were sending out thin tendrils of pale gray smoke against the blue afternoon sky, streaking southward, carrying the taint of sulfur.

"Used to be the Chickasaw Rustic Park, so folks reckon," Sullivan said, gesturing with the stem of his corncob pipe toward the odd little line of volcanoes.

Ryan was standing, letting the wind blow through his black curly hair, stretching his legs, and he pointed ahead of them. "Smudge along yonder. That Country Row?"

"See the billboard on the right. Be able to read it when we get a mile closer. Tell you everything you want to know about Country Row."

GERT WOLFRAM INC. Presents Country Row. For Your Enrichment And Pleasure. Country At Its Best. Old And New, Borrowed And Blue Songs. All You Ever Heard And All You've Ever Wanted To See.

There followed a series of smaller boards, listing some of the attractions that were on offer in Country Row: the car where Hank Williams had passed his last, lonely, dying hours; Dolly Parton's finest stage wardrobe, including her star-spangled underwear; Johnny Cash's guitar; Carl Perkins's blue suede shoes; Garth Brooks's top five Stetsons.

The list seemed endless and included displays of waxworks, living positronic-activated representations of some of the biggest and best.

Ryan recognized a lot of the names, but a number of them were obscure and meaningless.

Meanwhile, the smudge was growing closer and was resolving into a number of buildings. It was possible to make out a large rectangular block that Sullivan told them was the nerve center of Country Row, holding the main exhibitions. Clustered close around it were the bars and eateries, nearly all with country themes, with the tawdry glamour of sparkling lights twinkling around them in the fading evening dusk: the Lone Star, Green Coyote, Guitar an' Pick, Golden Mouth Harp, Alamo, Merle and Earle, Eggs'n'stuff, Blue Bayou, Lonesome Eats.

There seemed an endless array.

Sullivan throttled back. "Remember that warning about the kind of boys drink and eat in Country Row, Ryan," he said. "Take it serious."

Ryan nodded. "Always take warnings serious."

Chapter Twenty-Three

They parked the wags outside a roofless garage a couple of blocks from the Country Row Country Museums, Exhibition and Concert Hall.

Mike Sullivan called everyone together, checking where they were spending the night. A few had opted for one of the cheap flophouse hotels called the Flat Armadillo, but most were going to sleep in the cabs of the rigs.

Ryan and the others agreed that they'd stay close to the wags. It was a little after seven-thirty, with the light fading fast into a mild, velvety evening.

Sullivan passed by, spruced up, in polished crimson Western boots with silver scorpions embroidered across the toes. "Want to come along with me and some of the boys? Least we can do is watch your backs for you."

Ryan glanced around at the small circle of friends. "Reckon we might stay here awhile, then go take in the exhibition. Something different to do. After that...?" He shrugged. "See which way the dice roll."

The farmer nodded, turning as a highly polished and chromed 4x4 pulled into the parking lot, squealing to a halt by where the sawed-off stumps of the pumps still rusted. A couple of young blond men, in cutoff jeans and hand-printed T-shirts, jumped out. Both of them sported big Browning automatics on their hips, with bandoliers of ammo crossed over their muscular chests.

They looked over at the group, their attention immediately driving in on first Mildred, then Jak. It looked as if they were about to say something out loud, then they noticed the armory carried by the outlanders and contented themselves with a muttered comment and a snigger, turning their backs and striding away together.

"That's what we're talking about," Sullivan said quietly. "Keep close and keep watchful. You need to head anywhere on the run, come back here. There'll be some of the boys here on watch all night."

"Thanks. We'll do that."

Ryan watched the sturdy figure stalk away toward the bright lights of Country Row.

"YOU GOT THE JACK, then y'all come back. Your pockets are high, then walk on by. Best show of its kind in all of Deathlands. Nothing like it nowhere."

"Anywhere," Krysty whispered under her breath. "Gaia! Why can't people bother to speak properly?"

"We going in?" Mildred asked eagerly.

"Sure. It's what we came for." Ryan grinned. "Triple-red all the way."

"We head for the wags if there's trouble," J.B. said. "Gather there."

Ryan nodded. "Sure. And try and keep the blasters holstered. Fists and boots if it's controllable."

THE EXHIBITION WAS ALMOST deserted, its rooms and passages ringing to overamplified country music, songs riding over each other, Dolly drowning out Tammy, and George blaring across a crackling Carter Family album.

Ryan couldn't believe just how cheap and tawdry the whole place was. The glass cases that held some of the costumes were fly stained and dusty, several of them with hairline cracks disfiguring the faded labels.

A stout woman in a short cowgirl skirt and high-heeled boots was sitting on a chair in the first room, flicking through a pile of brittle old mags. She looked up as they entered, switching on a welcoming lip-sticked smile that was as real as everything else in the place.

Her voice was a flat, dull monotone. "Hi, y'all, country fans and a big howdy-doodee Country Row welcome. If you like, I can be your guide and show you the wonders and tell you the tales and play you the—"

"No, thanks," Krysty said. "Prefer to just look around on our own."

"Please yourself." The smile vanished like dew off a dawn meadow. The woman picked up the mag and carried on reading as though she'd never spoken to them.

They walked through, mostly in silence.

"Fake," Mildred said, looking at the car with an ill-dressed wax dummy slumped in the back seat. "Wrong model. Wrong color. I've seen pictures of the original. And that dummy looks like it weighs more than Hank ever did."

Jak was peering at a large display of the shirts of Conway Twitty, shaking his head. "If all his, how come lots different sizes?" he asked.

In another room a deep, portentous voice was reeling off a potted history of country, sprinkling the saga with the occasional anecdote.

"Music for the heart, not for the head. For the soul of decent folks. It's not smart music for bankers and lawyers, though some of the biggest fans have been professional men and women." There was a screen showing a succession of faces and scenes that had somehow gotten out of synch with the commentary, so a picture of the great Willie Nelson was identified as someone called Cornpone Cawson, the Hayseed Hick.

"Many greats of the industry, like Johnny Cash, worked as sharecroppers and came from dirt-poor families. Others, riding the high wave, tried to make similar claims. It was often said that the only cotton some of them picked was out of the top of aspirin bottles."

"I've had enough," Mildred said when they were about halfway through the echoing vault.

Doc cleared his throat. "I must admit that I have seldom if ever seen such a tarnished collection of rubbish and outright quackery and poodle-fakery. How they have the damned nerve to try to charge for people to come and admire this rubbish is quite beyond me."

"Because there's nothing else, Doc," Ryan said. "And when you got almost nothing, then even a real poor something's better than that."

"A philosophical truism, I suspect, my dear comrade," Doc agreed.

"Exit's over there," Jak said.

They passed a large display, behind chipped sec glass, of rare records, most of them in ancient vinyl, nearly all showing an aged yellow label and the word Sun.

Mildred peered at them, shading her eyes against the reflected light from the strips of harsh overhead neon, exclaiming at the rarity of some of the disks, then noticing the prices handprinted underneath.

"It's the album Waylon, Willie, Kris and Johnny cut together. I used to own this and nearly wore it out. Dates roughly from the 1990s. Title track's one of the finest country songs I ever heard. Jesus! Look at what they're asking for it."

J.B. joined her, taking off his glasses to read it more clearly. "Dark night! You could buy a pair of matched dragoons in the original box for that kind of jack."

Ryan laughed. "Least you buy blasters you can get to use them. Buy that record and what the triple-chill you going to play it on? Number of working players for that sort of disk that I've seen in Deathlands... Reckon that I could probably count them on the fingers of both hands."

"Yeah, but the really wealthy barons could probably afford one. Like this Countess Katya that Sullivan was talking about. Maybe we should buy her a record as a kind of peace offering for when we reach her ville."

"Day I buy presents for barons, male or female, is the day I head for the rocking chair on the porch, so I can sit and rest alongside old Mose," Ryan said.

"Who's old Mose?" Jak asked.

"Just sort of a name." Ryan scratched his head. "Don't rightly know where it came from, either. Guess there must once have been a real Mose who wanted a rocking chair."

NIGHT HAD FALLEN FULLY over Country Row as they stepped out of the exhibition, along a concrete corridor that smelled vaguely of piss, pushing open a swing-barred door into an alley off the main drag.

As the steel door swung shut behind them, it muffled the overbearing noise of the relentless music.

Mildred took a deep breath. "That was a serious disappointment," she said. "Country's such a great and positive force for good. Combine it with a little old-fashioned rock, and you've just about got my favorite music. But what they had in there..." She made a gesture of contempt. "Just a cheap way of getting a fast buck. Peddled like it all fell off the back of a wag and nobody gives a shit. What I'd like right now is to find a quiet bar and wash some of that taste out of my mouth."

"Sounds good," Jak said, clapping his long white hands softly.

Ryan led them out into the street. It was fairly quiet, with the various bars and eateries lining the strip. Most of them were ornamented with colored lights, some of them spelling out the names. Music filtered out from behind a variety of swing doors.

"Take your pick," he said.

"Quiet is a good choice," Mildred stated. "Less risk of real trouble."

They walked together along the center of the dusty, rutted street. Ryan's right hand rested gently on the butt of the SIG-Sauer, but he couldn't taste any threat in the air. A few townspeople strolled by, and several of the men lounging on the porches stared down at the outlanders. But it wasn't much more than the usual natural curiosity that would be encountered in any one of a thousand frontier pestholes, with their bars, gaudies, drunks and sluts.

"What an exercise in ingenuity has gone into thinking up some of these splendid names," Doc commented, pointing at some of them with the point of his cane: Flying Burrito, Palace of Sin, Satan's Golden Bar, Hank's Way, Wheels of Thunder, San Joaquin, Adelita's Muncheria, Gipsy Sharon's, My Place, Sam'n'Ella's.

"That last one sounds the kind of joint where you might pick up food poisoning," Mildred said, laughing at some private joke that none of the others understood.

"How about that?" Krysty asked, pointing to a small, dimly lit bar that stood on its own on the southern side of the street. "Nice name. Might get some good vibrations from it"

It was just called Harmony.

A YOUNG BEARDED GUITARIST sat on a stool on a tiny stage at the far end of the bar, singing a beautiful, mournful song about leaving an L.A. freeway. A tall woman with cropped black hair leaned on the counter, idly wiping a glass with a green-checkered cloth.

Ryan glanced around as soon as they were inside, trying to size up the atmosphere, feeling for any sense of danger. There were about a dozen people in Harmony, sitting at five or six tables. Four of them were playing a quiet game of poker, the rest were nursing schooners of beer and talking in low voices.

They were all men, in a variety of Western clothes, shirts, jeans and working boots.

Every head turned at the appearance of the six strangers, but Ryan had the feeling that their arrival in Country Row had already been noted by the locals. Nobody seemed at all surprised to see either Jak's stark white hair, blazing in the gloom like a beacon, or Mildred's black skin and beaded hair.

"What can I get you folks?" called the woman from behind the bar. "Come right on in. Don't stand in the doorway, blocking up the hall."

There was a large round table, its top scarred and ringed from years of cold glasses, and the companions sat at it, Ryan picking the seat that faced the main entrance. J.B. chose the chair that gave the best view of a rear door, which presumably opened into an alley at the back.

"We got beer, some local wine and some better stuff from out west. And we got fruit juices. Could even do you some coffee sub if you wanted."

Ryan looked up at the woman. "You do food?"

"Sure. Nothing fancy. Soup. Chili and beans. Got some ham and pork if you fancy that.

Ryan picked the chili and a long beer. Krysty followed his choice, as did Doc. J.B. chose a plate of ham and pork with a bottle of chilled wine, which he shared with Mildred. She didn't feel that hungry and ordered a bowl of the soup of the day, which turned out to be turnip, leek and bacon. Jak took a long time making up his mind, eventually opting for the soup, followed by chili with a side order of bread and cheese, washing it all down with two glasses of beer.

They had finished and were beginning a last round of drinks before going back to the wags to settle for the night, when the doors swung noisily open and in came the two young rednecks who owned the smart 4x4. They were both drunk, sweating heavily and still flaunting their Brownings and the ammo belts.

Ryan instantly tasted the bitter iron of danger and eased himself a little away from the table, his hand falling to the SIG-Sauer, seeing that each of the other friends was beginning to react in a similar way.

"Well, now, Albert, my man, you notice that nasty stink in this clean bar?"

"Sure do."

"Must be the stink of that black pussy and that scaredy little white rabbit I see there."

"Must be, Elmore. Must be that's what that nasty ol' stink is in here."

They stood side by side, facing Ryan and the others, sloppy grins leaking over their raw, fleshy faces, brutish and confident.

The woman behind the bar also had a nose for serious menace and she came out, wiping her hands on the cloth. "Now, we got a nice quiet bar here and everyone's having a good time. Let's try and keep it that way."

"Fuck you, slut! You serve freaks, muties and darkies. Sweet Jesus on the cross knows what them others might be, as well. But they shouldn't be in a place with decent folks."

One or two of the drinkers at the other tables were starting to take some notice, and to Ryan's dismay he caught the whispering of support for the two intruders.

"Yeah, shouldn't be blacks in with whites. Not the way in Country Row."

"Then we should mebbe all leave?" Ryan said, surprised at how calm and steady his voice sounded, not betraying the hot rage that was already surging through him, starting to cover his good combat sense.

Elmore thought about that for a little while, hands on his hips, inches away from the etched butts of the Brownings. For a moment Ryan sort of hoped that they might just be able to walk out of this without blood. Sort of hoped.

Then the redneck shook his mane of blond curls. "No. Not just like that."

"Let's do it," Ryan said.

Chapter Twenty-four

The Trader had been a man of many quotes, most of them dealing with the practical problems of surviving in the lethal boiling pit of Deathlands. What most of them came down to was simply a matter of getting in firstest with the mostest.

The collection of rednecks in the Harmony Bar in Country Row were mostly tough men who earned their livings by hard physical labor. And when it came to roughhousing, they would all have chosen themselves as winners against a group of outlanders composed of a one-eyed man, a good-looking redhead, a little guy with glasses and a faggot hat, an old man with a stick, a black woman and a freak kid with white hair.

Elmore and Albert were delighted when they saw that they'd managed to provoke the strangers into some kind of reaction. It would give them the icing on what had so far been a pleasant enough evening of drinking and whoring.

They both drew their Brownings, waving them around like old-time shooters, grinning with gap-toothed delight at the exquisite violence and chaos to come.

Ryan shot Elmore once through the throat, the bullet splintering and fragmenting against the cervical vertebrae, blowing an exit hole so large it very nearly took the head off his shoulders. The peckerwood never even had time to squeeze the triggers on his treasured blasters, dropping them with a clatter on the hardwood floor, going over backward in a spray of blood and a choked scream.

Mildred had been itching for Ryan's word to draw her ZKR 551, aiming and firing the Smith & Wesson .38 round in a single, smooth action.

But Ryan's speed and the instant destruction of Elmore started a chain of confusion. The blond racist's upright corpse staggered into Albert as it went down, knocking him off balance, so that Mildred's bullet hit him in the left shoulder instead of full through the middle of his face.

He let one of the Brownings drop from nerveless fingers, but began shooting with the other automatic, spraying a burst of lead around the small bar.

Ryan dived for the sawdust floor, followed moments later by the others, but the drinkers were slower, most of them rising to their feet, reaching for whatever weapons they were carrying. Albert's crazed volley took out three of them, killing one instantly with a bullet through the skull, hitting two others through the stomach and chest.

The bartender made the terminal error of not ducking. Standing still, she yelled for the shooting to stop as bottles exploded around her in shards of razored splinters. Albert shot her through the side of the neck, ripping out the big artery, sending her down in a welter of crimson, hands desperately trying to check the flow.

The air was filled with shouting, screams and the smell of gunfire and hot, fresh blood.

It was Krysty who finally took out Albert, rolling on one side from under the table and shooting him with her short-barreled Smith & Wesson double-action 640, the big bullets tearing into the man through his sweating, bare chest, one of them hitting the ammo bandolier and exploding a couple of the rounds in a burst of flame and noise.

He dropped without a sound, lying facedown in the spreading pool of dark blood that was still seeping from Elmore's shattered skull.

Ryan was up on his feet, covering the shocked survivors of the massacre, calling out above the cries of the wounded, trying to restore some kind of order.

"It's over!" The barrel of the SIG-Sauer moved from side to side like the head of a rattler. "Chilling's done. They got what they wanted. Sorry others of you got to pay the butcher's bill for them. Now we're leaving. Give us five clear minutes or we shoot anyone who sticks a head out. Then get all the help you can. And remember we didn't start this."

"Sure fuckin' finished it, mister," one of the patrons breathed in a shocked whisper.

"Yeah." He gestured for the others, guns all drawn, to move away toward the main entrance, then changed his mind. "No. Go out the back. Along the alley."

He turned back to the huddled survivors of the brief firefight. "Remember what I said. Five clear minutes, and then you can get help."

The gut-shot man was huddled on hands and knees, weeping in quiet desperation, tears streaking his face, mouth working in pain. "Gotta help me, mister," he panted.

"Five minutes," Ryan repeated, watching as the others walked safely out of the bar before following them, pausing a moment to make sure there wasn't going to be any more trouble. He slipped out as J.B. held the padded door open for him.

"Quiet," the Armorer said. "Looks like nobody heard the shooting."

"Only be a matter of time. We need to get out of here. Right now. Let's get to the wags."

His first plan had been to either persuade or force Sullivan into letting them take one of the lumbering grain wags. But he suddenly realized that there was a potentially much better option available to them.

"Take Albert and Elmore's 4x4," he called to Jak. "Hot-wire it."

"Sure." The teenager ran ahead, vanishing around a corner toward the abandoned garage.

The farmer wasn't there when they finally arrived, but his men were all on careful watch, covering Ryan and the others as they raced back.

"No time for talk. Got bad trouble in a bar. Like we were warned. Some folks on the last train west. We got a few minutes, then every honest citizen of Country Row's goin' to be lookin' for us with a rope in his hand."

The foreman, a tall, laconic Iowan called Webster, looked at Ryan warily. "You weren't thinkin' of takin' any of our wags, were you now?"

"Don't be a stupe. Two of the dead own that flash 4x4." The engine of which burst into roaring life as Jak finished hot-wiring it. "We're off in that."

"Fuel?"

"How's fuel, Jak?"

"Full."

Ryan shook the foreman's leathery hand. "Thanks for everything. Our best to Sullivan. See you all around one day. Watch your asses here."

The man grinned slowly. "Don't you worry none about us, Ryan Cawdor. Get goin' now."

There was a swift round of handshakes, then they piled into the chromed and polished wag, J.B. taking the wheel.

"Good luck," someone called.

They drove out into the main street of Country Row, between tumbling gateposts, stopping for a moment to check both ways. Other than the merry little lights and an odd staggering drunk, the place looked and sounded normal. The nearest bar was thundering out raucous music as they turned to the right and headed west.

IT WAS THE MOST overornamented wag that Ryan had ever encountered, reminding him of the florid pimpmobiles that he'd seen when riding with Trader in the gaudy sections of some of the larger pestholes.

The top of the windshield was festooned with all kinds of soft toys and junk: fluorescent green dice covered in fur; a pair of dogs with nodding heads and rolling idiot eyes; a flesh-colored Madonna that seemed to glow in the moonlight; a naked black doll, with a pregnant belly, holding a spear. Mildred tugged that off and threw it out the side window before they'd even reached the town marker for Country Row.

The only useful aid was a large compass, floating on a gyro, set in the middle of the dash.

As they drove west, J.B. gradually ripped everything off, reducing the vehicle to something more serviceable.

"Hit lucky with this wag," he said after they'd gone about fifteen bouncing miles. He pulled off onto the weed-grown soft shoulder and let the powerful engine idle, getting out to stare behind them.

Ryan joined him. "Nothing?"

The Armorer wiped his glasses. "Reckon they'd think twice about setting up a lynch mob, once they realize how well-tooled we are and that we got clean away. No profit in chasing us. Not like we robbed their bank."

Ryan patted his old friend on the back. "If we'd had another half hour, we could have done that, as well."

Jak climbed out of the rear of the three rows of seats, where he'd been perched with Doc. "Need a leak," he said. "Smart wag."

While he was pissing in the dry brush off the side of the highway, there was a rumble of thunder far ahead of them and a flash of pinkish silver lightning, threatening a chem storm somewhere down the line.

Seeing that they were going to have a short break, the others all got out of the wag and stretched their legs in the warm moonlight.

"More lightning," Mildred said. "Looks like we might run into that in a couple of hours."

Ryan glanced at his wrist chron, seeing that the tiny liquid-crystal display showed it was a little after eleven o'clock.

"What kind of tank she got?"

Krysty had been checking under the hood while they waited, whistling in admiration. "Those good old boys might have been shit at human relations, but they sure made a fine job of their wag. It's in as good condition as anything I ever saw. Must have been a kind of hobby for them."

Ryan knew that most of the predark wags had small fuel tanks. An average family car might only carry a dozen gallons. Now, with the roughly processed fuel costing lives, it wasn't any surprise to find that the 4x4 had a triple tank fitted to it that would hold around sixty gallons of crude gasoline, giving them a rough distance of five or six hundred miles. It was enough to get them to Memphis, and then all the way back to the redoubt.

Jak finished and they all climbed back into the vehicle, luxuriating in the soft-padded upholstery, feeling the solid thunk as the doors slammed shut.

"Upon my soul, but this is the way to travel," Doc said, sighing. "I do believe that a fellow could become used to this kind of stylish traveling."

"Shame that it cost men's lives," Krysty said.

Mildred snorted angrily. "You kidding me, Krysty? Those pig-ignorant sons of bitches had it coming. Leave the world a better and cleaner place. That's what I say. Come on, John, let's hit the road...and not come back here no more, no more. Graceland next stop."

BUT GRACELAND AND MEMPHIS still lay some distance over the western horizon. Sullivan had described to them some of the more radical changes in the eco-structure of that part of Tennessee. The shifts in the tectonic plates after skydark altered the face of the state. The highway now snaked across two rivers and a new range of jagged hills. There was also an area of flat land, around two hundred square miles, that had turned in the past hundred years into a smaller version of the bayous of Louisiana.

Since there was no sign at all of any pursuit for the chillings back in Country Row, Ryan figured that it should soon be possible to find somewhere safe to camp to catch up on their rest.

But there were still many miles to go before they would finally sleep.

And a surprising meeting.

Chapter Twenty-five

Ryan had taken over behind the wheel, picking his way slowly across the bleak land with the aid of some adequate low-beam lights. The moon had gone, slinking away behind a bank of thick cloud, leaving the trail difficult to navigate.

The original highway seemed to have almost totally disappeared, with only the occasional fairly level strip of pavement running for a couple of hundred yards, then doglegging off to either right or left.

The chem storm that they'd glimpsed ahead of them seemed to be moving slowly closer, with the lightning more frequent and the claps of thunder following more closely on its heels. The wind had risen, sighing dustily through the open windows of the cautiously advancing 4x4.

"Think we should stop?" Krysty asked, sitting on the far end of the spacious front seat, the occasional flashes bringing out the fiery reds and golds of her unique hair.

Ryan shook his head. "Haven't seen anything worth a spit for shelter for the rest of the night. Wag like this'll be strong enough to take any kind of weather. We get flash floods, then we just halt for a while until it subsides."

Doc had been sleeping in the back, snoring like a distant buzz saw. Now a bump from the front axle jerked him awake. "By the Three...! I thought myself in the famed city of Eldorado, reclining upon a couch of beaten gold while dusky maidens fed me iced grapes." He wiped ineffectually at the dusty window. "Are we there?" he asked. "Then again, I think that I am not certain just where 'there' is. Or whether it is the same as 'here.' Or whether both are metaphysical concepts being far beyond the reach of most Cro-Magnon anthropoids."

His weird, typically muddled pronouncement silenced everyone, and for the next three or four miles nobody spoke.

THE FIRST HEAVY DROPS of rain puddled on the windshield, drumming on the reinforced roof of the wag.

"Here it comes," Mildred said, leaning forward, resting her arms on the back of Krysty's seat. "Least it might lay the dust and clean the air a little. Been too hot and too dry for too long for me."

"Yeah, me too," Krysty agreed.

The storm intensified. "Hey, Ryan! Think we should—"

"Stop?" He eased off the gas and slipped the vehicle into Park, pulling on the brake and switching off the engine. "Yeah, I think we should stop."

The thunder was suddenly all around them, shaking the vehicle with its shocking force, and the lightning was so bright and constant that you could have read a book through it. Purple, pink and silver, in sheets and jagged daggers, it forked all around them, dropping the temperature by fifteen degrees and filling the air with the unforgettable stench of ozone.

And the rain came down in a pounding shroud, cutting visibility to less than ten feet. Ryan leaned forward and switched off the lights. "Might as well save the battery," he said. "Nothing to see out there."

THE WAG HAD BEEN BUILT to handle all sorts of rough, off-road terrain, but it wouldn't cope with suddenly slipping into a black hole in the highway or sliding off the gradient into some unseen foaming river.

The storm showed no signs of passing; indeed, it seemed to be still gathering strength. The wind was howling like a banshee, making the vehicle roll and rock from side to side, like an aspen in a hurricane. It felt as though some demonic forces were beneath it, trying to turn it over. Ryan could just make out a wide stream, inches deep, flowing beneath the wag, occasionally strong enough to move it a little. There seemed to be a sheer drop to the right, but he couldn't be certain.

The thunder was constant, the lightning slicing into the hills on both sides of the muddied trail.

And the rain sheeted down, in a ceaseless roar on the metal roof of the wag, streaming over the windows.

"Might as well try and get some sleep here," Ryan said. "We're going nowhere for a spell."

HE HAD BEEN in a dark dream, walking through a forest with no sunshine and a ceaseless drizzle of fine rain that soaked through the clothes and chilled the bones.

He blinked his good eye open, sitting upright for a moment, wondering what it was that had jerked him awake.

"Whoa," he whispered, glancing around in the dazzling bursts of lightning to make sure all the sec locks were snapped shut and everyone was fast asleep.

He checked the chron, seeing that it was a few minutes after one. He'd been asleep for less than a quarter hour, and the storm still raged all around them.

Nothing much seemed to be happening, and he readied himself to sleep again, trying to push back the prickling unease that had raised the short hairs at his nape.

He looked out of the windshield, wiping the driver's window, clearing away the cold condensation. The wag jerked a little, almost floating, with a recurrence of the same odd, insecure feeling of the wheels losing grip. And one side tilted slightly. Ryan peered out again, seeing that the 4x4 had definitely moved a good yard or more toward the drop on the right, away from the water-streaked face of the cliff on his side.

Even the worst wind and rain wouldn't do that to a massive six-seater like the 4x4—unless the whole highway was actually crumbling under them.

He was leaning to the right, trying to puzzle out what was going on, when there was a particularly savage flash of lightning that burned into his retina, the thunder pounding simultaneously at his hearing.

And he glimpsed something from the corner of his good eye, something low down, barely showing above the roll bar, something so hideous and grotesque that he knew that it had to have been a trick of the storm.

It was a face, tiny and distorted, like a rubber carnival mask, with every feature stretched, warped and scarred. The tiny eyes burned toward him, red in the chem lightning. The mutie had matted, straggling hair like coils of steel wire, a snuffling hole where the nose should have been and a slit of a mouth with a triple row of serrated teeth showing over the curved lips.

It was holding the roll bar with its long horned claws curling over, actually scratching away the paint as Ryan watched, peeling it away in strips that revealed the brightness of bare metal.

He blinked in a moment of blackness, seeing the ghastly afterimage seared into his vision, waiting for another flash of lightning, which came a couple of seconds later.

The road in front of the wag was empty, and the strange movement had ceased.

"Fireblast! Hey, wake up, friends. Looks like we got some company."

Simultaneously a jagged rock the size of a man's fist flew from the blackness and starred the middle window on the left side of the wag. But Elmore and Albert hadn't stinted on their pride and joy, and had used good-quality sec glass. So the window crazed, but held firm, unbroken.

"What?" J.B. said, holding the Uzi, peering into the teeming darkness, unable to see any kind of target.

"Muties," Ryan ducked as another rock thudded into the side door panel. "Spotted one. Not like anything I ever saw before. Kind of a bit like swampies but smaller."

"Could be what they call muddies. Heard of them. Tiny, with faces like living evil. Never saw them, but I recall Trader said he'd come across them a couple of times in bayou regions."

The 4x4 was ringing as the attack intensified, and it suddenly lifted on one side and shifted sideways toward the invisible drop.

"Underneath us," Jak yelled.

There was a certain security in the partly armored wag, but it was a false safety. It wouldn't take long to tip the whole vehicle over the side. And the six occupants could easily be trapped and helpless.

Ryan made the decision. "Out and chill them," he shouted, flicking the sec lock and diving through the open door into the deafening, blinding storm. He landed awkwardly in the soft torrent of slippery mud, rolling over on his hip and shoulder, coming up into a crouch about a dozen feet from the wag, close to the steep cliff.

The lightning gave plenty of illumination to one of the most macabre sights that Ryan had ever seen.

The sodden earth all around the wag was a mass of scurrying figures, just like the one he'd glimpsed hanging on the roll bar at the front of the 4x4.

They were less than four feet tall, most of them naked, covered in dank, thick hair, with the most hideous faces, gibbering and gesticulating toward him with their clawed hands.

One of them was wearing a strange silver disk around its thick little neck, which caught the multicolored flashes of lightning in a bizarre way.

Even as he started shooting, a small part of Ryan's concentration had slipped to that ornament, wondering at the sharp tug of memory that was triggered by it, trying to recall where he'd seen it before.

But the chilling swamped all other thoughts.

The muddies started to howl as the occupants of the wag tumbled into the rain all around them, pouring death from a variety of blasters.

The diminutive bodies were torn apart under the concentrated hail of lead, spinning and tumbling, sliding along in the river of liquid dirt.

With Ryan, Jak and J.B. on one side of the 4x4, and the others on the far side, the only danger was getting caught in the cross fire.

"Hold it!" Ryan yelled, seeing that the surviving muties had broken and run for it, all clawing their way over the steep slope and vanishing down into the stygian darkness, leaving only their dead and a few of their dying.

"Anyone hurt?" Krysty shouted.

"Little fucks never got to us," Jak called, standing up, his white face streaked with mud, hair plastered to the sides of his narrow skull, eyes glowing a fiery red in the lightning.

"Glad we got to them," Ryan said, quickly reloading his blaster.

Krysty and J.B. quickly terminated the squealing survivors, with single shots to the nape, bringing a silence to the heart of the storm.

"We chase them?" Jak asked, reloading.

Ryan shook his head, sending a spray of rain from his matted hair. "No. Best thing is to try and get moving again.'' He stared up at the sky, blinking against the flaring lightning. ''Pull her forward away from the edge, J.B., and we can get on. Take it slow and careful. Think it might be easing.''

He went to drag some of the stocky corpses away from the highway, pulling a face at the horrific expressions on the distorted heads. The others had finished reloading and lent a hand, clearing a path from the front of the vehicle while J.B. wired it back into life again.

The wag had edged clean, and J.B. leaned out of the cracked window. ''Ready when you are, friends.''

Krysty opened the middle door and slid in, wincing at the amount of mud she was smearing on the plush upholstery. Mildred joined J.B. in the front, and Jak and Doc sat in the back of the vehicle.

Ryan hesitated a moment, worrying that something was nagging at his memory, something that he'd noticed in the beginning of the brief fight and then forgotten.

''No,'' he said to himself. Whatever it was, it was gone. So it probably hadn't been important. He opened the passenger's door and joined Krysty in the middle section of the wag.

''Ready?'' J.B. asked, taking off his fedora and putting it on the seat at his side.

''Sure.''

They began to inch forward. The rain had eased, and the thunder and lightning had become more sporadic. Ryan looked out through the unbroken glass, squinting at the pile of muddies' corpses, seeing something glinting brightly among the bodies in a purple-pink flash of chem lightning.

"Hold it." He opened the door and jumped quickly into the mud. He splashed through and stooped over one of the dead muties, lifting the silver ornament and chain from around its stubby, bristly neck.

J.B. had put on the brake, stopping the 4x4, and now everyone piled out again, gathering around Ryan, peering at the disk that he held in his hand.

"It seems to me that I have seen that pretty bauble at another place and in another time," Doc said.

"Me, too." Mildred looked carefully at the engraved disk. "I know what it is!"

Ryan nodded before she even said the name. "I knew I recognized it. It belongs to Straub."

Chapter Twenty-Six

Straub was one of the most evil and dangerous men that Ryan had ever met, in a world that held far more than its share of dangerous and evil men and women.

He could visualize Straub without any trouble, recalling every detail of dress and appearance. He was about fifty years old, slender, a touch over six feet tall. His head was shaved clean, and he wore a large opal in his right ear and had a gold tooth at the front of his mouth. A beautiful necklace of raw turquoise hung around his throat.

He dressed totally in black: black shirt, silken, and black jeans with silver rivets; black Western boots, high-heeled, with a silver snake embroidered around them. Straub didn't carry a blaster, but wore a straight-edged razor with a carved ivory handle tucked into a soft leather sheath that hung down the back of his neck.

His skin was soft and smooth, like a much younger man's. His voice was low and insistent, a creepy, insinuating sort of voice that set the hairs prickling.

But the most remarkable thing about the man called Straub were his eyes.

It was possible that they might just have been a very dark brown, but the impression one had was of black, a deep, impenetrable sable with tiny flecks of silver light that seemed to whirl in them.

Straub was a successful hypnotist. Using the combination of his voice, his eyes and the whirling silver disk, he seemed able to overcome anyone, however strong their personality and resistance might be.

Power was Straub's goal, and he used his wicked and arcane skills to dominate and warp people to his own will.

It was Straub who had led the attack on Trader and Abe on that wave-swept, desolate beach some time ago, while Ryan and the others were helpless to assist Trader and his trusty companion. But events had moved on, and Ryan hadn't been able to witness the very last act of the dramatic tragedy and still didn't know whether the two men were actually dead.

But Straub would know.

And here was his silver hypnotism toy around the throat of a dead muddie, in the wilderness of Tennessee.

"It's hardly damaged at all," Mildred said, touching the smooth surface.

"Means that they took it off someone recently. Mebbe off Straub himself." Ryan rubbed a finger along the line of his chin. "Just a chance they have him prisoner. Lot of muties keep their captives awhile for sporting or sacrifice. Could even be planning to eat him." He stared down the ridge, where they could make out a narrow river. "Camp's that way. Muddies won't be looking for us to pursue them. Let's go take a look."

THEY LOCKED THE WAG, pulling it safely off the furrowed track into a narrow, wooded pullout a hundred yards west of the scene of the ambush.

The storm had finally passed on south, the thunder now a monotonous background rumble, the flashes of lightning few and far between. And the rain had stopped, leaving the highway awash with mud and streams. As the clouds cleared, the moon broke its way back through, giving them enough light to move after the muddies at reasonable speed.

The trampled trail was clear enough to follow through a lunar landscape of dismal gray pools and scummed ponds, with ragged, tilted trees scattered around.

The camp of the muddies was less than two miles into the swamp, in a part that lay under a cloud of thick mist, a stinking, whitish green fog that swirled around Ryan and the others as they crept closer.

"Smells primeval," Doc stated. "I wouldn't be that surprised to find dinosaurs browsing among this wilderness."

The camp was in an uproar, with the muddies squealing out in their own clicking language, undoubtedly telling one another about the massacre that had just taken place back on the road.

Ryan stopped when they were forty or fifty yards from the center of the squalid settlement of stunted thatched huts. "If they're holding Straub, where will that be? Can't go blundering in and search the place. Must be a hundred or more of the little bastards."

"Look!" Jak had the best night sight, and he pointed through the coiling tendrils of fog to a row of wooden stakes set in the ground on the far side of the clearing, beyond a smoldering fire. A figure was tied to one of them. Even at that distance it was possible to see that the man had a shaved head.

"Him," Ryan breathed. "Looks like he might still be this side of the black river."

"We waiting or going in?" J.B. asked. "My feeling is to hit them now, while they're still upset and disorganized."

"Agreed," Ryan said. "Jak, you and Krysty head straight for Straub. Cut him free and haul him back to the wag, fast and safe as you can. Rest of us charge at them, blasters firing. Drive them back, then establish a tight defensive perimeter. Hold it for no more than three minutes, maximum. Time for them to get Straub away. We pull in behind them. Loose skirmish, and try and hold the muddies off. Should work."

THE FOG GAVE THEM COVER over the first dangerous yards, and J.B. put the Uzi on full-auto, blasting out a stream of murderous 9 mm rounds that chopped into the heart of the throng of muties. Their little bodies danced and thrashed, tumbling into one another, the powerful blaster cutting off hands and legs. Ryan, Mildred and Doc were at J.B.'s side, picking their targets with more care, the Le Mat erupting in a cloud of black-powder smoke, with its 18-gauge shotgun round blowing a hole in the muddies' ranks.

The dwarfish muties fled their village, vanishing and splashing into the pools and the fog behind the settlement.

Ryan set the perimeter along the rear of the last row of huts, with Doc on his left and J.B. and Mildred on the right. Behind him, he glanced over his shoulder to make sure that Jak and Krysty had gotten through unharmed. They were kneeling by the row of torture stakes, working at severing the rawhide cords that tied the prisoner.

The numbers raced on the wrist chron. "Two minutes and ten seconds," he called.

A spear came from the mist, its flaked stone point digging into the dirt a yard or so from Ryan. He fired a couple of aimless shots into the gloom, but heard nothing.

"Got him, lover," Krysty yelled. "Unconscious. But it's Straub. Leaving with him now."

"One minute thirty-five," Ryan shouted. "Everyone still all right?"

The three friends confirmed that none of them had been harmed.

"Forty seconds. Looks like they're gathering out there. I can see them by that fallen mangrove."

Ryan didn't want to have to fight a running rearguard action all the way back to the highway, carrying an unconscious Straub, the vengeful muddies gathering at their heels.

More spears were thrown, one of them so close to Mildred that she had to parry it with her left arm. Somewhere in the rolling fog, a number of drums had started beating.

"I fear that they are gathering courage to attack us," Doc said. "Either that or they are summoning King Kong from his mountain fastness."

If it hadn't been for the rain soaking the crude huts, Ryan would have tried to start a diversionary fire.

On the spur of the moment he changed his plan. "Wait for them," he said. "If they want to summon up their nerve and try and charge us, then we let them. We got the firepower to hold them off at least one more time without blowing all the ammo. Beat them back, and they'll think a long time before they try us again. That's when we pull out and support Krysty and Jak back to the wag."

The drumming was growing louder, closer, the noise only slightly muffled by the thickening fog, and they could now hear a rhythmic chanting as the muddies worked themselves up to attack the outlanders.

Ryan glanced once more at the wrist chron, seeing Krysty and Jak already had a lead of nearly five minutes. Two miles across poor terrain would take a good half hour. Probably half as long as that again if they had to help Straub.

"Coming," J.B. said, setting the Uzi back onto single shot, aiming and firing carefully at the line of stocky figures that was creeping from the wall of mist.

Despite the poor light and the numbers of the muties, Ryan never felt that they were in serious danger. The blasters kept the muddies out of viable range for spears and knives, and the bodies dropped with a relentless regularity. There was time to pick a target and aim and fire, and even Doc, not the greatest marksman, was able to make good use of the revolver rounds of the Le Mat.

"This is plain and simple murder," the old man complained. "Why do they not retire and save themselves from further slaughter at our hands?"

"Because they got brains the size of peanuts," J.B. replied, slapping in another mag.

"They're folding," Mildred said. "Stop firing."

Ryan ignored her taking over his role by issuing such a command. She was right, and there was no point in making any kind of issue of it. The gunfire ceased and the swamps became quieter, with only weeping and cries from some of the wounded muddies lying twisting in the watery mud.

The drumming had stopped.

"Lets go," Ryan said. "Quick and quiet."

THERE WAS NO SOUND of pursuit, and they quickly caught up with Krysty and Jak, who were dragging the semiconscious prisoner between them. Ryan glanced at the bald-headed figure, making sure that it really was the infamous Straub that they'd taken the trouble to rescue. Just for a moment he wasn't certain, as the face was lined and pinched and seemed years older.

But the lids blinked open, showing the familiar black eyes, rolling and trying to focus. The mouth sagged, showing the tip of the reptilian tongue.

"The countess will thank you for saving her servant," he said in his unforgettably deep, rich voice. Then his eyes closed again and he slumped back, unconscious.

THE WAG WAS STILL THERE, safe and snug, and they slid Straub into the back seat, where Mildred sat with him. Ryan took the wheel, with Krysty at his side, and the others crowded into the middle seat of the vehicle.

The engine started and Ryan slid it into low gear, aware that the walking and fighting in the swamps had strained the wound in his thigh, leaving him with a dull ache. But it seemed to be healing well.

"Memphis and the countess," he said.

DAWN FOUND THEM out of the swamps, into a part of the state that looked relatively unchanged. A rolling green plain, with the blackened scar of a nameless township, squatted mute and dead a couple of miles to their north. Ahead the land rose slightly toward bluffs, and they found a beautiful narrow river flowing fast alongside the highway.

"Can we take a break?" Mildred asked. "Straub could do with some water. He's slipping in and out of consciousness. Be good to stabilize him."

"Sure," Ryan agreed, pulling onto a patch of lush grass, switching the engine off and throwing open the door to let in the fresh, cool morning air.

Straub was placed on his back while Mildred used a wet rag to wash his face and hands, trickling water into his open mouth. The man was barefoot, dressed in his usual black shirt and pants, though the encounter with the muddies had left them torn and crusted with dried blood.

"Looks in a poor state," Krysty observed. "Not the man he was when we saw him last."

The jewelry was gone, including the opal earring, which wasn't surprising, and there was a gap where the gold tooth had been knocked out. Ryan had already checked to make sure the man wasn't wearing any kind of concealed weapon, but he was clean. Presumably the muddies had stripped him of the ivory-hafted razor that he used to carry.

Straub's skin was very pale, and he'd lost a fair bit of weight, looking to be around one-thirty pounds. As they stood around him, the man's dark eyes opened again, and he looked up at the circle of his old enemies.

A slight smile curled his lips. "It wasn't a dream," he said. "I was taken by those grotesque little bastards and was preparing myself to die at their cruel claws. Then I was plucked away amid gunfire and darkness. And who should it be?" He looked puzzled. "The names escape me. Brian?"

"Ryan."

"Yes. Ryan Cordell."

"Cawdor." He wondered how much of this was genuine memory loss. It just didn't ring true with such a devious and cunning man as Straub.

"And Krysty Wroth. J. Rix."

"Dix. J. B. Dix," the Armorer said. "Come off it, Straub. You can't have forgotten. Not that long."

"You others…" He shook his head. "I'm sorry, but I've been through changes since we last met. Where was that? On the Greasy Grass of Montana? The red cliffs of Big Bend by the Grandee? In the haunted ruins of Los Alamos? I was there for some time, seeing what I could learn in those sterile, ticking corridors. But I've forgotten all of that, as well. I am grateful for your saving me from death, and the Countess Katya, who I serve willingly as her slave, will reward you."

"This is Jak Lauren, Mildred Wyeth and Doc Tanner," Ryan said. "We met before. Last time we saw you was on a cold beach, and you were attacking a good friend of ours. What happened to him?"

"Who?"

"Trader. Fireblast! Why are you playing this stupe game with us, Straub?"

The head shook slowly, and he seemed genuinely puzzled. "Never heard of this Trader. But since joining the countess, she's taught me to remember only what's important. What she wants is important. Nothing else. She edited my memory, marked me as hers and changed my body so that I no longer needed to be weak in lust."

He fumbled with his shirt, pulling it open.

"By the Three Kennedys!" Doc gasped. "What kind of . . . ?"

Straub's body was covered in tattoos. Silver chains had been etched around his wrists, around his arms, circling his chest. Both nipples had been pierced with steel rings, and a length of glittering chain linked them.

"She did that?" Ryan asked. "The countess did that and you let her?"

Straub rolled onto his stomach, smiling in delight at their reaction. "See how she claims me."

"I am the humble and valueless property of the Countess Katya, who may dispose of me in any way she wishes when I am no longer of use to her."

The words were tattooed in flowery letters of crimson, green and rich cobalt, covering him from shoulder to shoulder, down to his waist.

"Those are whip scars, lover," Krysty whispered, pointing to the seamed and welted surface of the man's skin.

Straub ignored their shock and horror. "But see how she rewarded me for a failure. I wasn't able to fulfill her deepest wish, so she has done this..."

He pulled down his pants, revealing his naked loins to their eyes.

He had been emasculated, his penis and genitals sliced away, leaving a neat, puckered scar and a narrow incision that also carried two silver rings and a linking chain.

"Dark night," J.B. whispered. "She did that?"

Straub giggled, and they all realized with a frisson of disgust that the man was now mad, his once-brilliant brain tilted by whatever had been done to him.

"She did," he said. "And we're close to her ville, so you can all meet her very soon."

"That'll be interesting," Krysty said. "I can hardly wait."

Chapter Twenty-Seven

"It is such a pleasure to have you as my guests in my ville. And to have the chance to thank you properly for rescuing my most valuable councillor, dear Straub."

Countess Katya Beausoleil was in her late thirties and was one of the most handsome women that Ryan had ever met. She was a couple of inches below six feet, with a luxuriant mane of tumbling hair as black as the sheen on a raven's wing. Her eyes were almost as green as Krysty's, hidden beneath hooded lids. Ryan noticed that her complexion was surprisingly pale, as though she spent very little time out of doors.

She wore a maroon pantsuit in some soft material that he guessed might be velvet. Her only concession to jewelry was a small silver brooch on her breast.

Straub had given them instructions how to get to the main building of the countess's ville, and they had driven there in three hours. It was to the east of Memphis, in what looked like an area that had once been very exclusive. The house was better described as a mansion, standing in grounds of a couple of hundred acres, and it had been extensively securitized with sec-steel shutters and heavy doors, as well as gun ports slashed into the walls and battlements erected along the line of the roof.

She had seemed pleased to welcome Straub, and he had fawned on her like a puppy, telling her who the visitors were and giving the impression that he had once been the closest of friends with them. It was a strange performance and seemed genuine enough. But Ryan, knowing the old Straub, was still deeply suspicious of the man's motives.

"We will be taking lunch shortly," Katya said, motioning toward the main hall. "The room at the far end. You will stay with us for a few days?" She placed her hand on Ryan's arm in a gesture that was noticed by Krysty.

"Like to."

"Good. I will have my people show you to rooms on the second floor. We eat in fifteen minutes."

THE SEC MEN WERE TACITURN, all seeming to be in their late twenties and early thirties. They were dressed in spotlessly clean casual clothes, well armed with matching chromed Ruger Redhawks, the .44 Magnum with a seven-and-a-half-inch barrel. The impression was of extreme alertness and a calm, self-contained efficiency. They were all very polite but never came anywhere close to being friendly. And that was something Ryan could admire.

The six companions were left alone in a large room, well-appointed in a classic predark country-house style: lots of padded furniture with flowered-print draperies and covers; polished bronze bowls of scented flowers on polished tables; an upright piano in the corner of the suite allocated to Ryan and Krysty; four-poster bed with heavy tapestry curtains around it; a bright fire blazing in the hearth and small silver and brass ornaments on the mantel. The walls were hung with a number of dark oil paintings, some showing stately galleons, others portraying old-fashioned men in ruffs solemnly skating on frozen polders.

"Tasteful," Mildred said. "Kind of thing you'd see in a *National Geographic* article on stately living in the country shires in England."

"Best-dressed ville I ever saw," J.B. agreed, sitting on a large sofa, sinking into the upholstery.

"How about Straub?" Ryan was looking out of the barred windows, across a neat herb garden, divided with a patterned box hedge.

"Man's mind's fucked," Jak said. "Lost it. Whole suit short of a deck. Only one round left in the chamber. One-way ticket to madsville."

Doc nodded. "I can only agree with our young friend. The Countess Katya Beausoleil has broken him in mind and spirit. He is totally in thrall to her."

There was general agreement that the evil mesmerist was a spent force. Ryan reluctantly went along with that. "I just wonder whether a snake can change its rattle. He was such a brilliant, swift and evil bastard. Is he playing a deep game?"

"Gaia, lover! You saw the way she's mutilated and castrated him. He's a broken man. I almost feel sorry for the poor devil."

There was a discreet knock on the door. "The countess would be obliged by your company," the sec man said in a muted Tennessee accent.

THE FOOD WENT with the house—excellent quality, yet bland and strangely oppressive.

They were served brown soup with beef to start, followed by broiled trout with a side salad that had been washed in a bland mayonnaise. Roast pork was next, with perfect carrots, baked potatoes and a tasteless gravy. Dessert was a steamed vanilla pudding with raisins, and sliced apple with a custard sauce. There was the faint hint of cinnamon with the apples, but that was almost the strongest flavor of the whole rich meal.

The countess served wines that had been imported from far-off France in the past ten years. The white was too sharp on the palate, and the red was as bland as the salad dressing.

They dined with the countess seated at the head of the long oak refectory table, Straub perched like a pet ape at the far end, keeping up a flow of fulsome praise for every course of the meal until he was silenced.

"Enough, Straub," Katya ordered, her voice cracking like a buggy whip, actually making Straub wince. He sat with head bowed, toying with his food, one hand playing with his retrieved silver disk around his throat.

"I must tell you a little about myself and about this ville," she said, turning to stare at Ryan, fixing him with her deep green eyes, largely ignoring the rest of the company.

"I inherited it from my father, Count Ricard Beausoleil. He had, in his turn, taken it over from his father, Count Emilion, and he from the first baron here, Count Fortdur Beausoleil. He built it in the bloody days after the long winters and made it largely what it is now."

She paused and Ryan felt that some comment was called for. "You aren't married?"

"I'll come to that, Ryan. My father had three sons and me, his weak ninny of a daughter." She gave a thin, contemptuous smile. "They're dead and I live and rule."

"Sickness, ma'am, or in battle?" Doc asked, helping himself from a silver tureen to more of the pudding and custard sauce.

"What? My brothers? An original Remington painting fell on the skull of Paul. Antoine drowned while cleaning out the carp pool. Georges was found dead in his bed, having choked while devouring a large bowl of lime gelatin."

"Ill luck," Doc said, shaking his head. "And there has not been a count to join you here?"

She laughed. "Oh, yes. I have had three husbands, my dear Dr. Tanner." She turned her smile onto Ryan, seated at her right. "And even more bad luck. I had hoped that one of them would supply me with the male heir that I need so much, but all of them failed. And having failed to get me with child, the fates snatched them away from me."

Straub giggled loudly. "The fates always operate at your command, my lady."

She didn't smile. "Just as with my brothers, all my husbands suffered extraordinary accidents. First was Nicholas. A sweet man. He was found dead in an old freezer chest in one of the outbuildings. He had been missing for several days. He was dressed in my underwear. Then came Robert. Built like a bull, but absent in the region of fatherhood. He had the unfortunate habit of smoking in bed. Little black cigars from the Caribbean. When someone finally heard his screams, the bed was totally ablaze and nothing could be done to save him."

"Chains don't melt," Straub said runically, getting an angry glare from the countess.

"The bald, cockless fool means the chains of love," she said smoothly.

"And your third husband?" Mildred prompted, pouring herself a crystal goblet of water.

"That was John. A tender lover. But when it came to the moment of most intense passion, I'm sorry to say that there wasn't much there. John flattered to deceive me."

"So he died?" Ryan asked.

"He died. I didn't know it, or he could have been saved, but the poor man took to walking in his sleep. Climbed to the attic turrets and slipped over the edge. We found him next morning, his thigh bones driven up through his shoulders."

"My God," Mildred breathed.

"Beware of blasphemy." Katya warned. "For He sees all and hears all."

"I'm sorry. But I have never heard a . . . a story to compare with that, Countess."

"That was a month ago. Since then, I have been distraught with grief. My clock is running out and I must, must, must have a son. So, we shall see what those fates provide."

Another snigger came from Straub, who was rolling his silver disk back and forth, so that it caught the light from the pendant-drop chandeliers.

Ryan glanced at it and found that it suddenly held his attention, seeming to lock in his mind. With a firm shake of his head he was able to free himself, but it set him wondering again about Straub.

The man seemed a crazed shell of what he'd been, yet there was something creepy, something that indicated that there might still be a river of power running quietly, far beneath the triple-mad exterior.

"Is there anything that any of you wish to visit while you stay here with us? Any attraction of old Memphis that we can escort you to and ensure your safety against local rowdies? Parts of the city are still there from pre-dark times."

Mildred half raised her hand, as though she were attracting the attention of a schoolteacher. "I've always had an interest in going to Graceland," she said hesitantly.

The countess nodded and smiled. "Others of our visitors have mentioned that place. The King's home. I have been there, and it is tawdry beyond belief. But if you like the songs of Elvis, then I suggest there is some fascination in visiting his home."

Though the request had come from Mildred, the ruler of the ville had ostentatiously addressed her reply to Ryan, leaning toward him so that the front of her dress cupped open and revealed the shadowed valley between her breasts.

Krysty caught his eye and shook her head in mock irritation, though Katya's interest in Ryan was so blatant it didn't seem to be offensive.

"We shall all go together," she declared. "Straub, make the arrangements and fix enough sec men."

"Of course, Countess. It will be a pleasure to do your bidding."

"Has everyone finished eating and drinking?" She waited only a nanosecond before standing and sweeping away toward the door. She stopped and turned to face her guests. "I am busy today and this evening. A ville of this size always requires my attention. Sadly I shall not meet you until tomorrow. But I look forward to that. Straub will help you in anything you need." The sec men at the door saluted as she strode past them, vanishing into the hall.

As the door closed, Straub was standing, leaning on the table with both hands. His face was split with a great beam showing the gap in his teeth.

"She is the most wonderful and powerful person that I have ever met," he said softly. "There is nothing in all Deathlands that the countess cannot have, if she wants it. She cannot be denied. And yet she is the essence of charm. What are your impressions of her, Ryan Cawdor? I felt that she liked you." He giggled again, covering his mouth with his hand.

Krysty was also standing. "She liked him the way the cat likes the cream," she said. "Long as she doesn't expect Ryan to be the one who provides her with her son and heir."

Straub stopped sniggering, his face hardening, lips tight. "You heard about all the bizarre accidents that have happened to her kinfolk? The countess has also had a string of lovers, and they've all failed her. Not many of them still walk around above ground. Best you don't make jokes about sons and heirs, Krysty."

"Doesn't it occur to her that the problem must lie with her and not with her banks of sperm donors?" Mildred said. "She ever had a proper gyno checkup?"

Straub looked around as though he'd suddenly heard the worm gnawing behind the arras, his black eyes twitching nervously, his voice an intense whisper. "That's an even better topic to get yourself on the last boat downriver, Dr. Wyeth. I'm your friend, and I have the ear of the mistress. But even I could do nothing to help you if she was to catch a mere breath of such a stupe and blasphemous suggestion."

Ryan was ready to go. "On the subject of your helping us, Straub?"

"Yeah?"

"Is Trader alive or dead?"

It was like watching a vanadium-steel sec shutter drop over tinted armaglass. The life seemed to disappear from the dark eyes. "Trader? You asked me before, and I can't remember. What's happened since then has wrapped an impenetrable shroud over my earlier memories. I can only recall clearly what's happened since I met the countess." His whole body shivered. "I can remember all of that, so well."

Ryan sighed, still unable to make his mind up about what was going on beneath that shaved skull. "Reckon time's our own now," he said. "Until tomorrow's trip to Graceland."

Chapter Twenty-Eight

The rest of that day passed amiably enough. Straub had offered himself as guide, but Ryan suggested that they would prefer to explore on their own. He was told that only the personal quarters of the countess were out-of-bounds to them.

"There's an armory?" J.B. asked. "Spent a lot of ammo getting you away from those shit-eating little muties."

Straub enthusiastically encouraged the six companions to visit the ville's store of weapons and ammunition and to help themselves to anything they found there.

THERE WAS A YOUNG GUARD on the door, crew cut, his hand resting casually on the butt of the Ruger Redhawk. "Welcome," he said. "Straub passed on the word from the countess that you could come and help yourself." He looked at their array of armaments and grinned in a friendly fashion. "Guess you know what you want without me having to come in. It's all labeled clear."

"Dark night," the Armorer breathed. "Here's a lady knows what she wants and has what she wants. Good an armory as I ever saw, even in a big frontier ville."

Jak had spotted a pedal-powered honing wheel and went straight to it, setting himself down to sharpen the edges on his beloved throwing knives.

Ryan handed over the eighteen-inch steel panga. "Can you hone that for me while you're at it, Jak?"

"Sure." Sparks flew as he pedaled furiously, making the large wheel hum.

"Doc, they even got some lead for your cannon," J.B. called. "Fill up your pockets while you can. Don't see many of those 18-gauge grapeshot rounds. And there's plenty of rounds for the revolver chamber." He pushed back the brim of his fedora and looked around the stone-walled room with its rows of chained rifles and scatterguns and the neatly labeled boxes of ammo of every caliber known to man. "This stuff's worth a baron's ransom," he said. "A serious fortune."

"Haven't got any fléchettes for the Smith & Wesson M-4000, have they?" Ryan asked.

J.B.'s unusual pistol-grip shotgun held eight rounds of Remington fléchettes, each round packed with twenty of the tiny, razored, inch-long darts.

"Yeah. Up here in this cabinet. Got plenty of those equaloy rounds and some caseless that would have done for your old Heckler & Koch, Ryan."

Ryan himself was scavenging for the 7.62 mm rounds he needed for the Steyr SSG-70 hunting rifle. To his delight he even found a brand-new baffle silencer, still in its factory-greased packing, that fitted the SIG-Sauer P-26 automatic. The original one had given up the ghost many months earlier. There were also three olive-green cases of 9 mm ammunition that fitted J.B.'s Uzi, as well as the SIG-Sauer.

"There are .38s over here, Mildred," Krysty called, stocking up for her double-action Smith & Wesson 640. Mildred's supremely accurate Czech target revolver also fired the Smith & Wesson .38 round.

Jak needed some .357s for his Colt Python, though he tended to use the blaster as little as possible, relying on his other weapons and his own skills.

"Those grens, John?" Mildred asked, looking into a row of open boxes.

"Yeah. Any you want? Always come in handy when you least expect it."

"Which are the ones that start fires?"

"Burners? Those. Next to the blue-and-scarlet implodes. What are you planning to burn, Millie?"

She smiled. "You never know what's going to come along just begging for someone to set it on fire."

The guard had been wandering around, occasionally checking out of one of the sec-steel barred windows, whistling an old predark song that Ryan recognized as "So Long, It's Been Good To Know You."

"Woody Guthrie," Doc said. "During the bleak time that I was held a hapless prisoner by the fiendish whitecoat scientists, before they fired me forward into Deathlands, I became very fond of folk music. Woody was one of my special favorites with his dust-bowl ballads."

"You got what you want?" the guard asked.

Ryan nodded. "Think so. You finished with that wheel, Jak? Yeah, then we're ready to go."

"What you goin' to do next, for the rest of the day? Check out the ville?" the guard asked, leaning against the frame of the sec door.

Ryan hadn't thought about it. "You got any ideas? Any good walks around in the grounds?"

The guard nodded vigorously. "Why, heck, do we? Countess is real keen on making things beautiful. Most important to her, apart from..." He looked around nervously. "Apart from you-know-what about having a son and all."

"Which way should we go?" Krysty asked.

"Out the rear entrance, past the stables and down over the terraces. Around the pin mill that stands at the end of the long fish pond. Follow a winding path across the flank of the steep valley, and that brings you to the viewing spot at the top of the gorge. Sight worth seeing."

"Thanks." Ryan looked around the armory again, thinking that the countess couldn't have seriously malign intentions toward them if she was allowing them this much freedom. There hadn't been even a hint that they might leave their blasters somewhere safe and collect them when they left.

"Have a nice day," the guard said.

THEY FOLLOWED his instructions, heading out into the sweet-scented gardens, where many of the plants had small metal labels attached to their stems to identify them. Near the house was a terrace of roses in all colors, sizes and shapes.

"This lemony one's beautiful," Krysty said, kneeling to catch the scent.

"I like the apricot-colored one." Mildred stooped to rub her fingers through a bush of flowering lavender, cupping her hands and breathing in deeply. "Lovely."

The still water of the large, rectangular pond was covered with waxen lilies, pink and ivory, and they could see gigantic carp moving slowly through the mysterious deeps, with smaller goldfish darting between the stems of the plants.

"There's path," said Jak, who had taken the lead, showing no interest in the array of shrubs, trees and flowers, eager to get on to the viewing spot so that he could see the river.

They passed along the side of a hill, richly planted, that dropped away into a steep valley, with gigantic pines at its bottom, and a narrow stream winding through under an ornamental wooden bridge.

"I believe that I can hear the river," Doc said, pausing to gather breath and sitting on a bench that overlooked the lovely valley.

There was a whispering sound, like surf on a distant beach, from somewhere ahead of them.

Jak was a long way in front, his flaring snow white hair leading them like a beacon along the twisting path. The ground leveled out, and the rich vegetation faded away until they were walking over bare rock.

"Noise is louder," Mildred said. "I thought that Old Miss was the only river running through Memphis."

"Probably was." Ryan paused and looked back, seeing the fortified mansion, standing on a promontory, perfectly placed for defense against any attackers. "But Tennessee was one of the states hardest hit by the earth shifts after the nuking. We've seen that already. Volcanoes and swamps. So a new river isn't much of a surprise."

"There's the viewing point that the guard mentioned," J.B. said.

It was a reinforced platform of concrete tied in with steel girders to the bedrock at the top of the cliffs. Ryan noticed that much of the stone all around the ville seemed oddly raw, as if it had been buried for aeons of time and had only been pushed out into daylight a hundred or so years earlier. The sides of the gorge down to the foaming ribbon of the river, several hundred feet below, were also fresh looking, with streaks of light stone among the darker gray.

Jak was hanging on to a wire fence that had been built around the edge of the platform, staring down into the deeps. "Can't dive straight into the river. Slopes away steep, then drops sheer for last hundred feet or so."

They all joined him, and Doc whistled softly between his excellent teeth. "Upon my soul, but that is a fine spectacle. To view it gives an odd tightening of the scrotum, if you will pardon my language, ladies."

Mildred tutted. "Keep your tight scrotum to yourself, will you, Doc?"

"But you know that feeling of part thrill and part primitive, atavistic terror of heights, madam. To go over there is to die, without a doubt."

Jak was swinging back and forth on the flimsy fence, oblivious to the fact that some of its base fastenings had come loose and it was only hanging in place by a few rusting pins. "If dived clean down be all right. Straight into river. Long as no shallows or rocks."

The Armorer was fanning himself with his hat, wiping sweat from his forehead with his sleeve. "Quite wrong, Jak."

"How?"

J.B. sniffed. "I saw a mag article once about high divers. Seems there's an optimum height, no matter how skillful you are, where your momentum gathers and you accelerate until hitting water's like hitting a sheet of marble."

"Thirty-two feet per second, per second," Mildred said. "One of the few facts I recall from high school physics. Rate of acceleration. Means in the first second you fall thirty-two feet. Sixty-four feet the next second. Ninety-six in the third second. And so on and on, faster and faster, until you reach maximum speed, whatever that is."

Krysty threw back her head, letting the strong breeze blow through her flaming hair. "I read that high divers also got punchy after a bit, because of the repeated damage to their brain. So keep away from the edge, Jak."

The teenager looked at the others, as if he wondered if he were being teased. He decided he wasn't and moved back a couple of paces from the brink.

"You all right, Doc?" Mildred asked, seeing that the old man was looking a little pale and had moved back out of the sun to sit on a shelf of shaded rock.

He was holding his stomach, biting his lip. "I believe it is just a passing attack of dyspepsia, thank you, Doctor. But rather sharp, I must confess."

"Maybe we should get back to the house, so you can have a rest. Put your feet up. Ryan?"

"Yeah, sure."

But the sight of the misty river, raging through the deep gorge, was hypnotic. The sensation drawing him toward it was strangely powerful and brought back to him the mesmeric powers of Straub.

He tore himself away from the platform, and they made their way back to the ville, Doc occasionally rubbing at his stomach while assuring them that he was feeling fine.

Ryan walked with J.B. and Krysty. "What do you make of Straub?" he asked.

"Mad and bad all the way through, lover. He glories in what that bitch's done to him. Like it was some sort of sick honor. Still wouldn't trust him as far as I could spit."

"J.B.?"

"Man's got a brain like a cunning, rabid rat. My guess is that he's got himself caught by someone as devious and power crazed as him. Now he's settling himself inside her nest. Become a councillor to her so she'll need him and trust him." The Armorer was polishing his glasses as they walked by the pool. A dragonfly, better than a foot in length, floated by them, a poem in iridescent turquoise and aquamarine. "And one day the Countess Katya Beausoleil gets to wake up dead."

Ryan paused to look at a gigantic carp, rainbow scaled, as it broke the surface of the pond to snap at a skimming water boatman. "Yeah," he said. "Like we think along the same lines. Wish he'd tell us the truth about Trader. Probably the only way we'll ever know how that final curtain came down."

THE HOUSE HAD A WONDERFUL library, and it was a pleasure for the companions to spend some time there during the afternoon. The weather had closed in, and a gray drizzle blew across the gardens from the gorge, beating on the shuttered windows. There was no sign of either the countess or of Straub himself.

They ate a perfectly cooked but exceedingly dull supper alone in the dining room.

A guard warned them as they prepared to go to their rooms for the night that the expedition for Graceland would be leaving around nine in the morning, so would they make sure they were down for breakfast by eight.

Chapter Twenty-Nine

The eggs were golden and perfectly circular. The bacon was lean and crisp, in long rashers. The tomatoes had been sliced precisely into halves and fried in salted butter. The hash browns had been sliced thin as a whisper and then cooked until their texture was exactly right. The bread was in uniform slices, and the grits were snowy, served in equal mounds on every plate.

And it was dull, dull, dull.

Krysty leaned across and whispered to Ryan, "Like the sort of food you see in old women's mags, brilliantly photographed so that it looks better than you could imagine. And when you eat it, then it somehow tastes like the paper the pix are printed on. I don't know how they do it."

The countess hadn't yet joined them, and Straub had told them that she was probably dining in her room alone.

"This is going to be so exciting. I just hope that we don't meet any muties or malcontents on the road."

"Is it far?" Ryan asked.

"I checked the maps last night. Sleep seems to evade me more than it once did. Few miles south of downtown Memphis. Whitehaven township in what was once called Shelby County. It's off Highway 51 South. On Elvis Presley Boulevard. One of the small number of streets in the whole region that keeps its predark name. Number 3764. I never saw it yet.''

''Is it still a popular attraction for tourists?'' Mildred asked, then shook her head. ''But you don't have such things as tourists now in Deathlands, do you?''

Straub smiled gently, like a wise uncle responding to a foolish but lovable niece. ''Tourists. I've read the word. People on vacation. I have asked the guards and most say it was once popular, but not many go now. Elvis Presley is fading away into the past like a vampire at dawn.''

Doc drained his coffee cup and wiped his mouth with a spotless linen napkin. ''Few names have survived, have they? Even I have heard of Elvis. We all have. Yet who can remember many of the main political figures in the world at the time the nukecaust broke across Earth?''

The door opened at the end of the dining hall, and the guards snapped to attention.

In came the Countess Katya Beausoleil, baron of her own powerful ville. She was wearing a pantsuit in maroon cotton, the pants tucked into a pair of black Western boots. Her only jewelry was a large uncut opal set in white gold, on a silver chain around her neck.

''Is everyone ready?'' she asked.

Straub leaped to his feet and bowed and nodded. ''Everyone is looking forward to the expedition, Countess.''

''Did I say you were coming?''

''No.''

"Do you wish to come?"

"Only if you wish me to come. If you wish me to stay, then I wish to stay."

"Creep," Mildred whispered loud enough for the man to hear. He turned toward her and for a moment the fawning devotion vanished, and she winced at the physical impact of the look of burning hatred that daggered in her direction. Then Straub blinked and the anger was totally gone, replaced with a bland smile.

"I wish you to come with us. I shall drive my own two-seater, and you will ride in the armawags with our guests and with the sec men. You think twenty will be enough?"

Straub thought about it for a moment, his black eyes closing as he considered the combat logistics. "There have been no reports of serious trouble from the city in months. The muddies keep to their own swamps. It was unfortunate that I was so far from home without an escort. And my thanks yet again to the outlanders for my salvation."

Katya looked around the room, then turned on her heel, hesitated and swung back. "I will take one of the outlanders with me in my wag." Her eyes roamed along the line of friends.

"Surprise me, bitch," Krysty mouthed just loud enough for Ryan to hear.

"Perhaps the old man would enjoy the trip?"

"Bullshit," Krysty muttered.

"No. My men would think it an honor to ride with me. Therefore, the honor must go to the leader of the group. That is you, is it not, Ryan Cawdor?"

"Best surprise, no surprise." Ryan was puzzled at the depth of genuine anger he detected in Krysty's whispering voice. It wasn't that important.

"Very well. Let's go."

THE CAR WAS a two-seater Mercedes sports car with gull-wing doors. The countess told him the model, but autowags didn't much interest Ryan. A something-or-other SL, he thought she said. Despite his lack of interest, Ryan had to admit that the vehicle, with cream upholstery, was in amazing condition.

The engine was smoother than anything he'd ever heard, and he wondered what she was paying for gas processed to that sort of standard. She touched the pedal, and he was pressed back in the soft seat. The car thundered onto the gravel driveway in front of the house and skidded to a halt. Three armored trucks waited there, and one of them set off in the lead at her signal.

"We go next."

Ryan saw Krysty sitting in the back of one of the other wags with Doc and Jak, and he lifted a hand in a wave. But she didn't respond.

THEY DROVE AT A GOOD speed. Despite the rain of the previous day, the roads had dried out and they moved at the center of a whirling dervish of reddish gray dust. Ryan tried to see where they were going, but it was impossible to make out any details from the Mercedes.

They had traveled a few miles in silence, when the countess started talking, asking him about everyone in the group, seeming to pay most attention to his relationship with Krysty.

How old is she? How long had they known each other? Were they married? Did they intend to get married?

"What are your thoughts about starting a family, Ryan? Settling down someplace?"

"We've talked about it."

"Does Krysty want children?"

"I already have a son, Dean, schooling up in the Rockies. He's closing in on twelve. Mother's long dead. I reckon that if we ever find that quiet place with sweet water and good land, then we might raise our own family. Me and Krysty. Talked about it. Almost since we first met. So hard to find a breathing time to walk away from the killing."

She nodded, shifting down as they encountered a section of highway that was particularly badly rutted.

"I can't tell you how much I want children, Ryan. I need them. Must have them. It's the greatest imperative, and it rules all my waking hours. My sleeping hours, too."

"I understand that."

She turned, and he saw tears glinting in the corners of her green eyes. "Do you? Do you, Ryan? No. Nobody does. Think I'm a stupe bitch, sliding toward an arid middle age. Then I'll get old and lose my grip on the ville with nobody to inherit. I must have a son."

"There must be any number of men who'd be more than happy to bed you and give you what you want."

"This part of Deathlands was badly nuked, and there's still a lot of residual hot spots."

Out of habit Ryan glanced down at the tiny rad-counter button on his lapel, as he'd been doing since they made the jump, as he did every hour or so, wherever they landed. The color was a clear, steady green.

"Not too bad here," he said cautiously.

The countess looked sideways at him, the wag swerving a little to the left. She corrected the movement automatically, wiping her sleeve across her eyes. "I say that it's the nuking that's affected all the men. They all have weak seed, and it won't grow within me and give me my son."

It was as if there was more she was going to say, but she held it back.

"NEARLY THERE, Ryan."

They were passing through a run-down, desolate suburb, with very little human habitation. Ryan had seen the crooked sign telling him they were actually on Highway 51 South, and he looked at the tumbled ruins of buildings that lined every such length of road across Deathlands: Shell, Taco Bell, Pizza Hut, Diego's Donuts, Fluff 'n' Fold, Shoney's Big Boy, Ma's Place. There were realtors and accountants, banks and thrift stores, used-car lots on both sides, some with rusting predark wrecks rotting where they stood. Most of the small, rectangular units had broken windows and doors kicked in, but it looked to Ryan as if it might have been one of the places where the Russkies had used neutron nukes that tended to destroy all life and spare the buildings.

A dusty, unbroken window on a nameless, signless store on the left of the highway still bore a scrawled message in white paint from a hundred years earlier: World Closing-Down Sale. Last Chance Bargains Before Eternity.

THE ARMAWAG WAS SLOWING, and Katya eased back on the gas. "Ryan?"

"Yeah?"

"Think about it for me."

"What?" Though he knew.

"You know."

There was no point in playing stupe. "You want me to try and father a child for you?"

"Please?"

"No. I'm sorry, but not me, Countess. Get yourself another stud bull."

"I could make you."

He shook his head. "I don't think so."

"We might explore that. You see what has happened to Straub, Ryan?"

He nodded slowly. "You think a threat like that could help to make me want to have sex with you, Countess? You think that, then I have to say you're missing a few shingles."

"Not many men speak to me like that," she said, her voice cold as Sierra meltwater.

"Can't help that." He looked ahead through the shield of the Mercedes. "We're stopping."

It was one of the most run-down areas that he'd ever seen. It was obvious that the region had recovered after the long winters, as the stores and eateries were in reasonable condition and one or two were still, just about, open. But most were closed and derelict.

"There," the countess said. "The opposite side of the highway." Her voice was calm and friendly, as though they'd never had the recent conversation.

He saw there was an oasis of green among the urban blight, with a number of tall trees, and a strange white gate of rusting wrought iron, with a guitar and musical notes built into it. A hand-painted sign was already weathered to near-illegibility: Car Park And Elvisly Souvenirs. An arrow pointed farther down the boulevard.

"We just stop here," the countess said. "Don't think there'll be any trouble."

The convoy halted and everyone climbed out. Ryan went straight to Krysty and took her by the arm, steering her away for a quick word, feeling the stiffness and resistance in her body.

"Not going to explain why I went with her," he said. "You might not like it, but you know there wasn't any choice."

"No?"

"No." He felt the throbbing pulse of her anger. "She wants me to father her a child. I said I wouldn't. She's totally locked into thinking that it's all the fault of the men."

"She would."

"Anyway, that's what's happening."

"How did she take it? Your refusal?" Krysty's attitude was softening, and Ryan felt his surge of rage easing into the background again.

"I think she's mad. Really gone right around the bend and back again. Has no concept of responsibility and the abuse of total power. Quite frightening the way

she can't see things she does are deeply wrong. Right
now she's normal as anything. Doesn't mean she'll stay
that way. Doesn't mean she's really taken in the fact
that I've refused her.''

They joined the others, surrounded by the posse of
sec men, the pale sunlight glinting on the polished
Ruger Redhawks in the greased holsters.

The gate swung open, and a chubby little lady in a
checked cotton dress, came out to greet them. ''You're
all so welcome,'' she trilled. ''Welcome to Graceland.''

Chapter Thirty

"This is dreadful," Mildred whispered to J.B. when they were about halfway through the tour. "Saddest thing I ever saw anyplace anytime."

It had very quickly become obvious that Graceland was an awful long way past its sell-by date. The place was filthy and neglected, with stains on carpets, and several of the florid displays of clothing and mementoes had deteriorated to such an extent they were actually rotting.

But their guide—Maybelline Blackwell—seemed totally oblivious to the ghostly charnel house that she showed them. Her commentary could have been written for her back in the predark days when Graceland was one of the most popular tourist attractions in the country, with hundreds of thousands of eager visitors thronging its rooms and gardens, soaking in the almost religious atmosphere of awe and respect.

"This was one of the King's favorite stage outfits, with the eagle decoration, the whole covered with precious and semiprecious jewels."

"Glass and paste," Doc muttered, peering at the faded frayed material and the discolored stones.

"The golden piano that you see ahead of you, past the beautiful bust of Elvis by a famed sculptor, was gilded for Elvis by Priscilla in 1968 as a gift on their first wedding anniversary. The instrument is a valuable 1928 Kimball concert grand.''

"Triple-ugly," was Jak's comment. "And got worm in legs."

"This is one of eleven teevee sets throughout Graceland, most of them gifts from the King's recording company, RCA Victor. In his latter days Elvis would sometimes have them all on, tuned to different channels—a habit he learned from President Johnson—while he moved around eating some of his favorite snack food."

They moved on to a room that was decorated in a kind of kitsch Polynesian style. The guide saw the expressions of amazement on their faces and took it for admiration.

"I see how impressed you are with Elvis's favorite room in the entire Graceland complex. The Jungle Room. Isn't it really just something?"

Krysty answered for them all. "Yeah, Maybelline, it's really just something."

"It was in this very room that Elvis recorded his best-selling album in 1976, entitled *From Elvis Presley Boulevard, Memphis, Tennessee.* Copies of some of his records can still be obtained on vinyl, cassette or ceedee at the Elvis souvenir stand across the way." She hesitated. "Though I'm not that certain it's open today. We don't get quite as many folks as we used to and..." The sentence trailed away like rainwater down a choked gutter.

The countess made her boredom obvious in the first ten minutes, always the first to leave a particular suite or room, eager to get on with the tour.

"Through this window you can glimpse Elvis's famous pink Cadillac. It is the 1955 Fleetwood Series Sixty that he bought for his beloved mother. Sadly the elements of weather have done some harm to the automobile."

"Can we visit the grave?" Mildred asked, wanting to get out of the choking atmosphere of the haunted mausoleum.

"I'm afraid not," Maybelline stated with well-rehearsed mock regret. "There has been a sorrowful increase in interference with the memorials, and we have had to limit access to nil access."

As they moved through the surprisingly small twenty-three rooms and eight bathrooms, Maybelline continued to flood them with facts and figures about Graceland: four hundred and sixty acres, built by Dr. Thomas Moore in 1939, bought, including nearly fourteen acres of surrounding land, for $102,500. Five times that had been spent on improvements in the first six months, the security wall of pink fieldstone costing $62,500 alone.

The Trophy Room included row upon row of Elvis's golden disks, more than one hundred and sixty of them, though there were gaps in the collection and several of the records were badly tarnished, with peeling labels.

"Sadly some damp has intruded here, and also callous thieves have made off with souvenirs from the collection," Maybelline complained.

Room after room, tired and sad, barely redolent of the hot house atmosphere of Graceland when its owner was in residence. Somehow the sorry spirit of Elvis haunted it, with the aura of physical and moral decay.

They finally reached the end of the tour.

Mildred had become more and more miserable, whispering her sorrow to J.B. as they trailed along. "It's pitiful. This isn't the memorial that Elvis Presley should have. A spider-veiled, mice-nibbled, worm-gnawed tomb that's rotting in on itself. Someone should do something. He really was the King, John. I feel like I should do something about it."

Once they were all out in the grounds, Maybelline was all rosy cheeks and bonhomie, trilling away in her little-girl voice. "Apart from the Meditation Garden, which is denied access, you may visit the grounds of Graceland. We hope you have enjoyed your visit here and will come back and see us again real soon. Tell your friends. Thank you very much."

Ryan muttered his thanks, and the others also nodded and mumbled. But all of them felt downcast at the sorry, run-down spectacle that Graceland had fallen to.

He looked around, suddenly noticing that Mildred was missing. "Anyone seen Mildred?"

J.B. had been standing polishing his spectacles and he started at the question, though Ryan knew him well enough to know that the Armorer was faking surprise.

"Millie?"

"Yeah?"

"Oh, she thought she might have left something behind and she just went back to get it."

"What?" Ryan pressed.

"What? How do you mean, bro?"

"What did she leave behind?"

Maybelline had finally tumbled that something had gone wrong and was hopping agitatedly from foot to foot. "Have we lost a member of our party? Oh, dear me!"

"I don't know what she thought she might have forgot," J.B. snapped. "Didn't tell me. Ask her yourself when she— Here she comes."

Mildred emerged from a side door a little farther up the gardens of Graceland, stopping in her tracks when she saw everyone staring at her.

"Where have you been?" Maybelline asked. "I just hope you haven't been pilfering. Oh, dear, we get so much of that these days. Now we have no security. From what I hear of the olden days..." Again her sentence trailed off into silence.

"Don't worry," Mildred said. "I didn't take anything from this place. Nothing I'd want to take." She turned to the others. "Sorry to keep you waiting. Can we go now?"

The countess had been tapping the toe of her foot restlessly on the stone flags of the garden path, arms folded, constantly checking the time on a platinum Rolex wristwatch. "I'm ready," she said.

Doc had been leaning on his swordstick, looking across the boulevard at the blighted, ugly stores. "I confess that this is a miserable place," he said. "And I—" He stopped suddenly, an expression of surprise crossing his face, his right hand touching himself low on the side of his stomach.

"What is it, Doc?" Jak asked. "All right?"

"Not very all right, as it happens, dear lad. A rather nasty stabbing pain in my belly. Quite ferocious, as if I'd swallowed a fox."

Mildred had been staring back at the house with an odd intensity, but Doc's voice brought her around. "You've gone real pale," she said.

"I am not at my best." He bit his lip, swaying to one side, steadied by Jak. "Perhaps if we might return to the house and I could lie down. Indigestion would be my most likely diagnosis. I think."

Mildred didn't say anything for a moment, studying him carefully. "Too low for indigestion," she said. "Stabbing, did you say?"

"Like a knife of fire, my dear Doctor. Indeed, I would be grateful if I could lie down in the back of the wag, or I fear that I might pass out. My hearing has gone rather fuzzy, and the world seems to be moving away from me."

"Get him in the wag," Mildred said to the guards. "Quickly."

She turned to the countess, who had showed very little interest in the small drama. "Can we move now?"

"Of course. Ryan. You'll drive with me again." It was a statement, not a question.

"No. I go with Doc. Sorry, Countess."

She nodded, her face like a mask hewn from living marble, showing no trace of emotion. "Very well. I understand, Ryan. Believe me, I do. Straub, I wish to talk to you. Come with me."

"Of course, Countess, delighted, delighted." He bowed and scraped in a parody of servility. "I am honored, honored."

She stalked off and one of the armed sec men opened the doors of the Mercedes. She got in, barely waiting for Straub before gunning the engine and roaring away in a cloud of smoking rubber.

"Thank you and goodbye, dear lady," Krysty said, touching Ryan on the arm.

Doc was moaning, sagging at the knees, supported by Jak on one side and by a guard on the other. Mildred was ushering them toward the rear of the nearest wag, telling them to lay him down, watching him safely installed. Then she walked back to Ryan and the others.

"I'll go with him," she said.

"Any idea what it is? Not having a heart attack, is he?" Ryan asked.

She shook her head. "Think not. I have an idea, but I'll need to examine him properly as soon as we're back at the ville. Then I'll know. Might be less than good news."

Mildred kept looking rather distractedly back at Graceland, as though she expected something to have happened. But she finally moved to the wag and climbed in.

"See you there," J.B. called.

"Sure, John." She made a decision. "John?"

"Yeah. What is it, Millie?"

"What's the maximum delay on an incendiary grenade?"

The Armorer's jaw sagged. "Dark night! What made you ask that? Maximum's twenty minutes on the ones that they had in the big house. But why do...? What have you...?"

The wag pulled away in an eruption of stinking exhaust smoke, taking Mildred, Doc and Jak with it.

Ryan guessed. ''Twenty minutes. I reckon we better get out. My guess is we got about five minutes.''

Krysty wasn't with it. ''I don't get it. Has Mildred set off a burner in Graceland?''

J.B. nodded, unable to conceal a smile of pride. ''Isn't she something? Said how much she hated what had happened to Elvis's home. Shameful. Wasn't worthy. Well, I guess she's gone and done something about it.''

Ryan beckoned the chief of the sec men. ''Need to get going back to the ville.''

''Sure. Everyone aboard.''

They were on the move away from Graceland in a couple of minutes, though one of the engines proved stubborn in starting, giving Ryan, Krysty and the Armorer a few nervous seconds before they were off and rolling.

The three friends sat together near the tailgate, looking behind them as the wag lumbered eastward.

J.B. had been checking his wrist chron. ''I make that past the twenty minutes maximum now, if that's what she set it for. Depends where she hid it, but we should be seeing some sign in the next minute or so. When they go, those babies really go.''

ALREADY THREE OR FOUR miles ahead, down the highway toward the ville, Countess Katya was talking with a cold ferocity to Straub, who nodded with increasing enthusiasm, then began to giggle, a hideous, bubbling noise, like boiling molasses.

"Yes, I can," he said. "Of course, most exalted one. Yes, of course."

"THERE," J.B. SAID, pointing behind them. The road had dipped, and a bunch of tattered palm trees were between them and Graceland. But they all saw the sudden flash of flame, rising fifty or sixty feet into the air, followed by a pillar of smoke, erupting much higher, until the southerly breeze started to tear its top apart.

They were more than a mile away, but all three of them felt the warm blast caress their faces from the explosion.

"That just one gren?" Krysty asked.

J.B. shook his head. "Don't know. But Millie must've placed it near the heating. Oil or gas, whatever. Whole place has gone. Did what she wanted."

Chapter Thirty-One

"Appendicitis."

"Sure?"

"Sure as can be. All the symptoms. Main thing is precisely where the pain's located. I can't think of anything else it could be."

Ryan whistled softly between his teeth. "Bad one. Known of a few people buy the farm with that."

Mildred was washing her hands. "But remember I'm not a general surgeon, Ryan. Freezing was my field, and I was real good at that. I did stuff like this when I was a student and then a junior resident. Long while ago. And I don't just mean the hundred years passed since skydark."

"So what can you do?" Krysty asked. All five friends were standing in the dimly lit corridor, outside the room where Doc had been sedated with a few drugs that were held in the ville's pharmacy.

"Infected and inflamed appendix means two things. It'll go down and get better, but maybe flare up again in a while. Days or weeks or months. Or never. Or it won't go down at all. Burst. Peritonitis and death."

They all stood silent. Since they'd gotten back to the fortified mansion they'd seen no sign of either the countess or of Straub. The sec men had been helpful, carrying Doc up to the room and showing Mildred the limited supplies of pharmaceuticals that were held in the ville.

Now it was decision time.

"How long wait?" Jak asked.

"Until it's too late?" Mildred sniffed. "I'm sort of sure it's bad news. Lot of pain. Fever. Intense, localized tenderness. If I'm going to try and operate to save the old buzzard, then I think I'll have to start within the hour. No longer."

"Someone should see the countess," Krysty said. "Tell her what's going on. Need her support. I can go." She looked doubtfully at Ryan.

"Better be me." He checked his chron. "Rest of you work with the sec men and get everything ready. See what tools and knives and stuff you can get, Mildred. Mebbe from the kitchens for the best blades. I'll go see the countess."

"HE WILL DIE if you don't operate on him?"

"We believe so."

"And the black woman is a real doctor?"

"Yeah. Just that we need your say-so to go ahead with it. Is that all right?"

"You come to me, Ryan, my dear man, with a request that only I can grant, which means life or death. Does this sound familiar to you and your friends?"

Ryan stood silent for a moment, seeing only too clearly what she meant. He decided in his mind that if she pushed it, then he would yield, agree to sleep with her if it meant the chance of saving Doc's life.

She waited a long minute. "Go and do this operation, Ryan Cawdor. It's not necessary to try and get what I want this way. The other options are more sure."

"What's that mean?"

"Nothing."

"Must mean something."

"Time will show us all, Ryan. Now, that same time is passing by and your friend could be on his way down the slippery slope. Go and save him."

"Thanks. Thanks a lot." For a moment he considered kissing her on the cheek, then decided against it.

MILDRED HAD ELECTED to try to operate down in the main kitchen area of the ville.

"Best lights. Large table we've had scrubbed and scrubbed. Some real good knives that Jak's been honing until they sing. Plenty of hot water. Can't ask for more."

"You want help?" Krysty asked.

"I'll use Jak. Got the longest, most agile fingers. Rest of you just keep well back." She wiped sweat from her forehead, reaching to tie a strip of white cotton around her temples. "Tell them to bring him down. And for Christ's sake, don't jog him."

"We'll do that. Me and Ryan," J.B. offered.

THE OLD MAN WAS DELIRIOUS, head rolling, eyes staring wildly. He looked through Ryan and J.B. as they bent over him, tucking in the bedclothes, ready to switch him to a stretcher that they'd borrowed.

"Turn the right flank, *mon commandant,* or we are lost! Save the Hussars and we save Moscow. It will take more than a French musketball to keep me from Corunna. Rally stouthearts, and let us seek glory in the cannon's mouth. Onward, onward!"

By the time they reached the kitchen with him, Doc had fallen into a deep sleep.

"Everything's ready," Mildred said, wearing a makeshift surgical mask, as was Jak, his narrow red eyes staring over the top of it.

The kitchen ovens were scorching hot, with caldrons of water bubbling and steaming. On a side table Mildred had laid out a number of silver needles, already threaded with stout cord, and an amazing array of different knives.

"One thing I don't have is any anesthetic," she said. "Have to go in quick and accurate. Ryan, hold his head still. J.B., you take Doc's feet. Krysty, try and keep his hands out of the way. Best we can do." She took a deep breath. "Let's do it."

She had three of the brighter sec men standing ready to help with swabs, cloth and water.

Behind them, a door opened and Straub entered, closely followed by Countess Katya Beausoleil, who gestured to Mildred to ignore her and get on with the operation.

"WOULD YOU LIKE LIQUOR to help take away the pain, Dr. Wyeth?" asked Katya.

"No. He's out cold. Probably come around, but I'm hoping it'll be quick."

Straub leaned forward, dark eyes fixed on Mildred. "I can use my silver disk and it will be easy."

She hesitated, knowing that the bald man spoke the truth. "No," she said. "Have to bring him around and that'll mean a lot of pain. Damned thing's about ready to burst as it is. I'm starting right now."

Ryan watched, unmoving, as she picked up one of the shorter, broad blades, bringing it close to Doc's wrinkled, taut stomach. He was holding the old man's head, tight in both hands, braced against any movement. At the far end of the whitewood table, the Armorer was leaning on his feet. Krysty was sprawled across his chest, both his hands held firmly in hers.

Doc seemed to be deeply unconscious, though his eyelids flickered and his lips were moving silently.

"Swab the blood, Jak," Mildred said as she made the first straight, deep cut. "Could do with clamps to hold the sides back. Have to do what I can."

It was amazingly fast. Ryan checked his chron as Mildred started the first incision. She made further cuts, then reached in to hold the gash while Jak went in, doing what he'd been told by her. He used the longest, thinnest flensing blade, cutting through something that gleamed a yellowish white, holding it up triumphantly in his right hand.

Then Mildred was suddenly busier than a one-legged man in a forest fire, sewing and swabbing the gushing tide of crimson that flowed from the wound, Jak at her elbow, following her hissed instructions.

"Done," she said, straightening and mopping sweat from her face.

"One minute and fifty-six seconds," Ryan said. "And Doc never even stirred."

At that precise moment the old man's blue eyes opened. "Thank you, Mama," he whispered. "The agony has somewhat abated." He fell back into the blackness.

Straub was softly clapping his hands. "That was quite brilliant, Dr. Wyeth. If you were to choose to stay here in the ville and serve the countess, then I'm certain your financial reward would be beyond your dreams."

"Never dream about jack, Straub," she replied. "But thanks for the offer."

"Sure, sure."

"He all right?" Ryan asked. "Breathing slow."

Mildred took his pulse and checked respiration. "Gone into clinical shock. Not surprised at that. Now he can relax." She held up the appendix, showing it around the room. "See the size and color. Doc was almost knock, knock, knocking on heaven's door. Another hour, and it might have burst and I'm not sure I could have saved him without proper facilities."

"Will you leave him here in the middle of my kitchen?" the countess asked. "I would prefer it if he could be moved to his own room."

Mildred looked at her. "'Course. Your roast pork and three vegetables comes before the health of a frail old man, doesn't it, Countess?"

"You hold your damned impudent tongue, or I'll have it hacked off at the roots and nailed to the door of the outside john."

"I don't think so," Ryan said quietly. "Not unless you wanted to be having a major burying party real soon."

She pointed a finger at him, turning toward the three watching sec men. "If I tell you, you're to chill all the outlanders. On my word."

Ryan shook his head, keeping his voice gentle and nonconfrontational. "Again I don't think so. By the time these boys draw the Rugers and get them into action, we'll have them down in the blood and dirt. Let's keep it calm, Countess."

Straub started to giggle once more. "The unstoppable up against the immovable. One must bend or break. Or both."

Mildred was washing her hands in a sink in the corner of the kitchen. "It's cool," she said. "Doc can be moved, carefully. Ryan, you and John do that."

Ryan nodded. "Sure. Mebbe we can all go up and take a break. Thanks a lot for the help and letting us save Doc's life down here, Countess. I appreciate it."

"How much?"

"Plenty."

"Enough to do what I asked?"

He shook his head slowly. "I'm real sorry. No. Not that. But we are truly grateful."

She bit her lip. "Go out of my sight, outlanders." She turned toward the door, then stopped. "We have caught a traitor among our sec men. He will be executed this afternoon at three, out back of the ville. I would want you to see how we punish those who are not faithful to us."

THEY WERE ALL GATHERED around Doc's bed when the old man finally blinked awake from his coma. He groaned, turning his head from side to side, the mane of silvery hair matted with sweat, his face lined with pain.

"The agony has not, after all, abated," he murmured. "Can you do nothing for me, Dr. Wyeth? What of your Hippocratic oath to aid the afflicted?"

"I've aided you, Doc," Mildred said.

"Then why am I still torn by the vultures while chained helpless to this mighty boulder?"

"Pain'll be bad right now, though they had some tablets in their pharmacy that should work. Herbal stuff. I got you to swallow them just after the operation."

"Operation?"

"Yeah."

"You mean that I have gone under the knife, and the knife was held by you, ma'am? My worst possible nightmare, and I didn't even know it was happening."

"You had real bad appendicitis," Ryan said. "Already had one foot on the westbound train."

Doc's eyes widened. "My appendix. Yes, that makes sense for the pain and where it lay." He touched himself gingerly, feeling the roll of bandages across his stomach. "And you operated and took it out, Doctor?"

"Sure did."

"And I yet live?"

Mildred grinned. "So far, so good, Doc."

He reached out a trembling hand, and she took it, holding it gently. "You and I have had many a falling-out over the long months together, Doctor. But I want you to know that it was all in jest." He paused. "Well, I would say that at least ninety percent of it was in jest." Another pause, and a leer showed that the old Doc was already making his comeback. "Eighty percent."

Mildred grinned broadly, shaking his hand. "Hell, Doc, I knew that."

DOC SLEPT MUCH of the time, as the natural healing processes took over.

"He all right?" Ryan asked.

"Tough old mountain goat," Mildred replied. "Another day and he'll be up and about. Couple of days and he should be ready to move. How's your leg?"

"Much better. Hardly notice it now."

They both turned as the door eased silently open, and the bald head of Straub appeared. "Countess is ready," he said softly. "All hands to witness punishment."

Chapter Thirty-Two

The mansion was totally silent, though they could hear the soft, rhythmic beating of a slack-skinned drum floating in through some of the open windows. There was no sign of any of the armed sec men patrolling the corridors.

"What's on, Straub?" Ryan asked.

"Traitor. Found out that one of the older sec sergeants had been stealing from the armory. Started with a fistful of ammo, then moved on to taking out submachine guns and LMGs in bits and pieces. One part at a time."

"Who'd he sell them to? Is there an antiville resistance?" J.B. asked.

Straub sniggered, playing with his silver pendant. "You ever know a ville in all Deathlands where there wasn't any resistance, John Barrymore Dix?"

"Guess not. But it seems like the countess has her heel on the neck of the region."

Straub clutched at his groin in a sudden wave of ecstasy. "Well put, Armorer. She has her heel on every part of the body corporate of the land around. And it can give supreme, exhilarating pain, as well as delicious pleasure."

"This resistance?"

"Young bloods in some of the outlying settlements. A little poaching of deer. Salmon from the ponds. Even prime carp. Nothing too serious. Ambushed a wag train last year and killed a couple of sec men. Countess sent out a raiding party and hung a few hostages. Quieted them."

"What going to happen this afternoon?" Jak asked as they reached the enormous armored sec doors at the front of the rambling house.

"Sergeant Gummer gets to pay the price for his treachery and his stupidity."

"Formal execution?" Krysty asked. "I don't really want to watch this."

Straub turned, and for a moment his habitual mask of slack semiidiocy slipped and he glared at her, the silver flecks whirling in his black eyes. "Do you think there's a choice, you stupe red-haired bitch?"

"Hey, back off," Ryan said, stepping in close to the man, hand gripping the butt of the SIG-Sauer. "If we don't want to watch, then we can all turn right around and go back to our rooms. You going to chill us all?"

"'Course not. And I apologize most humbly for losing control of my temper." He glanced to his right. "We must hurry. The countess will be here soon."

IT WAS AN ODD SIGHT.

Straub led them across the formal gardens, down into the bottom of the steep-sided valley they'd viewed the previous day, past the tinkling stream and toward a wilderness that looked as if it had once been used as a quarry.

The beating of the drum was louder, echoing all around them, muffled a little by the stark conifers that lined the stream. And then they saw the ranks of the sec men, lined up on three sides of a square beneath the high cliff that terminated the quarry, the ground covered with rocks of all sizes.

They were all in dress uniforms, with Rugers holstered at their hips.

"You will not have to participate in the execution," Straub said. "You can watch from here."

Ryan looked for a gallows or a headsman's block or some sign of a firing squad.

But there was nothing.

"How's he going to be sent off to buy the farm?" he asked Straub.

"A stoning."

"Stoning!" Mildred was unable to hide her shock and horror. And disgust. "That is unbelievably barbaric! If he has to be chilled, why not just put a bullet through the back of the poor bastard's neck. But to throw stones at him..."

"Barbaric, possibly, Dr. Wyeth. Even a little biblical as a form of killing. But everyone who betrays the countess knows that this is the fate that awaits them. This is, I believe, the first stoning of a traitor for more than three years, so you can appreciate that it is passing effective."

Krysty nudged Ryan. "Here she is," she whispered, "come to enjoy her afternoon."

The countess stalked toward them like a feral cat, elegant and in total control. She was wearing a golden ribbon, tying back her hair, and a deep purple pantsuit in rich velvet. Her boots were midcalf, in lilac leather, with stiletto heels. She had an escort of six of the younger sec men.

She stood over to the right, favoring her guests with a frosty bow.

"We may begin, Straub," she called.

"Excellency." He clapped his hands. "Bring out Sergeant Gummer."

The prisoner looked to be about thirty-five, powerfully built. He had been stripped naked, wearing only a ragged linen breechcloth that hardly covered his loins. He was barefoot. His hands were tied tightly behind his back, blood seeping around his nails from the pressure. His face was pale, and he stumbled between the two sec men who were almost holding him up, leading him to stand, swaying from side to side, at the bottom of the cliff, about twenty paces from the nearest of his fellows.

Mildred tugged at Straub's black clad arm. "You can ease him," she said. "Use your mesmeric toy to help him through the worst of the pain."

"I can," Straub agreed.

"Ask the countess," she urged him.

"She would listen to Ryan Cawdor."

Mildred turned. "Ask her if Straub can use his cunning to hypnotize the poor bastard."

"She won't listen to me."

Straub shook his head. "Oh, but she might. Katya has not given up hope of bending you to her will."

Ryan didn't hesitate. "Countess, why not show that justice can be tempered by mercy? Allow Straub to use his skills to ease the man's suffering. He will still die and be punished for his foolishness and treachery.''

Katya looked at him, a half smile playing around her lips. ''Why not?'' she said finally. ''Do it Straub, but make it fast. I am getting bored. And stop that incessant drumming!''

The drum fell silent as Straub moved forward to stand in front of Gummer, holding up the silver disk. The wind was soughing through the pines, and the stream chattered over smooth pebbles. But everyone was silent, listening to what the mesmerist was saying.

''Felix Gummer, hark to my words, and watch this bauble as it spins in front of you. Focus your eyes on it, and give me your attention. Listen well.''

The disgraced sec sergeant stared blankly as the disk began to spin, faster and faster, sending lances of colored light across his face.

''There will be no pain, no pain. Your body will resist and your mind will control it. You will go down under the stones, but the suffering will end quickly. Do you understand?''

Gummer's eyes were squeezed tight-shut, and his voice seemed to come from very far away. ''I understand, Master Straub. I will do as you say.''

Countess Katya called across impatiently, ''Enough. Straub, get back here and read the charge.''

The shaved-headed man did as he was bid, bowing low to her. ''I hear and obey, lady.'' He pulled a short scroll of parchment from one of his capacious pockets. ''Felix Gummer, you have been found guilty of stealing from Countess Katya Beausoleil, whose bondsman you were in body and soul. This is con-

strued as simple treachery with malice aforethought
and is punishable by death by stoning from your fellow sec men. Your body will be buried in the grave that
you dug yourself this morning, and no prayers will be
said. Do you have any last words?''

The man nodded.

Ryan hadn't seen the deep grave with the pile of raw
earth a few yards to the left of where Gummer stood,
gaping with a layer of gray clay, showing livid among
the orange earth.

Straub turned toward the countess. ''All is ready.''

''Begin.''

Straub called out orders to the men, as though it
were a military exercise, like presenting arms. ''Front
rank, bend and pick up one stone. Straighten. Second
rank, bend and pick up a stone, straighten. On the
word, first rank will throw their stones. Then on a
count of three, the second rank will do the same, while
the third rank bend to pick up stones. On a second
count of three, the second rank will throw their missiles and the first rank will pick up more stones. And
so on until the word is given by the countess to cease
the execution.

''Gaia, I've never seen anything like this,'' Krysty
whispered, touching Ryan on the arm.

''I have. Not that unusual as a sort of sun-king crop-
fertility ritual in some primitive frontier pestholes. Seen
one in a little place called Jackson, out in backwoods
Missouri, where they had a ceremony with the whole
ragged-assed community drawing stones from a bag.
Just once a year, early in the growing season. Person

got the black stone was the sacrifice for that year. But never seen it before as method of execution.''

"Begin," Straub yelped delightedly.

Most of the men had picked stones around the size of a baseball. But they were jagged flints, with cruel points and razored edges.

Each row consisted of eighteen men.

Ryan noticed immediately that their hearts weren't in the killing. Only four stones struck Gummer, mainly glancing blows on his chest and hips, making him stagger, a couple of them drawing threads of bright crimson blood.

The second row did little better. Five hits, only one of them carrying any weight, hitting Gummer on the thigh, bringing a gasp of shock, a trickle of blood and an instant bruise.

The countess wasn't a stupid woman, and she saw what was happening, calling out in a sharp, cold voice for the execution to stop.

"If I see any man aiming wide or not throwing with all his might, then that man will be tied to stand beside the wretched Gummer. And he will not have the benefit of Straub's mercy. You may begin again."

There was no doubting her intent.

The result when the stoning recommenced showed the power that she held over her ville and her men.

Krysty and Mildred both winced and looked away as nearly all the sharp rocks found their helpless target, thudding home, two of them hitting Gummer in the head. One slashed open his cheek, the white of bone showing for a moment before the flood of crimson veiled. The other hit him above the ear as he half turned, tearing the scalp, knocking him off his feet, leaving him huddled and weeping in the dirt.

"Your hypnotism helping the poor bastard?" Ryan said. "Still seems a lot of blood and pain."

"Be much worse if I hadn't hypnotized him. Countess didn't give me long enough to put him under deeply, but he's still going to find the passing easier."

Another volley of stones hissed in from the next row of sec men. Almost all found their sitting target, with sounds like a baseball bat striking a side of beef, wet and solid.

Three hit Gummer on the skull, and he slumped down, unconscious, feet twitching, the only sound in the quarry his bare toes scraping in the grit. His face was a pulped red mask.

"Why not chill him with a bullet?" the Armorer said. "Point's been made."

Straub shook his head, the sunlight glinting off the sweating, shaved pate. "Not the way of the ville," he said quietly. "During the time I've been with the countess, she's never failed to get her own way. Never. No matter what it takes."

He dropped his voice to a whisper. "Remember that, Ryan Cawdor. What she wants from you is a small favor. Refusal can bear a massively disproportionate price. Not just for you."

"How's that?"

Straub pulled his mouth into a grimace that might have been a smile. "All I can say. Last time I'll say it. Give it some serious thought, Ryan."

Another round of stones flew at the slumped, motionless figure, then Katya Beausoleil held up a gloved hand. "Enough," she said. "Tip the offal into his hole in the dirt."

Two of the sec men stepped forward and dragged Gummer across the bloodied sand and rolled him unceremoniously into the grave, picking up the spades and starting to bury him.

Mildred took a half step forward, then caught the flat, incurious eyes of the countess and moved back into line, shrugging her shoulders.

"What?" J.B. asked, as the hole rapidly filled up and the sec men prepared to march back to the mansion to resume their normal duties.

"Nothing. Best get back to see how Doc's getting on. Hope he's sleeping."

But the Armorer pressed her, knowing that there was something she wasn't saying. "Tell me, Millie."

"Well, that method of killing...executing... murdering...call it what you like. It was bad enough. Brutish and unbelievably cruel. But when it was over and they put him in the grave and filled it in..."

"Yeah. He was dead. Wasn't he?"

She looked at him, her dark eyes brimming with unshed tears. "His wounds were still bleeding freely. Meant he wasn't dead, John. The bitch had him buried alive."

Chapter Thirty-Three

Doc was still sleeping when they trudged back to the mansion. But he woke up, looking and sounding drugged, sighing at a sudden stab of pain, clutching at the bandages around his stomach. "If I die, Dr. Wyeth, then I shall never forgive you. Do they still have multimillion-dollar medical-malpractice suits here in Deathlands?"

"Don't think so, Doc," Mildred said, grinning. "Just have to come back and haunt me."

He smiled. "Truth be told, my dear madam, I think I am beginning to feel a little better. I could even manage a drop or two of clear soup, with a brace of coddled eggs. Or some steamed cod with a tiny portion of creamed potatoes. Thinly sliced bread and butter with the crusts cut off. A crystal dish of strawberry conserve. A well-cooked portion of veal Holstein and some lightly boiled cabbage with apple and cinnamon. Freshmade vanilla ice cream with stewed pears. A schooner of director's port." Doc stopped the list of food and drink as he realized that everyone else was grinning at him. "Well," he said defensively, "it is surely a welcome sign of my impending recovery, is it not?"

THE COUNTESS DIDN'T SHOW for supper that night, choosing to stay in her own quarters.

Straub took her place at the head of the table, in good spirits. "I am delighted to hear that the admirable Doc Tanner is recovering from the emergency operation."

"Should be up and about in a couple of days," Ryan said. "I'd hoped to be on our way before then, but... Guess we'll have to impose a while longer."

"Give you a little more time to change your mind about what she wants you to do for her." Straub was twiddling the silver disk around, and Ryan found his eye was caught by it, feeling sucked toward the whirling center, his mind becoming numb, his hearing fading into fuzziness.

Jak broke the spell and jerked him back to the dining room. "You got time tell us about end of Trader," he said. "Don't see much wrong your mind, Straub."

There was a clear threat, overlaid with anger, and it made the bald man start uneasily. His black eyes met Jak's crimson gaze. "Trader? He and I were on a beach with muties. Ignorant armies clashing by night. I recall that. Another man. Small, with a mustache."

"Abe," Ryan said, taking a couple of deep, slow breaths to bring himself back from the brink of mesmerism. The experience warned him yet again how dangerous Straub could be and how one ignored him at one's peril.

"Abe?" Straub tested the name as though it were an unusual cheese. "Perhaps."

"So, what happened? Don't believe you can't remember. Tell us, Straub."

Jak's threat was palpable, but it had little effect. "You must understand I have been through deep and mysterious changes in becoming slave to the countess. Not just in my body, but in every part of my brain. Presume not that I am the man I was, Jak Lauren. I can only operate at her will. Perhaps if she gave me permission to explore that closed room of memory..."

"You must know if Trader's dead or not," J.B. said, finishing the last spoonful of a steamed jam pudding with a white sauce that was flavored with too little nutmeg. "You were right there in his face."

Straub shook his head slowly. "I cannot help you. I see two scenes. One where Trader is butchered on that wet, shingled beach, surrounded by a mound of mutie corpses, faithful Abe dying at his feet from a score of wounds. Then I see him running away, wounded perhaps, but alive." He beamed. "And I do not know which is true. Perhaps neither."

EVERYONE RETIRED EARLY, exhausted from the rigors of a peculiarly strained day—Doc's sudden illness after the visit to Graceland and then the operation, followed by the grotesque horrors of the execution of the treacherous sec sergeant.

They all looked in on Doc before going to bed, delighted that the indomitable old-timer was already showing signs of returning to his crazed good health.

Mildred found that he was running a slight fever and gave him some drugs from the ville to try to reduce it. But it pushed his always fragile mind away over the brink.

He reverted to a time when he was living back on a cold winter's day in the nineteenth century, married to his beloved Emily. Doc was convinced that he had been out sleighing and skating and had caught influenza, which accounted for his temperature and general malaise.

"Keep darling Rachel and dear little Jolyon away from me, my beloved sweetheart," he said, eyes closed, breathing fast, cheeks flushed.

Krysty sat with him, holding his hand, giving him comfort in his isolation, talking quietly to him, trying to help him maintain a grip on real reality.

"You're fine, Doc, and you're with us. Soon be fighting-fit again."

He nodded, smiling. "Always one to look on the sunny side of the street, Emily my dove. If only I had refused to go on the horse-drawn sleigh with those confounded Ambersons. They think themselves so magnificent!"

IT WAS A LITTLE AFTER NINE when Ryan and Krysty went to their room and slid the bolt, undressed and climbed into their four-poster.

They lay together, side against side, watching the occasional flash of pinkish chem lightning through the mullioned windows on the east side of the room.

"How long before we leave this place, lover?"

Ryan rolled over to face her. "If it hadn't been for Doc's sickness, I was planning to move at dawn. Slip out and steal one of their wags and get going back northeast to the redoubt and jump on again."

"Countess would have come after you."

"No. She's arrogant beyond belief, but she isn't stupid. She knows that a full-scale knock-'em-down firefight would go against her. We got the power."

There was a long silence. Krysty's right hand reached out and feathered across Ryan's chest, touching him lower, waiting, caressing him very gently, waiting.

"No?" she whispered.

"Not tonight, I don't think. Just not in the right mood for it."

Krysty withdrew her hand. "Any reason?"

"Keep thinking about that bitch and her demands on me. Can't she see that if there's a biological problem, then it must lie with her? It gets to me the way she keeps looking at me. It's kind of scary."

"Why not do what she wants?"

Ryan sat up, startled. "How's that? You greasing my wheels, lover?"

"'Course not. You know me better than that, Ryan. Not a teasing matter. I truly wouldn't mind if you slept with her just the once. Take the pressure off all of us. I have this bad feeling. I can *see* it, lover. That she's going to cause some triple-bad trouble to try and get her own way. I see death."

Ryan sighed, fumbling down her arm until he could grip her hand tightly. "I know all that old-vid shit about a man's got to do what a man's got to do. I guess it wouldn't hurt, not in the cosmic scale of things, if I did it. But it *would* matter, Krysty. It's wrong. Trying to talk around it and justify it doesn't alter that. I can't ride around this one. Sorry. We can hold on for a couple more days. And then we'll be safe."

"Straub?"

Ryan sniffed. "Yeah. Man to watch. Might be worth chilling that cold-heart son of a bitch before we move on. I know he's got this weird change, and losing his cock and balls and all that. But there's still something deep-down, fundamentally evil about Straub. Caught him trying to get me under with that silver toy of his. Nearly managed it, too."

"Keep away from him until we break and run. The deaths that I see are linked to him."

"I couldn't do it with her. And that's all there is to it, lover. Couldn't." Ryan let go of Krysty's hand and rolled over onto his back again.

THEY SLEPT until the full fury of a chem storm broke around three in the morning, making the windows rattle, sending roof slates clattering into the courtyard. The room was brightly lit by the constant lightning, and demonically heavy rain pounded against the casements.

As it finally moved away toward the west, Ryan slid to the side of the bed, stroking Krysty's breast, feeling the nipple harden at his touch.

"You want to, lover?"

He took her right hand and guided it over the flat, muscular wall of his stomach, until she could check it for herself. He felt her smile as her strong fingers tightened around his hardness.

"I want to," he whispered.

IT WAS STILL RAINING steadily as they all went down for breakfast. Doc was dozing when they looked in on him, but his mind seemed to have returned to the present. He was aware of why he was ill and what had happened to him, asking for food, though Mildred urged caution for the time being.

To Ryan's surprise, they found that the countess was already seated at the head of the table, eating half of a honeydew melon, sugared, with a side dish of raspberries with clotted cream.

She smiled at them. "Awful storm last night. Done some damage to the roof and smashed a window in the east wing on the first floor." She gestured for them to help themselves from the row of silver chafing dishes on a long sideboard.

They served themselves from the usual array of eggs and meats and fish and fruit, sitting down and eating, mostly in silence, until the countess spoke again.

"Hope it didn't disturb you too much. The storm. How is the dear old Doc?"

"On the highway back to health," Mildred replied. "Could be up and moving in a couple of days if there's no infection."

"So, you'll be leaving us then?"

Ryan answered her. "I think so. Been good staying here, and we appreciate your hospitality. Thanks from all of us, Countess."

She nodded and smiled graciously. "We don't see many outlanders here who carry their own sense of power, Ryan. We have travelers and mercenaries and third-rate traders. Failures and losers. Mostly wanting free food and beds for a while. I turn them away. My only interest is in winners. Losers just get caught on the wrong side of the line. I don't know them. Don't want to know them."

During the short speech, her manner changed. The glossy, friendly mask slipped sideways, and the real nature of the ruthless woman peeked through. Her hooded eyes narrowed and her lips grew tight and thin. Her hands clenched, knuckles whitening around the silver spoon.

Straub shuffled in his seat, smiling nervously at Ryan and the others, trying to hide a small shrug of apology but terrified of showing it to his mistress.

"What are your plans for today?" he asked Ryan, seeking to ease past the moment.

"Thought I'd take a walk and look out over the gorge later," he said. "All this rain should have made the big river kind of spectacular."

The bald man nodded. "Sounds a good plan. Perhaps I'll come with you."

It was about the last thing that Ryan wanted, but he saw no reason to upset Straub, not when they would so soon be leaving the ville. "Sure."

"Too wet," Jak said.

"I'll stay and keep an eye on Doc." Mildred took a last sip of water from the goblet and stood. "You going to go out wet-walking, John?"

The Armorer shook his head. "Rain doesn't have much appeal for me, thanks. Take a rain check, I guess."

A joke from J.B. was as rare as a benevolent stickie, and Ryan grinned broadly. "Nice one, bro," he said, then turned to Krysty.

"How about you, lover?"

She looked across the dining room at the gray morning and the steady trickle of water across the windows from a blocked gutter. "You go, Ryan. I can find something to do around the house. Wouldn't mind some time in that library."

WHEN THEY FILED OUT, Ryan saw the countess standing by the front door, idly running her fingers across the pattern of a beautiful inlaid table, veneered with a dozen different colors of marble. She beckoned to him.

He gestured to the others to go along. "Be with you in a minute," he said. "Then I'll get myself ready to go out into the grounds."

Straub was suddenly at his shoulder, almost shepherding him toward the woman. "Before we go for our walk, Ryan, how about a small drink in my room to warm us? I have an excellent liqueur brewed from peaches and cherries. Just the stuff to keep away the cold and wet."

"Why not?"

The countess turned to face him, smiling, the mask back in place again. "A last question. And I promise I will not ask you again. I have never met a man who I more wanted to father a child for me. It is a small matter. A few minutes that may even prove enjoyable for both of us. Please, Ryan." She reached out with a studied impulsiveness and gripped his hand tightly and stared into his face. "I beg you."

He shook his head. "Not the way I live my life, Countess. I'm real honored, but you have to look elsewhere. Can't believe you wouldn't find a long line of men ready and willing and probably able. Sorry."

She nodded and let go of his hand, keeping her noble smile pasted firmly in place. "I understand. Just remember this moment, Ryan, and the price it may cost. Talk comes very cheap, but the price of action can be colossal."

The countess turned away without any further explanation, walking quickly along the hall until she vanished into the pool of shadows that melted at the bottom of the wide main staircase, leaving Ryan alone with Straub.

THE RAIN WAS still falling, sheeting gray and desolate across the trees and leaf-strewn lawns outside the window of Straub's room.

It was a large chamber, with an en suite bathroom. The walls were draped with black velvet, sprinkled with silver-and-gold stars and moons. A number of small round tables, inset with chalcedony and onyx, were set around the room, bearing crystal globes and odd-angled prisms. There was a sofa upholstered in deepest purple and a single bed, narrow and uncomfortable.

"Sit down," Straub said. "I'll get a couple of glasses for a sip of my sable nectar. Then we can brave the elements. It will be a fine sight."

The one thing that Ryan coped with badly was boredom. He needed to be up and moving, and the sudden illness of Doc had meant that they were hanging around the ville for longer than he wanted. He knew that without action his razored combat reflexes became blurred and his concentration wandered.

But a walk in the bracing rain would make him feel better, and a small drink with the bastard, Straub, couldn't do much harm.

He sipped at the tiny engraved glass, the jet black liqueur tasting oddly sweet and bitter. But there was the delicious flavor of tart cherries and summer-ripe peaches.

"To wishes fulfilled and enemies confounded," Straub said, raising his own glass. "Good, is it not, Ryan?"

"Excellent." It had a warming glow as it slipped down. He drained the glass, looking at the few sticky drops that remained in the bottom.

"Another?" He reached out to pour a second measure, smiling at Ryan as he did so.

Straub lit a number of long purple sticks of incense, filling the room with a heavy scent of lime and ginger. It seemed to be darker, and the bald man switched on a very bright overhead light that focused down onto the table where he and Ryan were sitting. Ryan closed his eye for a moment, blinking at the dazzle, aware that he was feeling more tired than he'd thought.

"You all right, Ryan? You look sleepy." Straub's voice sounded solicitous but oddly muffled, as if he were speaking from a far-off room.

"Fine. Fireblast! But my head is..."

"Open your eye, Ryan." There was a sharper note in the man's voice, snapping out the order.

Ryan swallowed hard, feeling the short hairs at his nape beginning to prickle with unease. His brain was puddled, like at the beginning of a jump, and his hearing was becoming more and more muffled. Unconsciously his hand began to reach for the butt of the SIG-Sauer, but it was missing, the holster empty.

"Open your eye, you fucking shit!"

Startled, Ryan did as Straub commanded, finding himself staring directly into the spinning silver disk that the bald man held in his right hand. It gripped his attention, though he made an effort to look away. It felt as if his brain were gripped in a vise, sucking him under.

Straub laughed, the voice echoing and echoing, filling the scented room. "So fucking easy, you triple-stupe arrogant bastard! It's cost you everything. Your friends are all prisoner now or already dead. After you've obliged the countess, then you will join them. It's over, Ryan. Over."

Chapter Thirty-Four

All that Ryan knew was the reality that Straub had showed him. His mind was bound in limitless shrouds of sweltering midnight linen, closing off all his perceptions.

Straub whispered in his ear as he sat there, motionless, paralyzed, explaining how he and the countess had worked out the only way to secure what she most wanted.

"Stiff-backed pride, Cawdor. Your downfall. As it was with that withered old fool called the Trader. He thought he was immortal until he faced death on that beach."

"Dead?" Ryan barely forced out the single word through gritted teeth.

Straub's face was close to his, so that he could taste the rotten odor of his breath, foul on his cheek. "You can go to your grave without ever being sure of that, you one-eyed, scum-sucking imbecile! But it might be you'll be meeting him again very soon. After you've performed your duty for my lady. But I only say mebbe. Why give you an inch of knowledge when you can more easily die ignorant?"

THE BALD MAN TOOK Ryan by the wrist, leading him unprotestingly through the shadowy passages of the huge, rambling mansion. It was oddly deserted, with no sec men at doors and cross corridors. There was no sign of any servants, nor of his friends. Ryan's feet seemed to float over the thick carpets, and his eye gazed incuriously around him.

"It was so easy. They chose to separate and go to different places. There was no need to be cunning. Simply to find them and slay them. Let me show you all your friends, outlander. All of your dead friends."

The combination of the powerful drug in the drink and the vicious skill of the bald man's mesmerism had robbed Ryan of all sense and reduced him to a feeble puppet in the hands of the sniggering Straub.

"First let us see your redheaded slut, Ryan. In the library, I think she said."

The door swung open silently, and Ryan and his captor drifted through into the dusty stillness.

"Smell the death, Ryan. Smell the spilled blood of your lover. See the way her hair melts into the flow of crimson from the slit throat, lying there, on the floor, with old books scattered around her corpse. See it."

Ryan saw it, exactly as Straub described it. Krysty was on her back, hands spread, fingers clenched, her fiery hair floating out around her shoulders, free and loose, the ends sodden in the lake of dull blood that still trickled from a deep gash that opened up the whiteness of bone in her throat.

Ryan blinked, stricken, feeling a vague surprise that her sentient hair hadn't coiled up defensively at the last. That was odd. But it was such a tiny, foolish detail.

"If you want to weep, then do it," Straub said, still grinning widely.

"No," Ryan said slowly. "After I've chilled you and the bitch . . . then . . . then . . ."

JAK HAD BEEN MURDERED in the armory. As they moved through the dark stillness, Straub had described what Ryan would see behind the hair-open door. And it was true.

The albino had been shot once through the back of the head, matting the fine, silken white hair with clots of pink-gray brain and splinters of bone. Even in the last, ghastly shock of dying, he'd managed to draw one of the throwing knives, holding it, unthrown in his hand.

J.B. AND MILDRED had returned to their bedroom to be close to Doc.

"Room still stinks of cordite," Straub said as they paused in the passage. "Sec men went in mob-handed on this one. Weren't taking any chances. Six of them, and it looks like they emptied their Rugers into the bodies. Kind of messy. Sure you want to see them?" He pushed Ryan through into the shambles.

The bodies were almost unrecognizable, and the room was filled with the biting fumes of the gunfire. It was just as Straub had said it would be. Mildred lay across the corpse of the Armorer, one arm blown off at the shoulder, most of the ragged wounds in her chest and stomach. J.B. stared at the ceiling, blank eyed, one lens of his glasses smashed like a star. Neither of them had had any chance of reaching their weapons.

"See," Straub said. "Just as I told you. They were such easy meat, and all because of your stubborn pride. Want to see the old man?"

"Yeah. See the butcher's bill that needs paying," Ryan said, grating out the harsh, helpless words. He barely hung on to the shreds of sanity at the realization that he had been completely defeated. All of his friends dead. All of them. And his own death only an hour or so away.

He felt physically beaten, hardly able to move, yet somehow movement was easy as Straub showed him everything that had happened. It was oddly dreamlike, with no sense of walking from place to place. The bald man clung to his arm and whispered it in his ear, and there it was.

"LOOKS PEACEFUL, DON'T HE?" Straub sneered. "Weak as a kitten, the lousy old prick."

"Why did you have to chill them all?" Ryan whispered, head spinning, feeling his stomach knotting with bitter bile. "Just take me."

"Not good enough for my lady. You spit in her face, and she couldn't just walk away from that."

Doc was on his back, eyes closed, the only sign of his violent passing his hands, clenched in front of his face as if he were trying to ward off a blow.

"How?" Ryan asked.

"Pillow. Didn't struggle too much."

TIME WAS STRETCHED and meaningless.

One moment Ryan was listening to Straub's painting the picture of Doc's bleak and lonely passing, then he was seeing it in every detail. And then he was back again in Straub's room, lying on the sofa, one hand absently rubbing at the wound in his thigh. He was vaguely aware of its prickling heat and how tender the flesh felt.

Straub was leaning over a large crystal, polishing it with a strip of aquamarine satin, breathing on it, his gleaming, skull-like face grotesquely distorted in the internal reflection of the globe.

He was whispering to himself in a childlike, crooning voice. Ryan heard the words and recognized that they had to make some sort of sense, but he still failed to understand them. Only snatches penetrated into his drugged, paralyzed mind.

"Feed her cream. Mebbe allow her the child. Take him under my wing. Use my powers to close the lady down. Careful and slow and gentle. Think of the enemies, all dismayed, creeping in the corridors, frightened of my shade."

Ryan slept, his mind brimming with the hideous, deathly images of his butchered comrades. His memory flicked back over adventures gone, never forgotten, looking out to the empty future, alone.

When he came back into the misty half world, Straub was still polishing, still whispering, hugging himself like an old woman against a bitter cold.

"Or pluck the flower from the nettle now? Let the plan run. Let the deaths come at her hands. Finish them all and finish the one-eyed rat king himself. You're such a fine, brave fellow, Straub, aren't you? You have two plans, and both are brilliant. Finest ever. Each one a glittering, flawless gem, with its own beautiful facets to cut and polish. You the best, Straub. The very, very best.''

THE COUNTESS WAS in the room, looking down at Ryan, stretched helpless on his sofa. She wore a knee-length white robe of embroidered silk, cut low across her swelling breasts, with a long crimson scarf wrapped around her neck. On her feet were boots of white Spanish leather.

''You are sure, Straub?''

The bald man was capering around, playing an imaginary flute, using a carved human femur as his instrument. ''Of course. First the drink and the potion. Then my little silver pendant to draw him and bind him and keep him. Now he sees only the pictures that I paint for him and does what I command.''

''I wish him to do what I command.''

Straub giggled again. ''But of course. My plans are for you, Mistress.''

Ryan watched as she drifted in slow motion across the thick carpet and touched the man softly on the cheek with her long fingernail, drawing it across the taut skin, leaving a needle-thin thread of scarlet.

''Yes,'' she hissed, the syllable dragging on and on like an angry cobra.

''Where will you take him, Mistress?'' Straub asked, ignoring the bead of blood that dangled from his chin.

''My room.''

''Not here?'' A note of faint disappointment crept into the unctuous voice.

''No.'' She paused. ''In fact I think it should be more special. Perhaps that is why I have been failing. The setting has not been right for the fathering of a fine son. Not a dull bedroom in a dull house. The attic of the old mill above the gardens. With its fine view. On the way to the ob platform over the gorge.''

Straub laughed. ''The one-eyed stupe had said he wanted to see the river. Why not show it to him after he has fulfilled your requirements, Mistress?''

The woman smiled and nodded at him, turning her face toward Ryan, who unaccountably shuddered, unaccountably since none of the words being spoken made any sense to his crazed, fogged mind.

THEY WERE OUTSIDE in a fine drizzle, with a light breeze whipping through the tops of a gigantic pair of live oaks near the rear entrance to the ville.

Straub had seen them off, bowing to the countess and slapping Ryan gently and contemptuously across the cheek. ''I pray it will be success.''

''I know it will. And after, I shall follow your idea and send him to view the river.''

''And I go into the house, Mistress, to make everything he saw into reality.''

SHE HELD HIM BY THE HAND as they strolled like lovers across the terracing, down the side of the long pool toward the squat building. Ryan could hear a faint roaring sound in the background, like ferocious animals trapped deep underground. He had no idea what it might be.

''Soon, lover,'' she said. ''It will take time, so that I am properly satisfied, but I shall tell you what to do. Anything I want, anything. And your seed will fill me, and I will rule on here through my son, through eternity. Soon, Ryan.''

STRAUB WENT FIRST into the room where Doc lay on his back on the bed, eyes closed, motionless. He looked around the room and picked up a large stuffed cushion from an armchair, hefting it and moving silently across the room.

"So long, you babbling old fool," he whispered, bending low over the frail figure beneath the coverlet.

"So long," Doc said, squeezing the trigger on the concealed Le Mat and blowing Straub's guts out through his spine.

Chapter Thirty-Five

Straub died without saying a word, sitting against the wall, hands pressed together to try to hold his stomach together. The 18-gauge scattergun round had cut the cord on his silver amulet, which rolled beneath a long mahogany table and lay in the shadows.

The shot had set fire to the bedcover, and Doc laid the blaster down, quickly beating out the smoldering material. He looked up unworriedly as the door burst open and J.B. jumped into the room, holding the Uzi, with Mildred at his heels, the ZKR 551 cocked and ready in her right fist.

"Doc! Dark night, what . . . ?"

"Caught a rat sneaking in trying to do a princes-in-the-tower job on me. Shut me up with that cushion." He pointed to it with the smoking muzzle of the blaster. "One thing that traveling with you and dear Ryan has emphasized to me is that caution is ever-constant and the eye never sleeps. The blade is never sheathed. The pistol never unloaded. The spirit always ready. But I digress. I heard the door creak and squinted out and saw Straub there. So I shot him. It looks as though things must be moving elsewhere for him to try that. Should we not find Ryan and the others?"

Mildred looked at him as he started to get out of bed. "Doc! You aren't well enough for this." But the doubt in her voice showed that she also realized that things were indeed moving quickly against them.

"I'm well. Well enough, Dr. Wyeth."

J.B. bit his lip. "I'll get our things. Collect the Steyr. Find Ryan and the others. Think Krysty went into the library. Jak said something about the armory. Ryan? Don't know."

THERE WAS A BALCONY on the top floor of the mill, and the countess stood proudly there, arm in arm with the hero who would father her long-needed son and heir.

"It is a shame you are so stupe-stubborn," she said, smiling into his blank, puzzled face. "We could have rid ourselves of that mongrel Straub once the baby was born. And you could have ruled with me. Obeyed me. Though I think that Straub might leave us sooner rather than later. Yes, very soon for the sick bastard. Once he has finished cleaning."

Far below them they could see the lily-fringed lake, with the shadows of the giant carp moving sinuously below the rain-speckled surface.

But it made no sense to Ryan. His lips moved and he said, "All dead. Krysty, all dead." But no sound came out of his mouth. The drizzle ran over his stubbled cheeks, mingling with the invisible salt tears.

After a few moments the woman shuddered. "Time to go in and get warm, my strong love," she said.

KRYSTY WAS LOUNGING in a padded chair by the window of the library, looking out over the damp, streaming, melancholy gardens of the ville, flipping through some bound issues of a travel magazine from the 1990s, bound in bright yellow covers. She'd seen them scattered around Deathlands, but never in such clean condition, giving an amazing peephole into the late months before skydark and the long winters.

She looked up as Mildred came in, helping Doc, who was moving slowly and painfully.

"What's up?"

"Weird. Shit's hitting the fan somehow. Straub tried to waste Doc, so he chilled him. But he was alone. No sign of the sec men anywhere. Place is deserted. Countess isn't anywhere. But we're finding the others and getting out. John's getting Jak from the armory. Where's Ryan?"

"Said he was going for a walk to the river."

"Oh, yeah, I remember."

Krysty stood, looking worried. "Something's triple-bad, Mildred. Few minutes ago I almost saw him in here, with Straub. Felt them as strong as if they were standing by the door, but the room was empty. One of the oddest, most powerful feelings I ever had. Something real bad."

She looked out of the window, seeing the ornamental mill just visible through the drifting, misty rain, with its wrought-iron balcony that looked out over the fish pool. She narrowed her eyes, seeing a flicker of movement. Someone stood there in white. Two people? She rubbed her eyes and looked again, but the balcony was empty.

J.B. rushed into the room draped in blasters, followed by Jak.

Krysty spun, overwhelmed by a feeling of total, heart-stopping disaster. "The mill . . . river . . . out that way," she gasped. "Now!"

"KNEEL DOWN." The voice was a harsh, gasping parody of seductive lust.

Ryan did as he was told, wincing at the sharp pain it caused his healing thigh. The woman towered over him, her white boots smeared with mud and dulled with rain, inches from his hands. She was so close he could smell the rutting scent of her body, hot and urgent and deeply unattractive to him.

His mind was flooded with pain, unbalanced by Straub's evil genius.

Krysty was dead.

John Dix was dead.

Doc, Jak and Mildred were all dead. Perhaps he was also dead and this was a form of Hell, like the Bible thumpers used to preach at the river-crossing meetings.

"First, your tongue." Slowly she lifted her skirt, revealing her knees, then her thighs, almost touching his face. She wore no underclothes, and her coiling hair was moist and matted with her utterly overpowering need. "Taste me."

He ignored her for a moment, though he knew he was soon going to do what she wanted. That was inexorably charted by the steel locks of Straub's will, and nothing could stop him. But the bitterness of bereavement held him back from obeying for a handful of crucial seconds.

"Do it, you weak-willed prick!" she screamed, losing control. She stepped back half a pace and kicked him with all her vicious anger.

The sharp toe of her boot cracked hard into his right thigh, squarely on the wound.

Ryan screamed, once, high and thin, like a stallion at the gelding pole.

KRYSTY WAS HALFWAY across the top terrace, skidding on the wet turf as she heard a faint cry of anguish somewhere ahead and below them.

"Ryan!"

THE PAIN WAS UNIMAGINABLE, far worse than the original wound had been.

As he screamed, Ryan flung himself forward against the countess, knocking her flat on her back, the skirt riding higher, her head cracking against an antique oak blanket chest at the bottom of the bed.

Part of him felt the warmth of blood flowing freely down his leg, and part of him felt a terrible, surging anger throwing off the mental shackles. This woman and the man Straub had murdered all his friends, enslaved him to make him their creature. Now that was over.

"Fireblast!" he groaned. "Fucking over!"

The woman blinked, half-stunned, looking across the room at the crouching man, seeing his lips tugged back from his teeth in a feral snarl of burning hatred, the wide, shocked eyes and the hands, clawing toward her.

"Don't," she pleaded.

"Kill you, bitch..."

"They're not..." she began, but he lunged at her, clumsy, off balance from the agonizing injury, his fingers barely brushing the hem of her dress.

The countess was on her feet, kicking past him, diving for the stairs that led out of the cozy attic. She was down and out in a single tumbling, panicked movement into the drenched gardens, hearing him screaming behind her, feet pounding, hands clutching.

The house was uphill and she needed speed. She turned around and raced onto the narrow path along the flank of the steep valley, heading toward the view point over the tumbling gorge.

KRYSTY COULD FEEL the blank horror in her lover's mind, as well as hear his yells of demonic rage, inhuman and piercing, ringing through the waterlogged grounds of the ville like a maddened banshee.

"Faster," she panted, sliding around the corner onto the flat ground by the pool. She was unable to see any sign of Ryan, but still heard the noise of pursuit from the rear of the mill, overlaid by the sound of the swollen river.

Jak was right on her heels, followed closely by J.B. Mildred was ten paces behind, pausing to stop and help Doc who was still making the most valiant efforts to keep up with the others.

"River!" Krysty yelled.

THE PATH ACROSS THE SIDE of the tree-lined valley seemed endless to the terrified woman. If only she'd thought to bring a blaster, she could have gunned down the madman who pursued her with such relentless ferocity. But she'd trusted Straub.

As she ran and dodged, water showering off overhanging branches, the countess swore a dreadful oath to herself to slaughter Straub, slowly and in the utmost agony, for what he had done to her.

Ryan was about thirty yards behind, clumsy with the wounded leg, unable to run flat out. His arms were outstretched in front of him, fingers aching to grasp the slender white neck and tear, mangle and throttle it, to force the life from the protruding eyes and smile at the purpled tongue.

At least there would be that.

But the woman raced ahead, arms and legs pumping, heading toward the end of the path and the platform over the gorge.

A hundred yards away.

SHE WAS BACKED against the raw face of the cliff, trembling, her fingers knotted into the flimsy wire fence, her weight against it, making it sway back and forth. Ryan faced her, blocking the exit back toward the ville, his spine touching the rusting supports. Behind him was the drop of hundreds of feet, the last hundred or so sheer down to the thread of foaming water below.

"You didn't have to butcher them all," he yelled, his voice torn from his throat in a scream. "It was just you and me."

She made a move toward him, her mouth working. "Listen to me," she began. "Straub played..."

Ryan swung at her, feeling the satisfying force of the impact as the woman's cheekbone splintered, the force of the punch knocking her down against the rocks, the back of her head cut and bleeding. Her bright eyes half closed for a moment.

"Get the fuck up, bitch," he whispered, inaudible above the thunderous roaring. "I'm going to beat you to a bloody pulp and then drop you over the edge. One way all the way down. Pay a fraction the price. Then Straub."

Her eyes blinked open, and he stooped and swung her up, gripping the torn material of her dress, holding her balanced while he measured the next punch.

Krysty was in sight, and she stopped and cupped her hands. "Ryan! Hey, Ryan!"

Ryan started to turn, disbelief stark on his face, his mouth sagging open. He blinked through the driving rain, seeing a blurred vision of a tall woman with a shock of bright, fiery hair. Another figure, hair like snow, was at her side. Three others were farther back, staring at him.

"Krysty..." he whispered, a rush of knowledge paralyzing him for a moment.

Katya Beausoleil pushed against him with all her failing strength, catching him off balance, pushing him hard into the frail fencing. He heard rusting iron creak and snap, and he was staggering backward, feet brushing air, falling away.

Krysty screamed once.

He was over, pushing the limp body of the countess from him, rolling onto a steep slope of treacherous mud.

Ryan's fingers reached, grasped, failing to find any grip. He spread himself, arms and legs wide, hopeless, around and around, head down, somersaulting over and over.

He glimpsed the white dress below him, vanishing over the last sheer brink and tumbling into the water, vanishing from his sight.

Ryan reached the final frontier himself, skidding over, hopelessly out of control.

Flying, falling, spinning, hitting the surface of the flooded river with a fearsome impact, trying to keep his body straight, blacking out. The shock of the icy, raging torrent brought him around for a snatched moment.

The force of the current was unimaginable, filled with sucking maelstroms and murderous smooth boulders. Ryan was sucked under and spit out into the air, then drawn deep under once more, into the welcoming darkness.

His eye closed.

**Gold Eagle Presents
a special three-book in-line continuity**

THE RED DRAGON TRILOGY

Beginning in June 1996, Gold Eagle brings you
another action-packed three-book in-line continuity,
The Red Dragon Trilogy.

In THE EXECUTIONER #210—FIRE LASH, book 1 of The
Red Dragon Trilogy, The Triads and the Red Chinese
have struck a bargain sealed in hell—with a quick payoff
in escalating terrorism, murder and heroin traffic. But
long-range plans include a conspiracy of terrifying
global consequence.

Don't miss the first book of this new trilogy, available in
June at your favorite retail outlet.

Or order your copy now by sending your name, address, zip or postal code, along
with a check or money order (please do not send cash) for $3.75 for each book
ordered ($4.25 in Canada), plus 75¢ postage and handling ($1.00 in Canada), payable
to Gold Eagle Books, to:

In the U.S.	In Canada
Gold Eagle Books	Gold Eagle Books
3010 Walden Ave.	P.O. Box 636
P.O. Box 9077	Fort Erie, Ontario
Buffalo, NY 14269-9077	L2A 5X3

Please specify book title with your order.
Canadian residents add applicable federal and provincial taxes.

DT96-1

TAKE 'EM FREE

4 action-packed novels plus a mystery bonus

NO RISK

NO OBLIGATION TO BUY

SPECIAL LIMITED-TIME OFFER

Mail to: Gold Eagle Reader Service
3010 Walden Ave,
P.O. Box 1394
Buffalo, NY 14240-1394

YEAH! Rush me 4 FREE Gold Eagle novels and my FREE mystery gift. Then send me 4 brand-new novels every other month as they come off the presses. Bill me at the low price of just $14.80* for each shipment—a saving of 12% off the cover prices for all four books! There is NO extra charge for postage and handling! There is no minimum number of books I must buy. I can always cancel at any time simply by returning a shipment at your cost or by returning any shipping statement marked "cancel." Even if I never buy another book from Gold Eagle, the 4 free books and surprise gift are mine to keep forever.

164 BPM ANQZ

Name	(PLEASE PRINT)	
Address		Apt. No.
City	State	Zip

Signature (if under 18, parent or guardian must sign)

* Terms and prices subject to change without notice. Sales tax applicable in NY. This offer is limited to one order per household and not valid to present subscribers. Offer not available in Canada.

GE-94

An old enemy develops a deadly
new train of thought...

THE Destroyer

#103 Engines of Destruction

Created by
WARREN MURPHY
and RICHARD SAPIR

The railways have become the fastest—and surest—way
to get from here to eternity. Could the repeated sightings
of a ghostly samurai swordsman be linked to the
high-speed derailments that are strewing the rails with
headless victims? Suspecting the train terror is merely a
decoy, Remo Williams and Master Chiun become
involved, only to find they may literally lose their heads
over an old enemy.

Available in July at your favorite retail outlet or order your copy now by sending your
name, address, zip or postal code, along with a check or money order (please do not
send cash) for $5.50 ($6.50 in Canada) for each book ordered, plus 75¢ postage and
handling ($1.00 in Canada), payable to Gold Eagle Books, to:

In the U.S.	In Canada
Gold Eagle Books	Gold Eagle Books
3010 Walden Ave.	P.O. Box 636
P.O. Box 9077	Fort Erie, Ontario
Buffalo, NY 14269-9077	L2A 5X3

DEST103

Please specify book title with your order.
Canadian residents add applicable federal and provincial taxes.